THE RED THUMB MARK

T0040246

A DR. THORNDYKE MYSTERY

R. AUSTIN FREEMAN

Skyhorse Publishing

A Herman Graf Book

First Skyhorse Publishing edition 2016

Skyhorse Publishing books may be purchased in bulk at special discounts for sales promotion, corporate gifts, fund-raising, or educational purposes. Special editions can also be created to specifications. For details, contact the Special Sales Department, Skyhorse Publishing, 307 West 36th Street, 11th Floor, New York, NY 10018 or info@skyhorsepublishing.com.

Skyhorse® and Skyhorse Publishing® are registered trademarks of Skyhorse Publishing, Inc.®, a Delaware corporation.

Visit our website at www.skyhorsepublishing.com.

10 9 8 7 6 5 4 3 2 1

Library of Congress Cataloging-in-Publication Data is available on file.

Cover design by Elise Chapdelaine
Cover illustration credit iStock

Print ISBN: 978-1-5107-0773-3
Ebook ISBN: 978-1-5107-0775-7

Printed in the United States of America

TABLE OF CONTENTS

PREFACE

In writing the following story, the author has had in view no purpose other than that of affording entertainment to such readers as are interested in problems of crime and their solutions; and the story itself differs in no respect from others of its class, excepting in that an effort has been made to keep within the probabilities of ordinary life, both in the characters and in the incidents.

Nevertheless it may happen that the book may serve a useful purpose in drawing attention to certain popular misapprehensions on the subject of finger-prints and their evidential value; misapprehensions the extent of which may be judged when we learn from the newspapers that several Continental commercial houses have actually substituted finger-prints for signed initials.

The facts and figures contained in Mr. Singleton's evidence, including the very liberal estimate of the population of the globe, are, of course, taken from Mr. Galton's great and important work on finger-prints; to which the reader who is interested in the subject is referred for much curious and valuable information.

In conclusion, the author desires to express his thanks to his friend Mr. Bernard E. Bishop for the assistance rendered to him in certain photographic experiments, and to those officers of the Central Criminal Court who very kindly furnished him with details of the procedure in criminal trials.

CHAPTER ONE

MY LEARNED BROTHER

"Conflagratam An° 1677. Fabricatam An° 1698. Richardo Powell Armiger Thesaurar." The words, set in four panels, which formed a frieze beneath the pediment of a fine brick portico, summarized the history of one of the tall houses at the upper end of King's Bench Walk, and as I, somewhat absently, read over the inscription, my attention was divided between admiration of the exquisitely finished carved brickwork and the quiet dignity of the building, and an effort to reconstitute the dead and gone Richard Powell, and the stirring times in which he played his part.

I was about to turn away when the empty frame of the portico became occupied by a figure, and one so appropriate, in its wig and obsolete habiliments, to the old-world surroundings that it seemed to complete the picture, and I lingered idly to look at it. The barrister had halted in the doorway to turn over a sheaf of papers that he held in his hand, and as he replaced the red tape that bound them together, he looked up and our eyes met. For a moment we regarded one another with the incurious gaze that casual strangers bestow on one another; then there was a flash of mutual recognition; the impassive and rather severe face of the lawyer softened into a genial smile, and the figure, detaching itself from its frame, came down the steps with a hand extended in cordial greeting.

"My dear Jervis," he exclaimed, as we clasped hands warmly, "this is a great and delightful surprise. How often have I thought of my old comrade and wondered if I should ever see him again, and lo! here he is, thrown up on the sounding beach of the Inner Temple, like the proverbial bread cast upon the waters."

"Your surprise, Thorndyke, is nothing to mine," I replied, "for your bread has at least returned as bread; whereas I am in the position of a man who, having cast his bread upon the waters, sees it return in the form of a buttered muffin or a Bath bun. I left a respectable medical practitioner, and I find him transformed into a bewigged and begowned limb of the law."

Thorndyke laughed at the comparison.

"Liken not your old friend unto a Bath bun," said he. "Say, rather, that you left him a chrysalis and come back to find him a butterfly. But the change is not so great as you think. Hippocrates is only hiding under the gown of Solon, as you will understand when I explain my metamorphosis; and that I will do this very evening, if you have no engagement."

"I am one of the unemployed at present," I said, "and quite at your service."

"Then come round to my chambers at seven," said Thorndyke, "and we will have a chop and a pint of claret together and exchange autobiographies. I am due in court in a few minutes."

"Do you reside within that noble old portico?" I asked.

"No," replied Thorndyke. "I often wish I did. It would add several inches to one's stature to feel that the mouth of one's burrow was graced with a Latin inscription for admiring strangers to ponder over. No; my chambers are some doors further down—number 6A"—and he turned to point out the house as we crossed toward Crown Office Row.

At the top of Middle Temple Lane we parted, Thorndyke taking his way with fluttering gown toward the Law Courts, while I directed my steps westward toward Adam Street, the chosen haunt of the medical agent.

The soft-voiced bell of the Temple clock was telling out the hour of seven in muffled accents (as though it apologized for breaking the studious silence) as I emerged from the archway of Mitre Court and turned into King's Bench Walk.

The paved footway was empty save for a single figure, pacing slowly before the doorway of number 6A, in which, though the wig had now given place to a felt hat and the gown to a jacket, I had no difficulty in recognizing my friend.

"Punctual to the moment, as of old," said he, meeting me half-way. "What a blessed virtue is punctuality, even in small things. I have just been taking the air in Fountain Court, and will now introduce you to my chambers. Here is my humble retreat."

We passed in through the common entrance and ascended the stone stairs to the first floor, where we were confronted by a massive door, above which my friend's name was written in white letters.

"Rather a forbidding exterior," remarked Thorndyke, as he inserted the latchkey, "but it is homely enough inside."

The heavy door swung outward and disclosed a baize-covered inner door, which Thorndyke pushed open and held for me to pass in.

"You will find my chambers an odd mixture," said Thorndyke, "for they combine the attractions of an office, a museum, a laboratory, and a workshop."

"And a restaurant," added a small, elderly man, who was decanting a bottle of claret by means of a glass syphon: "you forgot that, sir."

"Yes, I forgot that, Polton," said Thorndyke, "but I see you have not." He glanced toward a small table that had been placed near the fire and set out with the requisites for our meal.

"Tell me," said Thorndyke, as we made the initial onslaught on the products of Polton's culinary experiments, "what has been happening to you since you left the hospital six years ago?"

"My story is soon told," I answered, somewhat bitterly. "It is not an uncommon one. My funds ran out, as you know, rather unexpectedly. When I had paid my examination and registration fees, the coffer was absolutely empty, and though, no doubt, a medical diploma contains—to use Johnson's phrase—the potentiality of wealth beyond the dreams of avarice, there is a vast difference in practice between the potential and the actual. I have, in fact, been earning a subsistence, sometimes as an assistant, sometimes as a *locum tenens*. Just now I've got no work to do, and so have entered my name on Turcival's list of eligibles."

Thorndyke pursed up his lips and frowned.

"It's a wicked shame, Jervis," said he presently, "that a man of your abilities and scientific acquirements should be frittering away his time on odd jobs like some half-qualified wastrel."

"It is," I agreed. "My merits are grossly undervalued by a stiffnecked and obtuse generation. But what would you have, my learned brother? If poverty steps behind you and claps the occulting bushel over your thirty-thousand-candle-power luminary, your brilliancy is apt to be obscured."

"Yes, I suppose that is so," grunted Thorndyke, and he remained for a time in deep thought.

"And now," said I, "let us have your promised explanation. I am positively frizzling with curiosity to know what chain of circumstances has converted John Evelyn Thorndyke from a medical practitioner into a luminary of the law."

Thorndyke smiled indulgently.

"The fact is," said he, "that no such transformation has occurred. John Evelyn Thorndyke is still a medical practitioner."

"What, in a wig and gown!" I exclaimed.

"Yes, a mere sheep in wolf's clothing," he replied. "I will tell you how it has come about. After you left the hospital, six years ago, I stayed on, taking up any small appointments that were going—assistant demonstrator—or curatorships and such like—hung about the chemical and physical laboratories, the museum and post mortem room, and meanwhile took my MD and DSc. Then I got called to the bar in the hope of getting a coronership, but soon after this, old Stedman retired unexpectedly—you remember Stedman, the lecturer on medical jurisprudence—and I put in for the vacant post. Rather to my surprise, I was appointed lecturer, whereupon I dismissed the coronership from my mind, took my present chambers, and sat down to wait for anything that might come."

"And what has come?" I asked.

"Why, a very curious assortment of miscellaneous practice," he replied. "At first I only got an occasional analysis in a doubtful poisoning case, but, by degrees, my sphere of influence has extended until it now includes all cases in which a special knowledge of medicine or physical science can be brought to bear upon law."

"But you plead in court, I observe," said I.

"Very seldom," he replied. "More usually I appear in the character of that *bête noir* of judges and counsel—the scientific witness. But in most instances I do not appear at all; I merely direct investigations, arrange and analyze the results, and prime the counsel with facts and suggestions for cross-examination."

"A good deal more interesting than acting as understudy for an absent g.p.," said I, a little enviously. "But you deserve to succeed, for you were always a deuce of a worker, to say nothing of your capabilities."

"Yes, I worked hard," replied Thorndyke, "and I work hard still; but I have my hours of labor and my hours of leisure, unlike you poor devils of general practitioners, who are liable to be dragged away from the dinner table or roused out of your first sleep by—confound it all! Who can that be?"

For at this moment, as a sort of commentary on his self-congratulation, there came a smart rapping at the outer door.

"Must see who it is, I suppose," he continued, "though one expects people to accept the hint of a closed oak."

He strode across the room and flung open the door with an air of by no means gracious inquiry.

"It's rather late for a business call," said an apologetic voice outside, "but my client was anxious to see you without delay."

"Come in, Mr. Lawley," said Thorndyke, rather stiffly, and as he held the door open, the two visitors entered. They were both men— one middle-aged, rather foxy in appearance and of a typically legal aspect, and the other a fine, handsome young fellow of very prepossessing exterior, though at present rather pale and wild-looking, and evidently in a state of profound agitation.

"I am afraid," said the latter, with a glance at me and the dinner table, "that our visit—for which I am alone responsible—is a most unseasonable one. If we are really inconveniencing you, Dr. Thorndyke, pray tell us, and my business must wait."

Thorndyke had cast a keen and curious glance at the young man, and he now replied in a much more genial tone—

"I take it that your business is of a kind that will not wait, and as to inconveniencing us, why, my friend and I are both doctors, and as you are aware, no doctor expects to call any part of the twenty-four hours his own unreservedly."

I had risen on the entrance of the two strangers, and now proposed to take a walk on the Embankment and return later, but the young man interrupted me.

"Pray don't go away on my account," he said. "The facts that I am about to lay before Dr. Thorndyke will be known to all the world by this time tomorrow, so there is no occasion for any show of secrecy."

"In that case," said Thorndyke, "let us draw our chairs up to the fire and fall to business forthwith. We had just finished our dinner and were waiting for the coffee, which I hear my man bringing down at this moment."

We accordingly drew up our chairs, and when Polton had set the coffee on the table and retired, the lawyer plunged into the matter without preamble.

CHAPTER TWO

THE SUSPECT

"I had better," said he, "give you a general outline of the case as it presents itself to the legal mind, and then my client, Mr. Reuben Hornby, can fill in the details if necessary, and answer any questions that you may wish to put to him.

"Mr. Reuben occupies a position of trust in the business of his uncle, John Hornby, who is a gold and silver refiner and dealer in precious metals generally. There is a certain amount of outside assay work carried on in the establishment, but the main business consists in the testing and refining of samples of gold sent from certain mines in South Africa.

"About five years ago, Mr. Reuben and his cousin Walter—another nephew of John Hornby—left school, and both were articled to their uncle, with the view to their ultimately becoming partners in the house; and they have remained with him ever since, occupying, as I have said, positions of considerable responsibility.

"And now for a few words as to how business is conducted in Mr. Hornby's establishment. The samples of gold are handed over at the docks to some accredited representative of the firm—generally either Mr. Reuben or Mr. Walter—who has been dispatched to meet the ship, and conveyed either to the bank or to the works according to circumstances. Of course every effort is made to have as little gold as possible on the premises, and the bars are always removed to the bank at the earliest opportunity; but it happens unavoidably that samples of considerable value have often to remain on the premises all night, and so the works are furnished with a large and powerful safe or strong room for their reception. This safe is situated in the private office under the eye of the principal, and as an additional precaution, the caretaker, who acts as night-watchman, occupies a room directly over the office and patrols the building periodically through the night.

"Now a very strange thing has occurred with regard to this safe. It happens that one of Mr. Hornby's customers in South Africa is interested in a diamond mine, and although transactions in precious stones form no part of the business of the house, he has, from time to time, sent parcels of rough diamonds addressed to Mr. Hornby, to be either deposited in the bank or handed on to the diamond brokers.

"A fortnight ago Mr. Hornby was advised that a parcel of stones had been dispatched by the *Elmina Castle*, and it appeared that the parcel was an unusually large one and contained stones of exceptional size and value. Under these circumstances Mr. Reuben was sent down to the docks at an early hour in the hope the ship might arrive in time for the stones to be lodged in the bank at once. Unfortunately, however, this was not the case, and the diamonds had to be taken to the works and locked up in the safe."

"Who placed them in the safe?" asked Thorndyke.

"Mr. Hornby himself, to whom Mr. Reuben delivered up the package on his return from the docks."

"Yes," said Thorndyke, "and what happened next?"

"Well, on the following morning, when the safe was opened, the diamonds had disappeared."

"Had the place been broken into?" asked Thorndyke.

"No. The place was all locked up as usual, and the caretaker, who had made his accustomed rounds, had heard nothing, and the safe was, outwardly, quite undisturbed. It had evidently been opened with keys and locked again after the stones were removed."

"And in whose custody were the keys of the safe?" inquired Thorndyke.

"Mr. Hornby usually kept the keys himself, but, on occasions, when he was absent from the office, he handed them over to one of his nephews—whichever happened to be in charge at the time. But on this occasion the keys did not go out of his custody from the time when he locked up the safe, after depositing the diamonds in it, to the time when it was opened by him on the following morning."

"And was there anything that tended to throw suspicion upon anyone?" asked Thorndyke.

"Why, yes," said Mr. Lawley, with an uncomfortable glance at his client, "unfortunately there was. It seemed that the person who abstracted the diamonds must have cut or scratched his thumb or finger in some way, for there were two drops of blood on the bottom of the safe and one or two bloody smears on a piece of paper, and, in addition, a remarkably clear imprint of a thumb."

"Also in blood?" asked Thorndyke.

"Yes. The thumb had apparently been put down on one of the drops and then, while still wet with blood, had been pressed on the paper in taking hold of it or otherwise."

"Well, and what next?"

"Well," said the lawyer, fidgeting in his chair, "to make a long story short, the thumb-print has been identified as that of Mr. Reuben Hornby."

"Ha!" exclaimed Thorndyke. "The plot thickens with a vengeance. I had better jot down a few notes before you proceed any further."

He took from a drawer a small paper-covered notebook, on the cover of which he wrote "Reuben Hornby," and then, laying the book open on a blotting-pad, which he rested on his knee, he made a few brief notes.

"Now," he said, when he had finished, "with reference to this thumb-print. There is no doubt, I suppose, as to the identification?"

"None whatever," replied Mr. Lawley. "The Scotland Yard people, of course, took possession of the paper, which was handed to the director of the finger-print department for examination and comparison with those in their collection. The report of the experts is that the thumb-print does not agree with any of the thumb-prints of criminals in their possession; that it is a very peculiar one, inasmuch as the ridge-pattern on the bulb of the thumb—which is a remarkably distinct and characteristic one—is crossed by the scar of a deep cut, rendering identification easy and infallible; that it agrees in every respect with the thumb-print of Mr. Reuben Hornby, and is, in fact, his thumb-print beyond any possible doubt."

"Is there any possibility," asked Thorndyke, "that the paper bearing the thumb-print could have been introduced by any person?"

"No," answered the lawyer. "It is quite impossible. The paper on which the mark was found was a leaf from Mr. Hornby's memorandum block. He had penciled on it some particulars relating to the diamonds and laid it on the parcel before he closed up the safe."

"Was anyone present when Mr. Hornby opened the safe in the morning?" asked Thorndyke.

"No, he was alone," answered the lawyer. "He saw at a glance that the diamonds were missing, and then he observed the paper with the thumb-mark on it, on which he closed and locked the safe and sent for the police."

"Is it not rather odd that the thief did not notice the thumb-mark, since it was so distinct and conspicuous?"

"No, I think not," answered Mr. Lawley. "The paper was lying face downward on the bottom of the safe, and it was only when he picked it up and turned it over that Mr. Hornby discovered the thumb-print. Apparently the thief had taken hold of the parcel, with the paper on it, and the paper had afterward dropped off and fallen with the marked surface downward—probably when the parcel was transferred to the other hand."

"You mentioned," said Thorndyke, "that the experts at Scotland Yard have identified this thumb-mark as that of Mr. Reuben Hornby. May I ask how they came to have the opportunity of making the comparison?"

"Ah!" said Mr. Lawley. "Thereby hangs a very curious tale of coincidences. The police, of course, when they found that there was so simple a means of identification as a thumb-mark, wished to take thumb-prints of all the employees in the works; but this Mr. Hornby refused to sanction—rather quixotically, as it seems to me—saying that he would not allow his nephews to be subjected to such an indignity. Now it was, naturally, these nephews in whom the police were chiefly interested, seeing that they alone had had the handling of the keys, and considerable pressure was brought to bear upon Mr. Hornby to have the thumb-prints taken.

"However, he was obdurate, scouting the idea of any suspicion attaching to either of the gentlemen in whom he had reposed such complete confidence and whom he had known all their lives, and so the matter would probably have remained a mystery but for a very odd circumstance.

"You may have seen on the bookstalls and in shop windows an appliance called a 'Thumbograph,' or some such name, consisting of a small book of blank paper for collecting the thumb-prints of one's friends, together with an inking pad."

"I have seen those devices of the Evil One," said Thorndyke, "in fact, I have one, which I bought at Charing Cross Station."

"Well, it seems that some months ago, Mrs. Hornby, the wife of John Hornby, purchased one of these toys—"

"As a matter of fact," interrupted Reuben, "it was my cousin Walter who bought the thing and gave it to her."

"Well, that is not material," said Mr. Lawley (though I observed that Thorndyke made a note of the fact in his book); "at any rate, Mrs. Hornby became possessed of one of these appliances and proceeded to fill it with the thumb-prints of her friends, including her two nephews. Now it happened that the detective in charge of this case called yesterday at Mr. Hornby's house when the latter was absent from home, and took the opportunity of urging her to induce her husband to consent to have the thumb-prints of her nephews taken for the inspection of the experts at Scotland Yard. He pointed out that the procedure was really necessary, not only in the interests of justice but in the interests of the young men themselves, who were regarded with considerable suspicion by the police, which suspicion would be completely removed if it could be shown by actual comparison that the thumb-print could not have been made by either of them. Moreover, it seemed that both the young men had expressed their willingness to have the test applied, but had been forbidden by their uncle. Then Mrs. Hornby had a brilliant idea. She suddenly remembered the 'Thumbograph' and, thinking to set the question at rest once for all, fetched the little book and showed it to the detective. It contained the prints of both thumbs of Mr. Reuben (among others), and as the detective had with him a photograph of the incriminating mark, the comparison was made then and there; and you may imagine Mrs. Hornby's horror and amazement when it was made clear that the print of her nephew Reuben's left thumb corresponded in every particular with the thumb-print that was found in the safe.

"At this juncture Mr. Hornby arrived on the scene and was, of course, overwhelmed with consternation at the turn events had taken. He would have liked to let the matter drop and make good the loss of the diamonds out of his own funds, but as that would have amounted practically to compounding a felony, he had no choice but to prosecute. As a result, a warrant was issued for the arrest of Mr. Reuben, and was executed this morning, and my client was taken forthwith to Bow Street and charged with the robbery."

"Was any evidence taken?" asked Thorndyke.

"No. Only evidence of arrest. The prisoner is remanded for a week, bail having been accepted in two sureties of five hundred pounds each."

Thorndyke was silent for a space after the conclusion of the narrative. Like me, he was evidently not agreeably impressed by the lawyer's manner, which seemed to take his client's guilt for granted, a position indeed not entirely without excuse, having regard to the circumstances of the case.

"What have you advised your client to do?" Thorndyke asked presently.

"I have recommended him to plead guilty and throw himself on the clemency of the court as a first offender. You must see for yourself that there is no defense possible."

The young man flushed crimson, but made no remark.

"But let us be clear how we stand," said Thorndyke. "Are we defending an innocent man or are we endeavoring to obtain a light sentence for a man who admits that he is guilty?"

Mr. Lawley shrugged his shoulders.

"That question can be best answered by our client himself," said he.

Thorndyke directed an inquiring glance at Reuben Hornby, remarking—

"You are not called upon to incriminate yourself in any way, Mr. Hornby, but I must know what position you intend to adopt."

Here I again proposed to withdraw, but Reuben interrupted me.

"There is no need for you to go away, Dr. Jervis," he said. "My position is that I did not commit this robbery and that I know nothing whatever about it or about the thumb-print that was found in the safe. I do not, of course, expect you to believe me in the face of the overwhelming evidence against me, but I do, nevertheless, declare in the most solemn manner before God, that I am absolutely innocent of this crime and have no knowledge of it whatever."

"Then I take it that you did not plead 'guilty'?" said Thorndyke.

"Certainly not; and I never will," replied Reuben hotly.

"You would not be the first innocent man, by very many, who has entered that plea," remarked Mr. Lawley. "It is often the best policy, when the defense is hopelessly weak."

"It is a policy that will not be adopted by me," rejoined Reuben. "I may be, and probably shall be, convicted and sentenced, but I shall continue to maintain my innocence, whatever happens. Do you think," he added, turning to Thorndyke, "that you can undertake my defense on that assumption?"

"It is the only assumption on which I should agree to undertake the case," replied Thorndyke.

"And—if I may ask the question—" pursued Reuben anxiously, "do you find it possible to conceive that I may really be innocent?"

"Certainly I do," Thorndyke replied, on which I observed Mr. Lawley's eyebrows rise perceptibly. "I am a man of facts, not an advocate, and if I found it impossible to entertain the hypothesis of your innocence, I should not be willing to expend time and energy in searching for evidence to prove it. Nevertheless," he continued, seeing the light of hope break out on the face of the unfortunate young man, "I must impress upon you that the case presents enormous difficulties and that we must be prepared to find them insuperable in spite of all our efforts."

"I expect nothing but a conviction," replied Reuben in a calm and resolute voice, "and can face it like a man if only you do not take my guilt for granted, but give me a chance, no matter how small, of making a defense."

"Everything shall be done that I am capable of doing," said Thorndyke; "that I can promise you. The long odds against us are themselves a spur to endeavor, as far as I am concerned. And now, let me ask you, have you any cuts or scratches on your fingers?"

Reuben Hornby held out both his hands for my colleague's inspection, and I noticed that they were powerful and shapely, like the hands of a skilled craftsman, though faultlessly kept. Thorndyke set on the table a large condenser such as is used for microscopic work, and taking his client's hand, brought the bright spot of light to bear on each finger in succession, examining their tips and the parts around the nails with the aid of a pocket lens.

"A fine, capable hand, this," said he, regarding the member approvingly, as he finished his examination, "but I don't perceive any trace of a scar on either the right or left. Will you go over them, Jervis? The robbery took place a fortnight ago, so there has been time for a small cut or scratch to heal and disappear entirely. Still, the matter is worth noting."

He handed me the lens, and I scrutinized every part of each hand without being able to detect the faintest trace of any recent wound.

"There is one other matter that must be attended to before you go," said Thorndyke, pressing the electric bell-push by his chair. "I will take one or two prints of the left thumb for my own information."

In response to the summons, Polton made his appearance from some lair unknown to me, but presumably the laboratory, and, having received his instructions, retired, and presently returned carrying a box, which he laid on the table. From this receptacle Thorndyke drew forth a bright copper plate mounted on a slab of hard wood, a small printer's roller, a tube of finger-print ink, and a number of cards with very white and rather glazed surfaces.

"Now, Mr. Hornby," said he, "your hands, I see, are beyond criticism as to cleanliness, but we will, nevertheless, give the thumb a final polish."

Accordingly he proceeded to brush the bulb of the thumb with a well-soaked badger-hair nail-brush, and, having rinsed it in water, dried it with a silk handkerchief, and gave it a final rub on a piece of chamois leather. The thumb having been thus prepared, he squeezed out a drop of the thick ink on to the copper plate and spread it out with the roller, testing the condition of the film from time to time by touching the plate with the tip of his finger and taking an impression on one of the cards.

When the ink had been rolled out to the requisite thinness, he took Reuben's hand and pressed the thumb lightly but firmly on to the inked plate; then, transferring the thumb to one of the cards, which he directed me to hold steady on the table, he repeated the pressure, when there was left on the card a beautifully sharp and clear impression of the bulb of the thumb, the tiny papillary ridges being shown with microscopic distinctness, and even the mouths of the sweat glands, which appeared as rows of little white dots on the black lines of the ridges. This maneuver was repeated a dozen times on two of the cards, each of which thus received six impressions. Thorndyke then took one or two rolled prints, *i.e.* prints produced by rolling the thumb first on the inked slab and then on the card, by which means a much larger portion of the surface of the thumb was displayed in a single print.

"And now," said Thorndyke, "that we may be furnished with all the necessary means of comparison, we will take an impression in blood."

The thumb was accordingly cleansed and dried afresh, when Thorndyke, having pricked his own thumb with a needle, squeezed out a good-sized drop of blood on to a card.

"There," said he, with a smile, as he spread the drop out with the needle into a little shallow pool, "it is not every lawyer who is willing to shed his blood in the interests of his client."

He proceeded to make a dozen prints as before on two cards, writing a number with his pencil opposite each print as he made it.

"We are now," said he, as he finally cleansed his client's thumb, "furnished with the material for a preliminary investigation, and if you will now give me your address, Mr. Hornby, we may consider our business concluded for the present. I must apologize to you, Mr. Lawley, for having detained you so long with these experiments."

The lawyer had, in fact, been viewing the proceedings with hardly concealed impatience, and he now rose with evident relief that they were at an end.

"I have been highly interested," he said mendaciously, "though I confess I do not quite fathom your intentions. And, by the way, I should like to have a few words with you on another matter, if Mr. Reuben would not mind waiting for me in the square just a few minutes."

"Not at all," said Reuben, who was, I perceived, in no way deceived by the lawyer's pretense. "Don't hurry on my account; my time is my own—at present." He held out his hand to Thorndyke, who grasped it cordially.

"Good-bye, Mr. Hornby," said the latter. "Do not be unreasonably sanguine, but at the same time, do not lose heart. Keep your wits about you and let me know at once if anything occurs to you that may have a bearing on the case."

The young man then took his leave, and as the door closed after him, Mr. Lawley turned toward Thorndyke.

"I thought I had better have a word with you alone," he said, "just to hear what line you propose to take up, for I confess that your attitude has puzzled me completely."

"What line would you propose?" asked Thorndyke.

"Well," said the lawyer, with a shrug of his shoulders, "the position seems to be this: our young friend has stolen a parcel of diamonds and has been found out; at least, that is how the matter presents itself to me."

"That is not how it presents itself to me," said Thorndyke drily. "He may have taken the diamonds or he may not. I have no means of judging until I have sifted the evidence and acquired a few more facts. This I hope to do in the course of the next day or two, and I suggest that we postpone the consideration of our plan of campaign until I have seen what line of defense it is possible to adopt."

"As you will," replied the lawyer, taking up his hat, "but I am afraid you are encouraging the young rogue to entertain hopes that will only make his fall the harder—to say nothing of our own position. We don't want to make ourselves ridiculous in court, you know."

"I don't, certainly," agreed Thorndyke. "However, I will look into the matter and communicate with you in the course of a day or two."

He stood holding the door open as the lawyer descended the stairs, and when the footsteps at length died away, he closed it sharply and turned to me with an air of annoyance.

"The 'young rogue,'" he remarked, "does not appear to me to have been very happy in his choice of a solicitor. By the way, Jervis, I understand you are out of employment just now?"

"That is so," I answered.

"Would you care to help me—as a matter of business, of course—to work up this case? I have a lot of other work on hand, and your assistance would be of great value to me."

I said, with great truth, that I should be delighted.

"Then," said Thorndyke, "come round to breakfast tomorrow and we will settle the terms, and you can commence your duties at once. And now let us light our pipes and finish our yarns as though agitated clients and thick-headed solicitors had no existence."

CHAPTER THREE

A LADY IN THE CASE

When I arrived at Thorndyke's chambers on the following morning, I found my friend already hard at work. Breakfast was laid at one end of the table, while at the other stood a microscope of the pattern used for examining plate-cultures of micro-organisms, on the wide stage of which was one of the cards bearing six thumb-prints in blood. A condenser threw a bright spot of light on the card, which Thorndyke had been examining when I knocked, as I gathered from the position of the chair, which he now pushed back against the wall.

"I see you have commenced work on our problem," I remarked as, in response to a double ring of the electric bell, Polton entered with the materials for our repast.

"Yes," answered Thorndyke. "I have opened the campaign, supported, as usual, by my trusty chief-of-staff; eh! Polton?"

The little man, whose intellectual, refined countenance and dignified bearing seemed oddly out of character with the tea tray that he carried, smiled proudly, and, with a glance of affectionate admiration at my friend, replied—

"Yes, sir. We haven't been letting the grass grow under our feet. There's a beautiful negative washing upstairs and a bromide enlargement, too, which will be mounted and dried by the time you have finished your breakfast."

"A wonderful man that, Jervis," my friend observed as his assistant retired. "Looks like a rural dean or a chancery judge, and was obviously intended by Nature to be a professor of physics. As an actual fact he was first a watchmaker, then a maker of optical instruments, and now he is mechanical factotum to a medical jurist. He is my right hand, is Polton; takes an idea before you have time to utter it—but you will make his more intimate acquaintance by-and-by."

"Where did you pick him up?" I asked.

"He was an in-patient at the hospital when I first met him, miserably ill and broken, a victim of poverty and undeserved misfortune. I gave him one or two little jobs, and when I found what class of man he was, I took him permanently into my service. He is perfectly devoted to me, and his gratitude is as boundless as it is uncalled for."

"What are the photographs he was referring to?" I asked.

"He is making an enlarged *facsimile* of one of the thumb-prints on bromide paper and a negative of the same size in case we want the print repeated."

"You evidently have some expectation of being able to help poor Hornby," said I, "though I cannot imagine how you propose to go to work. To me his case seems as hopeless a one as it is possible to conceive. One doesn't like to condemn him, but yet his innocence seems almost unthinkable."

"It does certainly look like a hopeless case," Thorndyke agreed, "and I see no way out of it at present. But I make it a rule, in all cases, to proceed on the strictly classical lines of inductive inquiry—collect facts, make hypotheses, test them, and seek for verification. And I always endeavor to keep a perfectly open mind.

"Now, in the present case, assuming, as we must, that the robbery has actually taken place, there are four conceivable hypotheses: One, that the robbery was committed by Reuben Hornby; two, that it was committed by Walter Hornby; three, that it was committed by John Hornby; or four, that it was committed by some other person or persons.

"The last hypothesis I propose to disregard for the present and confine myself to the examination of the other three."

"You don't think it possible that Mr. Hornby could have stolen the diamonds out of his own safe?" I exclaimed.

"I incline at present to no one theory of the matter," replied Thorndyke. "I merely state the hypotheses. John Hornby had access to the diamonds, therefore it is possible that he stole them."

"But surely he was responsible to the owners."

"Not in the absence of gross negligence, which the owners would have difficulty in proving. You see, he was what is called a gratuitous bailee, and in such a case no responsibility for loss lies with the bailee unless there has been gross negligence."

"But the thumb-mark, my dear fellow!" I exclaimed. "How can you possibly get over that?"

"I don't know that I can," answered Thorndyke calmly; "but I see you are taking the same view as the police, who persist in regarding a finger-print as a kind of magical touchstone, a final proof, beyond which inquiry need not go. Now, this is an entire mistake. A finger-print is merely a fact—a very important and significant one,

I admit—but still a fact, which, like any other fact, requires to be weighed and measured with reference to its evidential value."

"And what do you propose to do first?"

"I shall first satisfy myself that the suspected thumb-print is identical in character with that of Reuben Hornby—of which, however, I have very little doubt, for the finger-print experts may fairly be trusted in their own speciality."

"And then?"

"I shall collect fresh facts, in which I look to you for assistance, and, if we have finished breakfast, I may as well induct you into your new duties."

He rose and rang the bell, and then, fetching from the office four small, paper-covered notebooks, laid them before me on the table.

"One of these books," said he, "we will devote to data concerning Reuben Hornby. You will find out anything you can—anything, mind, no matter how trivial or apparently irrelevant—in any way connected with him and enter it in this book." He wrote on the cover "Reuben Hornby" and passed the book to me. "In this second book you will, in like manner, enter anything that you can learn about Walter Hornby, and, in the third book, data concerning John Hornby. As to the fourth book, you will keep that for stray facts connected with the case but not coming under either of the other headings. And now let us look at the product of Polton's industry."

He took from his assistant's hand a photograph ten inches long by eight broad, done on glazed bromide paper and mounted flatly on stiff card. It showed a greatly magnified *facsimile* of one of the thumb-prints, in which all the minute details, such as the orifices of the sweat glands and trifling irregularities in the ridges, which, in the original, could be seen only with the aid of a lens, were plainly visible to the naked eye. Moreover, the entire print was covered by a network of fine black lines, by which it was divided into a multitude of small squares, each square being distinguished by a number.

"Excellent, Polton," said Thorndyke approvingly; "a most admirable enlargement. You see, Jervis, we have photographed the thumbprint in contact with a numbered micrometer divided into square twelfths of an inch. The magnification is eight diameters, so that the squares are here each two-thirds of an inch in diameter. I have a number of these micrometers of different scales, and I find them invaluable in examining checks, doubtful signatures, and such like. I see you have packed up the camera and the microscope, Polton; have you put in the micrometer?"

"Yes, sir," replied Polton, "and the six-inch objective and the low-power eyepiece. Everything is in the case; and I have put 'special rapid' plates into the dark-slides in case the light should be bad."

"Then we will go forth and beard the Scotland Yard lions in their den," said Thorndyke, putting on his hat and gloves.

"But surely," said I, "you are not going to drag that great microscope to Scotland Yard, when you only want eight diameters. Haven't you a dissecting microscope or some other portable instrument?"

"We have a most delightful instrument of the dissecting type, of Polton's own make—he shall show it to you. But I may have need of a more powerful instrument—and here let me give you a word of warning: whatever you may see me do, make no comments before the officials. We are seeking information, not giving it, you understand."

At this moment the little brass knocker on the inner door—the outer oak being open—uttered a timid and apologetic *rat-tat.*

"Who the deuce can that be?" muttered Thorndyke, replacing the microscope on the table. He strode across to the door and opened it somewhat brusquely, but immediately whisked his hat off, and I then perceived a lady standing on the threshold.

"Dr. Thorndyke?" she inquired, and as my colleague bowed, she continued, "I ought to have written to ask for an appointment but the matter is rather urgent—it concerns Mr. Reuben Hornby, and I only learned from him this morning that he had consulted you."

"Pray come in," said Thorndyke. "Dr. Jervis and I were just setting out for Scotland Yard on this very business. Let me present you to my colleague, who is working up the case with me."

Our visitor, a tall, handsome girl of twenty or thereabouts, returned my bow and remarked with perfect self-possession, "My name is Gibson—Miss Juliet Gibson. My business is of a very simple character and need not detain you many minutes."

She seated herself in the chair that Thorndyke placed for her, and continued in a brisk and businesslike manner—

"I must tell you who I am in order to explain my visit to you. For the last six years, I have lived with Mr. and Mrs. Hornby, although I am no relation to them. I first came to the house as a sort of companion to Mrs. Hornby, though, as I was only fifteen at the time, I need hardly say that my duties were not very onerous; in fact, I think Mrs. Hornby took me because I was an orphan without the proper means of getting a livelihood, and she had no children of her own.

"Three years ago I came into a little fortune which rendered me independent; but I had been so happy with my kind friends that I asked to be allowed to remain with them, and there I have been ever since in the position of an adopted daughter. Naturally, I have seen a great deal of their nephews, who spend a good part of their time at the house, and I need not tell you that the horrible charge against Reuben has fallen upon us like a thunderbolt. Now, what I have come to say to you is this: I do not believe that Reuben stole those diamonds. It is entirely out of character with all my previous experience of him. I am convinced that he is innocent, and I am prepared to back my opinion."

"In what way?" asked Thorndyke.

"By supplying the sinews of war," replied Miss Gibson. "I understand that legal advice and assistance involves considerable expense."

"I am afraid you are quite correctly informed," said Thorndyke.

"Well, Reuben's pecuniary resources are, I am sure, quite small, so it is necessary for his friends to support him, and I want you to promise me that nothing shall be left undone that might help to prove his innocence if I make myself responsible for any costs that he is unable to meet. I should prefer, of course, not to appear in the matter, if it could be avoided."

"Your friendship is of an eminently practical kind, Miss Gibson," said my colleague, with a smile. "As a matter of fact, the costs are no affair of mine. If the occasion arose for the exercise of your generosity, you would have to approach Mr. Reuben's solicitor through the medium of your guardian, Mr. Hornby, and with the consent of the accused. But I do not suppose the occasion will arise, although I am very glad you called, as you may be able to give us valuable assistance in other ways. For example, you might answer one or two apparently impertinent questions."

"I should not consider any question impertinent that you considered necessary to ask," our visitor replied.

"Then," said Thorndyke, "I will venture to inquire if any special relations exist between you and Mr. Reuben."

"You look for the inevitable motive in a woman," said Miss Gibson, laughing and flushing a little. "No, there have been no tender passages between Reuben and me. We are merely old and intimate friends; in fact, there is what I may call a tendency in another direction—Walter Hornby."

"Do you mean that you are engaged to Mr. Walter?"

"Oh, no," she replied; "but he has asked me to marry him—he has asked me, in fact, more than once; and I really believe that he has a sincere attachment to me."

She made this latter statement with an odd air, as though the thing asserted were curious and rather incredible, and the tone was evidently noticed by Thorndyke as well as me for he rejoined—

"Of course he has. Why not?"

"Well, you see," replied Miss Gibson, "I have some six hundred a year of my own and should not be considered a bad match for a young man like Walter, who has neither property nor expectations, and one naturally takes that into account. But still, as I have said, I believe he is quite sincere in his professions and not merely attracted by my money."

"I do not find your opinion at all incredible," said Thorndyke, with a smile, "even if Mr. Walter were quite a mercenary young man—which, I take it, he is not."

Miss Gibson flushed very prettily as she replied—

"Oh, pray do not trouble to pay me compliments; I assure you I am by no means insensible of my merits. But with regard to Walter Hornby, I should be sorry to apply the term 'mercenary' to him, and yet—well, I have never met a young man who showed a stronger appreciation of the value of money. He means to succeed in life, and I have no doubt he will."

"And do I understand that you refused him?"

"Yes. My feelings toward him are quite friendly, but not of such a nature as to allow me to contemplate marrying him."

"And now, to return for a moment to Mr. Reuben. You have known him for some years?"

"I have known him intimately for six years," replied Miss Gibson.

"And what sort of character do you give him?"

"Speaking from my own observation of him," she replied, "I can say that I have never known him to tell an untruth or do a dishonorable deed. As to theft, it is merely ridiculous. His habits have always been inexpensive and frugal, he is unambitious to a fault, and in respect to the 'main chance' his indifference is as conspicuous as Walter's keenness. He is a generous man, too, although careful and industrious."

"Thank you, Miss Gibson," said Thorndyke. "We shall apply to you for further information as the case progresses. I am sure that you will help us if you can, and that you can help us if you will, with your clear head and your admirable frankness. If you will leave us your card, Dr. Jervis and I will keep you informed of our prospects and ask for your assistance whenever we need it."

After our fair visitor had departed, Thorndyke stood for a minute or more gazing dreamily into the fire. Then, with a quick glance at his watch, he resumed his hat and, catching up the microscope, handed the camera case to me and made for the door.

"How the time goes!" he exclaimed, as we descended the stairs; "but it hasn't been wasted, Jervis, hey?"

"No, I suppose not," I answered tentatively.

"You suppose not!" he replied. "Why here is as pretty a little problem as you could desire—what would be called in the jargon of the novels, a psychological problem—and it is your business to work it out, too."

"You mean as to Miss Gibson's relations with these two young men?"

Thorndyke nodded.

"Is it any concern of ours?" I asked.

"Certainly it is," he replied. "Everything is a concern of ours at this preliminary stage. We are groping about for a clue and must let nothing pass unscrutinized."

"Well, then, to begin with, she is not wildly infatuated with Walter Hornby, I should say."

"No," agreed Thorndyke, laughing softly, "we may take it that the canny Walter has not inspired a grand passion."

"Then," I resumed, "if I were a suitor for Miss Gibson's hand, I think I would sooner stand in Reuben's shoes than in Walter's."

"There again I am with you," said Thorndyke. "Go on."

"Well," I continued, "our fair visitor conveyed to me the impression that her evident admiration of Reuben's character was tempered by something that she had heard from a third party. That expression of hers, 'speaking from my own observation,' seemed to imply that her observations of him were not in entire agreement with somebody else's."

"Good man!" exclaimed Thorndyke, slapping me on the back, to the undissembled surprise of a policeman whom we were passing; "that is what I had hoped for in you—the capacity to perceive the essential underneath the obvious. Yes; somebody has been saying something about our client, and the thing that we have to find out is, what is it that has been said and who has been saying it. We shall have to make a pretext for another interview with Miss Gibson."

"By the way, why didn't you ask her what she meant?" I asked foolishly.

Thorndyke grinned in my face. "Why didn't you?" he retorted.

"No," I rejoined, "I suppose it is not politic to appear too discerning. Let me carry the microscope for a time; it is making your arm ache, I see."

"Thanks," said he, handing the case to me and rubbing his fingers, "it is rather ponderous."

"I can't make out what you want with this great instrument," I said. "A common pocket lens would do all that you require. Besides, a six-inch objective will not magnify more than two or three diameters."

"Two, with the draw-tube closed," replied Thorndyke, "and the low-power eyepiece brings it up to four. Polton made them both for me for examining checks, banknotes and other large objects. But you will understand when you see me use the instrument, and remember, you are to make no comments."

We had by this time arrived at the entrance to Scotland Yard, and were passing up the narrow thoroughfare, when we encountered a uniformed official who halted and saluted my colleague.

"Ah, I thought we should see you here before long, doctor," said he genially. "I heard this morning that you have this thumb-print case in hand."

"Yes," replied Thorndyke; "I am going to see what can be done for the defense."

"Well," said the officer as he ushered us into the building, "you've given us a good many surprises, but you'll give us a bigger one if you can make anything of this. It's a foregone conclusion, I should say."

"My dear fellow," said Thorndyke, "there is no such thing. You mean that there is a *prima facie* case against the accused."

"Put it that way if you like," replied the officer, with a sly smile, "but I think you will find this about the hardest nut you ever tried your teeth on—and they're pretty strong teeth, too, I'll say that. You had better come into Mr. Singleton's office." And he conducted us along a corridor and into a large, barely furnished room, where we found a sedate-looking gentleman seated at a large writing table.

"How-d'ye-do, doctor?" said the latter, rising and holding out his hand. "I can guess what you've come for. Want to see that thumb-print, eh?"

"Quite right," answered Thorndyke, and then, having introduced me, he continued: "We were partners in the last game, but we are on opposite sides of the board this time."

"Yes," agreed Mr. Singleton, "and we are going to give you check-mate."

He unlocked a drawer and drew forth a small portfolio, from which he extracted a piece of paper that he laid on the table. It appeared to be a sheet torn from a perforated memorandum block, and bore the penciled inscription: "Handed in by Reuben at 7.3 p.m., 9.3.01. J. H." At one end was a dark, glossy bloodstain, made by the falling of a good-sized drop, and this was smeared slightly, apparently by a finger or thumb having been pressed on it. Near to it were two or three smaller smears and a remarkably distinct and clean print of a thumb.

Thorndyke gazed intently at the paper for a minute or two, scrutinizing the thumb-print and the smears in turn, but making no remark, while Mr. Singleton watched his impassive face with expectant curiosity.

"Not much difficulty in identifying that mark," the official at length observed.

"No," agreed Thorndyke; "it is an excellent impression and a very distinctive pattern, even without the scar."

"Yes," rejoined Mr. Singleton; "the scar makes it absolutely conclusive. You have a print with you, I suppose?"

"Yes," replied Thorndyke, and he drew from a wide flap-pocket the enlarged photograph, at the sight of which Mr. Singleton's face broadened into a smile.

"You don't want to put on spectacles to look at that," he remarked; "not that you gain anything by so much enlargement; three diameters is ample for studying the ridge-patterns. I see you have divided it up into numbered squares—not a bad plan; but ours—or rather Galton's, for we borrowed the method from him—is better for this purpose."

He drew from the portfolio a half-plate photograph of the thumb-print, which appeared magnified to about four inches in length.

The print was marked by a number of figures written minutely with a fine-pointed pen, each figure being placed on an "island," a loop, a bifurcation, or some other striking and characteristic portion of the ridge-pattern.

"This system of marking with reference numbers," said Mr. Singleton, "is better than your method of squares, because the numbers are only placed at points which are important for comparison, whereas your squares or the intersections of the lines fall arbitrarily on important or unimportant points according to chance. Besides, we can't let you mark our original, you know, though, of course, we can give you a photograph, which will do as well."

"I was going to ask you to let me take a photograph presently," said Thorndyke.

"Certainly," replied Mr. Singleton, "if you would rather have one of your own taking. I know you don't care to take anything on trust. And now I must get on with my work, if you will excuse me. Inspector Johnson will give you any assistance you may require."

"And see that I don't pocket the original," added Thorndyke, with a smile at the inspector who had shown us in.

"Oh, I'll see to that," said the latter, grinning; and, as Mr. Singleton returned to his table, Thorndyke unlocked the microscope case and drew forth the instrument.

"What, are you going to put it under the microscope?" exclaimed Mr. Singleton, looking round with a broad smile.

"Must do something for my fee, you know," replied Thorndyke, as he set up the microscope and screwed on two extra objectives to the triple nosepiece.

"You observe that there is no deception," he added to the inspector, as he took the paper from Mr. Singleton's table and placed it between two slips of glass.

"I'm watching you, sir," replied the officer, with a chuckle; and he did watch, with close attention and great interest, while Thorndyke laid the glass slips on the microscope stage and proceeded to focus.

I also watched, and was a good deal exercised in my mind by my colleague's proceedings. After a preliminary glance with the six-inch glass, he swung round the nosepiece to the half-inch objective and slipped in a more powerful eyepiece, and with this power he examined the bloodstains carefully, and then moved the thumb-print into the field of vision. After looking at this for some time with deep attention, he drew from the case a tiny spirit lamp, which was evidently filled with an alcoholic solution of some sodium salt, for when he lit it, I recognized the characteristic yellow sodium flame. Then he replaced one of the objectives by a spectroscopic attachment, and having placed the little lamp close to the microscope mirror, adjusted the spectroscope. Evidently my friend was fixing the position of the "D" line (or sodium line) in the spectrum.

Having completed the adjustments, he now examined afresh the blood smears and the thumb-print, both by transmitted and reflected light, and I observed him hurriedly draw one or two diagrams in his notebook. Then he replaced the spectroscope and lamp in the case and brought forth the micrometer—a slip of rather thin glass about three inches by one and a half—which he laid over the thumb-print in the place of the upper plate of glass.

Having secured it in position by the clips, he moved it about, comparing its appearance with that of the lines on the large photograph, which he held in his hand. After a considerable amount of adjustment and readjustment, he appeared to be satisfied, for he remarked to me—

"I think I have got the lines in the same position as they are on our print, so, with Inspector Johnson's assistance, we will take a photograph which we can examine at our leisure."

He extracted the camera—a quarter-plate instrument—from its case and opened it. Then, having swung the microscope on its stand into a horizontal position, he produced from the camera case a slab of mahogany with three brass feet, on which he placed the camera, and which brought the latter to a level with the eyepiece of the microscope.

The front of the camera was fitted with a short sleeve of thin black leather, and into this the eyepiece end of the microscope was now passed, the sleeve being secured round the barrel of the microscope by a stout India rubber band, thus producing a completely light-tight connection.

Everything was now ready for taking the photograph. The light from the window having been concentrated on the thumb-print by means of a condenser, Thorndyke proceeded to focus the image on the ground-glass screen with extreme care and then, slipping a small leather cap over the objective, introduced the dark slide and drew out the shutter.

"I will ask you to sit down and remain quite still while I make the exposure," he said to me and the inspector. "A very little vibration is enough to destroy the sharpness of the image."

We seated ourselves accordingly, and Thorndyke then removed the cap, standing motionless, watch in hand, while he exposed the first plate.

"We may as well take a second, in case this should not turn out quite perfect," he said, as he replaced the cap and closed the shutter.

He reversed the dark slide and made another exposure in the same way, and then, having removed the micrometer and replaced it by a slip of plain glass, he made two more exposures.

"There are two plates left," he remarked, as he drew out the second dark slide. "I think I will take a record of the bloodstain on them."

He accordingly made two more exposures—one of the larger bloodstain and one of the smaller smears.

"There," said he, with an air of satisfaction, as he proceeded to pack up what the inspector described as his "box of tricks." "I think we have all the data that we can squeeze out of Scotland Yard, and I am very much obliged to you, Mr. Singleton, for giving so many facilities to your natural enemy, the counsel for the defense."

"Not our natural enemies, doctor," protested Mr. Singleton. "We work for a conviction, of course, but we don't throw obstacles in the way of the defense. You know that perfectly well."

"Of course I do, my dear sir," replied Thorndyke, shaking the official by the hand. "Haven't I benefited by your help a score of times? But I am greatly obliged all the same. Good-bye."

"Good-bye, doctor. I wish you luck, though I fear you will find it 'no go' this time."

"We shall see," replied Thorndyke, and with a friendly wave of the hand to the inspector, he caught up the two cases and led the way out of the building.

CHAPTER FOUR

CONFIDENCES

During our walk home, my friend was unusually thoughtful and silent, and his face bore a look of concentration under which I thought I could detect, in spite of his habitually impassive expression, a certain suppressed excitement of a not entirely unpleasurable kind. I forbore, however, from making any remarks or asking questions, not only because I saw that he was preoccupied, but also because, from my knowledge of the man, I judged that he would consider it his duty to keep his own counsel and to make no unnecessary confidences even to me.

On our arrival at his chambers, he immediately handed over the camera to Polton with a few curt directions as to the development of the plates, and lunch being already prepared, we sat down at the table without delay.

We had proceeded with our meal in silence for some time when Thorndyke suddenly laid down his knife and fork and looked into my face with a smile of quiet amusement.

"It has just been borne in upon me, Jervis," said he, "that you are the most companionable fellow in the world. You have the heaven-sent gift of silence."

"If silence is the test of companionability," I answered, with a grin, "I think I can pay you a similar compliment in even more emphatic terms."

He laughed cheerfully and rejoined—

"You are pleased to be sarcastic, I observe; but I maintain my position. The capacity to preserve an opportune silence is the rarest and most precious of social accomplishments. Now, most men would have plied me with questions and babbled comments on my proceedings at Scotland Yard, whereas you have allowed me to sort out, without interruption, a mass of evidence while it is still fresh and impressive, to docket each item and stow it away in the pigeonholes of my brain. By the way, I have made a ridiculous oversight."

"What is that?" I asked.

"The 'Thumbograph.' I never ascertained whether the police have it or whether it is still in the possession of Mrs. Hornby."

"Does it matter?" I inquired.

"Not much; only I must see it. And perhaps it will furnish an excellent pretext for you to call on Miss Gibson. As I am busy at the hospital this afternoon and Polton has his hands full, it would be a good plan for you to drop in at Endsley Gardens—that is the address, I think—and if you can see Miss Gibson, try to get a confidential chat with her, and extend your knowledge of the manners and customs of the three Messieurs Hornby. Put on your best bedside manner and keep your weather eye lifting. Find out everything you can as to the characters and habits of those three gentlemen, regardless of all scruples of delicacy. Everything is of importance to us, even to the names of their tailors."

"And with regard to the 'Thumbograph'?"

"Find out who has it, and if it is still in Mrs. Hornby's possession, get her to lend it to us or—what might, perhaps, be better—get her permission to take a photograph of it."

"It shall be done according to your word," said I. "I will furbish up my exterior, and this very afternoon make my first appearance in the character of Paul Pry."

About an hour later, I found myself upon the doorstep of Mr. Hornby's house in Endsley Gardens, listening to the jangling of the bell that I had just set in motion.

"Miss Gibson, sir?" repeated the parlormaid in response to my question. "She *was* going out, but I am not sure whether she has gone yet. If you will step in, I will go and see."

I followed her into the drawing room and, threading my way amongst the litter of small tables and miscellaneous furniture by which ladies nowadays convert their special domain into the semblance of a broker's shop, let go my anchor in the vicinity of the fireplace to await the parlormaid's report.

I had not long to wait, for in less than a minute Miss Gibson herself entered the room. She wore her hat and gloves, and I congratulated myself on my timely arrival.

"I didn't expect to see you again so soon, Dr. Jervis," she said, holding out her hand with a frank and friendly manner, "but you are very welcome all the same. You have come to tell me something?"

"On the contrary," I replied, "I have come to ask you something."

"Well, that is better than nothing," she said, with a shade of disappointment. "Won't you sit down?"

I seated myself with caution on a dwarf chair of scrofulous aspect, and opened my business without preamble.

"Do you remember a thing called a 'Thumbograph'?"

"Indeed I do," she replied with energy. "It was the cause of all this trouble."

"Do you know if the police took possession of it?"

"The detective took it to Scotland Yard that the finger-print experts might examine it and compare the two thumb-prints; and they wanted to keep it, but Mrs. Hornby was so distressed at the idea of its being used in evidence that they let her have it back. You see, they really had no further need of it, as they could take a print for themselves when they had Reuben in custody; in fact, he volunteered to have a print taken at once, as soon as he was arrested, and that was done."

"So the 'Thumbograph' is now in Mrs. Hornby's possession?"

"Yes, unless she has destroyed it. She spoke of doing so."

"I hope she has not," said I, in some alarm, "for Dr. Thorndyke is extremely anxious, for some reason, to examine it."

"Well, she will be down in a few minutes, and then we shall know. I told her you were here. Have you any idea what Dr. Thorndyke's reason is for wanting to see it?"

"None whatever," I replied. "Dr. Thorndyke is as close as an oyster. He treats me as he treats everyone else—he listens attentively, observes closely, and says nothing."

"It doesn't sound very agreeable," mused Miss Gibson; "and yet he seemed very nice and sympathetic."

"He *is* very nice and sympathetic," I retorted with some emphasis, "but he doesn't make himself agreeable by divulging his clients' secrets."

"I suppose not, and I regard myself as very effectively snubbed," said she, smiling, but evidently somewhat piqued by my not very tactful observation.

I was hastening to repair my error with apologies and self-accusations, when the door opened and an elderly lady entered the room. She was somewhat stout, amiable, and placid of mien, and impressed me (to be entirely truthful) as looking rather foolish.

"Here is Mrs. Hornby," said Miss Gibson, presenting me to her hostess; and she continued, "Dr. Jervis has come to ask about the 'Thumbograph.' You haven't destroyed it, I hope?"

"No, my dear," replied Mrs. Hornby. "I have it in my little bureau. What did Dr. Jervis wish to know about it?"

Seeing that she was terrified lest some new and dreadful surprise should be sprung upon her, I hastened to reassure her.

"My colleague, Dr. Thorndyke, is anxious to examine it. He is directing your nephew's defense, you know."

"Yes, yes," said Mrs. Hornby. "Juliet told me about him. She says he is a dear. Do you agree with her?"

Here I caught Miss Gibson's eye, in which was a mischievous twinkle, and noted a little deeper pink in her cheeks.

"Well," I answered dubiously, "I have never considered my colleague in the capacity of a dear, but I have a very high opinion of him in every respect."

"That, no doubt, is the masculine equivalent," said Miss Gibson, recovering from the momentary embarrassment that Mrs. Hornby's artless repetition of her phrase had produced. "I think the feminine expression is more epigrammatic and comprehensive. But to return to the object of Dr. Jervis's visit. Would you let him have the 'Thumbograph,' aunt, to show to Dr. Thorndyke?"

"Oh, my dear Juliet," replied Mrs. Hornby, "I would do anything—anything—to help our poor boy. I will never believe that he could be guilty of theft—common, vulgar theft. There has been some dreadful mistake—I am convinced there has—I told the detectives so.

I assured them that Reuben could not have committed the robbery, and that they were totally mistaken in supposing him to be capable of such an action. But they would not listen to me, although I have known him since he was a little child and ought to be able to judge, if anyone is. Diamonds, too! Now, I ask you, what could Reuben want with diamonds? And they were not even cut."

Here Mrs. Hornby drew forth a lace-edged handkerchief and mopped her eyes.

"I am sure Dr. Thorndyke will be very much interested to see this little book of yours," said I, with a view to stemming the tide of her reflections.

"Oh, the 'Thumbograph,'" she replied. "Yes, I will let him have it with the greatest pleasure. I am so glad he wishes to see it; it makes one feel hopeful to know that he is taking so much interest in the case. Would you believe it, Dr. Jervis, those detective people actually wanted to keep it to bring up in evidence against the poor boy. My 'Thumbograph,' mind you. But I put my foot down there and they had to return it. I was resolved that they should not receive any assistance from me in their efforts to involve my nephew in this horrible affair."

"Then, perhaps," said Miss Gibson, "you might give Dr. Jervis the 'Thumbograph,' and he can hand it to Dr. Thorndyke."

"Of course I will," said Mrs. Hornby; "instantly; and you need not return it, Dr. Jervis. When you have finished with it, fling it into the fire. I wish never to see it again."

But I had been considering the matter, and had come to the conclusion that it would be highly indiscreet to take the book out of Mrs. Hornby's custody, and this I now proceeded to explain.

"I have no idea," I said, "for what purpose Dr. Thorndyke wishes to examine the 'Thumbograph,' but it occurs to me that he may desire to put it in evidence, in which case it would be better that it should not go out of your possession for the present. He merely commissioned me to ask for your permission to take a photograph of it."

"Oh, if he wants a photograph," said Mrs. Hornby, "I could get one done for him without any difficulty. My nephew Walter would take one for us, I am sure, if I asked him. He is so clever, you know—is he not, Juliet, dear?"

"Yes, aunt," replied Miss Gibson quickly, "but I expect Dr. Thorndyke would rather take the photograph himself."

"I am sure he would," I agreed. "In fact, a photograph taken by another person would not be of much use to him."

"Ah," said Mrs. Hornby in a slightly injured tone, "you think Walter is just an ordinary amateur; but if I were to show you some of the photographs he has taken, you would really be surprised. He is remarkably clever, I assure you."

"Would you like us to bring the book to Dr. Thorndyke's chambers?" asked Miss Gibson. "That would save time and trouble."

"It is excessively good of you—" I began.

"Not at all. When shall we bring it? Would you like to have it this evening?"

"We should very much," I replied. "My colleague could then examine it and decide what is to be done with it. But it is giving you so much trouble."

"It is nothing of the kind," said Miss Gibson. "You would not mind coming with me this evening, would you, aunt?"

"Certainly not, my dear," replied Mrs. Hornby, and she was about to enlarge on the subject when Miss Gibson rose and, looking at her watch, declared that she must start on her errand at once. I also rose to make my adieux, and she then remarked—

"If you are walking in the same direction as I am, Dr. Jervis, we might arrange the time of our proposed visit as we go along."

I was not slow to avail myself of this invitation, and a few seconds later we left the house together, leaving Mrs. Hornby smiling fatuously after us from the open door.

"Will eight o'clock suit you, do you think?" Miss Gibson asked as we walked up the street.

"It will do excellently, I should say," I answered. "If anything should render the meeting impossible, I will send you a telegram. I could wish that you were coming alone, as ours is to be a business conference."

Miss Gibson laughed softly—and a very pleasant and musical laugh it was.

"Yes," she agreed. "Dear Mrs. Hornby is a little diffuse and difficult to keep to one subject; but you must be indulgent to her little failings; you would be if you had experienced such kindness and generosity from her as I have."

"I am sure I should," I rejoined; "in fact, I am. After all, a little diffuseness of speech and haziness of ideas are no great faults in a generous and amiable woman of her age."

Miss Gibson rewarded me for these highly correct sentiments with a little smile of approval, and we walked on for some time in silence. Presently she turned to me with some suddenness and a very earnest expression, and said—

"I want to ask you a question, Dr. Jervis, and please forgive me if I beg you to put aside your professional reserve just a little in my favor. I want you to tell me if you think Dr. Thorndyke has any kind of hope or expectation of being able to save poor Reuben from the dreadful peril that threatens him."

This was a rather pointed question, and I took some time to consider it before replying.

"I should like," I replied at length, "to tell you as much as my duty to my colleague will allow me to; but that is so little that it is hardly worth telling. However, I may say this without breaking any confidence: Dr. Thorndyke has undertaken the case and is working hard at it, and he would, most assuredly, have done neither the one nor the other if he had considered it a hopeless one."

"That is a very encouraging view of the matter," said she, "which, had, however, already occurred to me. May I ask if anything came of your visit to Scotland Yard? Oh, please don't think me encroaching; I am so terribly anxious and troubled."

"I can tell you very little about the results of our expedition, for I know very little; but I have an idea that Dr. Thorndyke is not dissatisfied with his morning's work. He certainly picked up some facts, though I have no idea of their nature, and as soon as we reached home, he developed a sudden desire to examine the 'Thumbograph.'"

"Thank you, Dr. Jervis," she said gratefully. "You have cheered me more than I can tell you, and I won't ask you any more questions. Are you sure I am not bringing you out of the way?"

"Not at all," I answered hastily. "The fact is, I had hoped to have a little chat with you when we had disposed of the 'Thumbograph,' so I can regard myself as combining a little business with a great deal of pleasure if I am allowed to accompany you."

She gave me a little ironical bow as she inquired—

"And, in short, I may take it that I am to be pumped?"

"Come, now," I retorted. "You have been plying the pump handle pretty vigorously yourself. But that is not my meaning at all. You see, we are absolute strangers to all the parties concerned in this case, which, of course, makes for an impartial estimate of their characters. But, after all, knowledge is more useful to us than impartiality. There is our client, for instance. He impressed us both very favorably, I think; but he might have been a plausible rascal with the blackest of records. Then you come and tell us that he is a gentleman of stainless character and we are at once on firmer ground."

"I see," said Miss Gibson thoughtfully; "and suppose that I or someone else had told you things that seemed to reflect on his character. Would they have influenced you in your attitude toward him?"

"Only in this," I replied; "that we should have made it our business to inquire into the truth of those reports and ascertain their origin."

"That is what one should always do, I suppose," said she, still with an air of deep thoughtfulness, which encouraged me to inquire—

"May I ask if anyone to your knowledge has ever said anything to Mr. Reuben's disadvantage?"

She pondered for some time before replying, and kept her eyes bent pensively on the ground. At length she said, not without some hesitation of manner—

"It is a small thing and quite without any bearing on this affair. But it has been a great trouble to me, since it has to some extent put a barrier between Reuben and me; and we used to be such close friends. And I have blamed myself for letting it influence me—perhaps unjustly—in my opinion of him. I will tell you about it, though I expect you will think me very foolish.

"You must know, then, that Reuben and I used, until about six months ago, to be very much together, though we were only friends, you understand. But we were on the footing of relatives, so there was nothing out of the way in it. Reuben is a keen student of ancient and mediaeval art, in which I also am much interested, so we used to visit the museums and galleries together and get a great deal of pleasure from comparing our views and impressions of what we saw.

"About six months ago, Walter took me aside one day and, with a very serious face, asked me if there was any kind of understanding between Reuben and me. I thought it rather impertinent of him, but nevertheless, I told him the truth, that Reuben and I were just friends and nothing more.

"If that is the case,' said he, looking mighty grave, 'I would advise you not to be seen about with him quite so much.'

"And why not?' I asked very naturally.

"Why, the fact is,' said Walter, 'that Reuben is a confounded fool. He has been chattering to the men at the club and seems to have given them the impression that a young lady of means and position has been setting her cap at him very hard, but that he, being a high-souled philosopher above the temptations that beset ordinary mortals, is superior both to her blandishments and her pecuniary attractions. I give you the hint for your own guidance,' he continued, 'and I expect this to go no farther. You mustn't be annoyed with Reuben. The best of young men will often behave like prigs and donkeys, and I have no doubt the fellows have grossly exaggerated what he said; but I thought it right to put you on your guard.'

"Now this report, as you may suppose, made me excessively angry, and I wanted to have it out with Reuben then and there. But Walter refused to sanction this—'There was no use in making a scene,' he said—and he insisted that the caution was given to me in strict confidence; so what was I to do? I tried to ignore it and treat Reuben as I always had done, but this I found impossible; my womanly pride was much too deeply hurt. And yet I felt it the lowest depth of meanness to harbor such thoughts of him without giving him the opportunity to defend himself. And although it was most unlike Reuben in some respects, it was very like him in others; for he has always expressed the utmost contempt for men who marry for a livelihood. So I have remained on the horns of a dilemma and am there still. What do you think I ought to have done?"

I rubbed my chin in some embarrassment at this question. Needless to say, I was most disagreeably impressed by Walter Hornby's conduct, and not a little disposed to blame my fair companion for giving an ear to his secret disparagement of his cousin; but I was obviously not in a position to pronounce, offhand, upon the merits of the case.

"The position appears to be this," I said, after a pause, "either Reuben has spoken most unworthily and untruthfully of you, or Walter has lied deliberately about him."

"Yes," she agreed, "that is the position; but which of the two alternatives appears to you the more probable?"

"That is very difficult to say," I answered. "There is a certain kind of cad who is much given to boastful rodomontade concerning his conquests. We all know him and can generally spot him at first sight, but I must say that Reuben Hornby did not strike me as that kind of man at all. Then it is clear that the proper course for Walter to have adopted, if he had really heard such rumors, was to have had the matter out with Reuben, instead of coming secretly to you with whispered reports. That is my feeling, Miss Gibson, but, of course, I may be quite wrong. I gather that our two young friends are not inseparable companions?"

"Oh, they are very good friends, but you see, their interests and views of life are quite different. Reuben, although an excellent worker in business hours, is a student, or perhaps rather what one would call a scholar, whereas Walter is more a practical man of affairs— decidedly long-headed and shrewd. He is undoubtedly very clever, as Mrs. Hornby said."

"He takes photographs, for instance," I suggested.

"Yes. But not ordinary amateur photographs; his work is more technical and quite excellent of its kind. For example, he did a most beautiful series of microphotographs of sections of metalliferous rocks which he reproduced for publication by the collotype process, and even printed off the plates himself."

"I see. He must be a very capable fellow."

"He is, very," she assented, "and very keen on making a position; but I am afraid he is rather too fond of money for its own sake, which is not a pleasant feature in a young man's character, is it?"

I agreed that it was not.

"Excessive keenness in money affairs," proceeded Miss Gibson oracularly, "is apt to lead a young man into bad ways—oh, you need not smile, Dr. Jervis, at my wise saws; it is perfectly true, and you know it. The fact is, I sometimes have an uneasy feeling that Walter's desire to be rich inclines him to try what looks like a quick and easy method of making money. He had a friend—a Mr. Horton—who is a dealer on the Stock Exchange and who 'operates' rather largely—'operate' I believe is the expression used, although it seems to be nothing more than common gambling—and I have more than once suspected Walter of being concerned in what Mr. Horton calls 'a little flutter.'"

"That doesn't strike me as a very long-headed proceeding," I remarked, with the impartial wisdom of the impecunious, and therefore untempted.

"No," she agreed, "it isn't. But your gambler always thinks he is going to win—though you mustn't let me give you the impression that Walter is a gambler. But here is my destination. Thank you for escorting me so far, and I hope you are beginning to feel less like a stranger to the Hornby family. We shall make our appearance tonight at eight punctually."

She gave me her hand with a frank smile and tripped up the steps leading to the street door; and when I glanced back, after crossing the road, she gave me a little friendly nod as she turned to enter the house.

CHAPTER FIVE

THE "THUMBOGRAPH"

"So your net has been sweeping the quiet and pleasant waters of feminine conversation," remarked Thorndyke when we met at the dinner table and I gave him an outline of my afternoon's adventures.

"Yes," I answered, "and here is the catch cleaned and ready for the consumer."

I laid on the table two of my notebooks in which I had entered such facts as I had been able to extract from my talk with Miss Gibson.

"You made your entries as soon as possible after your return, I suppose?" said Thorndyke—"while the matter was still fresh?"

"I wrote down my notes as I sat on a seat in Kensington Gardens within five minutes after leaving Miss Gibson."

"Good!" said Thorndyke. "And now let us see what you have collected."

He glanced quickly through the entries in the two books, referring back once or twice, and stood for a few moments silent and abstracted. Then he laid the little books down on the table with a satisfied nod.

"Our information, then," he said, "amounts to this: Reuben is an industrious worker at his business and, in his leisure, a student of ancient and medieval art; possibly a babbling fool and a cad or, on the other hand, a maligned and much-abused man.

"Walter Hornby is obviously a sneak and possibly a liar; a keen man of business, perhaps a flutterer round the financial candle that burns in Throgmorton Street; an expert photographer and a competent worker of the collotype process. You have done a very excellent day's work, Jervis. I wonder if you see the bearing of the facts that you have collected."

"I think I see the bearing of some of them," I answered; "at least, I have formed certain opinions."

"Then keep them to yourself, *mon ami*, so that I need not feel as if I ought to unbosom myself of my own views."

"I should be very much surprised if you did, Thorndyke," I replied, "and should have none the better opinion of you. I realize fully that your opinions and theories are the property of your client and not to be used for the entertainment of your friends."

Thorndyke patted me on the back playfully, but he looked uncommonly pleased, and said, with evident sincerity, "I am really grateful to you for saying that, for I have felt a little awkward in being so reticent with you who know so much of this case. But you are quite right, and I am delighted to find you so discerning and sympathetic. The least I can do under the circumstances is to uncork a bottle of Pommard and drink the health of so loyal and helpful a colleague. Ah! Praise the gods! Here is Polton, like a sacrificial priest accompanied by a sweet savor of roasted flesh. Rump steak, I ween," he added, sniffing, "food meet for the mighty Shamash (that pun was fortuitous, I need not say) or a ravenous medical jurist. Can you explain to me, Polton, how it is that your rump steak is better than any other steak? Is it that you have command of a special brand of ox?"

The little man's dry countenance wrinkled with pleasure until it was as full of lines as a ground-plan of Clapham Junction.

"Perhaps it is the special treatment it gets, sir," he replied. "I usually bruise it in the mortar before cooking, without breaking up the fiber too much, and then I heat up the little cupel furnace to about six hundred C, and put the steak in on a tripod."

Thorndyke laughed outright. "The cupel furnace, too," he exclaimed. "Well, well, 'to what base uses'—but I don't know that it is a base use after all. Anyhow, Polton, open a bottle of Pommard and put a couple of ten by eight 'process' plates in your dark slides. I am expecting two ladies here this evening with a document."

"Shall you bring them upstairs, sir?" inquired Polton, with an alarmed expression.

"I expect I shall have to," answered Thorndyke.

"Then I shall just smarten the laboratory up a bit," said Polton, who evidently appreciated the difference between the masculine and feminine view as to the proper appearance of working premises.

"And so Miss Gibson wanted to know our private views on the case?" said Thorndyke, when his voracity had become somewhat appeased.

"Yes," I answered; and then I repeated our conversation as nearly as I could remember it.

"Your answer was very discreet and diplomatic," Thorndyke remarked, "and it was very necessary that it should be, for it is essential that we show the backs of our cards to Scotland Yard; and if to

Scotland Yard, then to the whole world. We know what their trump card is and can arrange our play accordingly, so long as we do not show our hand."

"You speak of the police as your antagonists; I noticed that at the 'Yard' this morning, and was surprised to find that they accepted the position. But surely their business is to discover the actual offender, not to fix the crime on some particular person."

"That would seem to be so," replied Thorndyke, "but in practice it is otherwise. When the police have made an arrest, they work for a conviction. If the man is innocent, that is his business, not theirs; it is for him to prove it. The system is a pernicious one—especially since the efficiency of a police officer is, in consequence, apt to be estimated by the number of convictions he has secured, and an inducement is thus held out to him to obtain a conviction, if possible; but it is of a piece with legislative procedure in general. Lawyers are not engaged in academic discussions or in the pursuit of truth, but each is trying, by hook or by crook, to make out a particular case without regard to its actual truth or even to the lawyer's own belief on the subject. That is what produces so much friction between lawyers and scientific witnesses; neither can understand the point of view of the other. But we must not sit over the table chattering like this; it has gone half-past seven, and Polton will be wanting to make this room presentable."

"I notice you don't use your office much," I remarked.

"Hardly at all, excepting as a repository for documents and stationery. It is very cheerless to talk in an office, and nearly all my business is transacted with solicitors and counsel who are known to me, so there is no need for such formalities. All right, Polton; we shall be ready for you in five minutes."

The Temple bell was striking eight as, at Thorndyke's request, I threw open the iron-bound "oak"; and even as I did so, the sound of footsteps came up from the stairs below. I waited on the landing for our two visitors, and led them into the room.

"I am so glad to make your acquaintance," said Mrs. Hornby, when I had done the honors of introduction; "I have heard so much about you from Juliet—"

"Really, my dear aunt," protested Miss Gibson, as she caught my eye with a look of comical alarm, "you will give Dr. Thorndyke a most erroneous impression. I merely mentioned that I had intruded on him without notice and had been received with undeserved indulgence and consideration."

"You didn't put it quite in that way, my dear," said Mrs. Hornby, "but I suppose it doesn't matter."

"We are highly gratified by Miss Gibson's favorable report of us, whatever may have been the actual form of expression," said Thorndyke, with a momentary glance at the younger lady, which covered her with smiling confusion, "and we are deeply indebted to you for taking so much trouble to help us."

"It is no trouble at all, but a great pleasure," replied Mrs. Hornby; and she proceeded to enlarge on the matter until her remarks threatened, like the rippling circles produced by a falling stone, to spread out into infinity. In the midst of this discourse Thorndyke placed chairs for the two ladies and, leaning against the mantelpiece, fixed a stony gaze upon the small handbag that hung from Mrs. Hornby's wrist.

"Is the 'Thumbograph' in your bag?" interrupted Miss Gibson, in response to this mute appeal.

"Of course it is, my dear Juliet," replied the elder lady. "You saw me put it in yourself. What an odd girl you are. Did you think I should have taken it out and put it somewhere else? Not that these handbags are really very secure, you know, although I daresay they are safer than pockets, especially now that it is the fashion to have the pocket at the back. Still, I have often thought how easy it would be for a thief or a pickpocket or some other dreadful creature of that kind, don't you know, to make a snatch and—in fact, the thing has actually happened. Why, I knew a lady—Mrs. Moggridge, you know, Juliet—no, it wasn't Mrs. Moggridge, that was another affair, it was Mrs.—Mrs.—dear me, how silly of me!—now, what was her name? Can't you help me, Juliet? You must surely remember the woman. She used to visit a good deal at the Hawley-Johnsons'—I think it was the Hawley-Johnsons', or else it was those people, you know—"

"Hadn't you better give Dr. Thorndyke the 'Thumbograph'?" interrupted Miss Gibson.

"Why, of course, Juliet, dear. What else did we come here for?" With a slightly injured expression, Mrs. Hornby opened the little bag and commenced, with the utmost deliberation, to turn out its contents on to the table. These included a laced handkerchief, a purse, a card-case, a visiting list, a packet of *papier poudré*, and when she had laid the last-mentioned article on the table, she paused abruptly and gazed into Miss Gibson's face with the air of one who has made a startling discovery.

"I remember the woman's name," she said in an impressive voice. "It was Gudge—Mrs. Gudge, the sister-in-law of—"

Here Miss Gibson made an unceremonious dive into the open bag and fished out a tiny parcel wrapped in notepaper and secured with a silk thread.

"Thank you," said Thorndyke, taking it from her hand just as Mrs. Hornby was reaching out to intercept it. He cut the thread and drew from its wrappings a little book bound in red cloth, with the word "Thumbograph" stamped upon the cover, and was beginning to inspect it when Mrs. Hornby rose and stood beside him.

"That," said she, as she opened the book at the first page, "is the thumb-mark of a Miss Colley. She is no connection of ours. You see it is a little smeared—she said Reuben jogged her elbow, but I don't think he did; at any rate he assured me he did not, and, you know—"

"Ah! Here is one we are looking for," interrupted Thorndyke, who had been turning the leaves of the book regardless of Mrs. Hornby's rambling comments; "a very good impression, too, considering the rather rough method of producing it."

He reached out for the reading lens that hung from its nail above the mantelpiece, and I could tell by the eagerness with which he peered through it at the thumb-print that he was looking for something. A moment later I felt sure that he had found that something he had sought, for, though he replaced the lens upon its nail with a quiet and composed air and made no remark, there was a sparkle of the eye and a scarcely perceptible flush of suppressed excitement and triumph which I had begun to recognize beneath the impassive mask that he presented to the world.

"I shall ask you to leave this little book with me, Mrs. Hornby," he said, breaking in upon that lady's inconsequent babblings, "and, as I may possibly put it in evidence, it would be a wise precaution for you and Miss Gibson to sign your names—as small as possible—on the page which bears Mr. Reuben's thumb-mark. That will anticipate any suggestion that the book has been tampered with after leaving your hands."

"It would be a great impertinence for anyone to make any such suggestion," Mrs. Hornby began; but on Thorndyke's placing his fountain pen in her hand, she wrote her signature in the place indicated and handed the pen to Miss Gibson, who signed underneath.

"And now," said Thorndyke, "we will take an enlarged photograph of this page with the thumb-mark; not that it is necessary that it should be done now, as you are leaving the book in my possession; but the photograph will be wanted, and as my man is expecting us and has the apparatus ready, we may as well dispatch the business at once."

To this both the ladies readily agreed (being, in fact, devoured by curiosity with regard to my colleague's premises), and we accordingly proceeded to invade the set of rooms on the floor above, over which the ingenious Polton was accustomed to reign in solitary grandeur.

It was my first visit to these mysterious regions, and I looked about me with as much curiosity as did the two ladies. The first room that we entered was apparently the workshop, for it contained a small woodworker's bench, a lathe, a bench for metal work, and a number of mechanical appliances that I was not then able to examine; but I noticed that the entire place presented to the eye a most unwork-manlike neatness, a circumstance that did not escape Thorndyke's observation, for his face relaxed into a grim smile as his eye traveled over the bare benches and the clean-swept floor.

From this room we entered the laboratory, a large apartment, one side of which was given up to chemical research, as was shown by the shelves of reagents that covered the wall, and the flasks, retorts, and other apparatus that were arranged on the bench, like ornaments on a drawing-room mantelpiece. On the opposite side of the room was a large, massively constructed copying camera, the front of which, carrying the lens, was fixed, and an easel or copyholder traveled on parallel guides toward, or away, from it, on a long stand.

This apparatus Thorndyke proceeded to explain to our visitors while Polton was fixing the "Thumbograph" in a holder attached to the easel.

"You see," he said, in answer to a question from Miss Gibson, "I have a good deal to do with signatures, checks, and disputed documents of various kinds. Now a skilled eye, aided by a pocket-lens, can make out very minute details on a check or banknote; but it is not possible to lend one's skilled eye to a judge or juryman, so that it is often very convenient to be able to hand them a photograph in which the magnification is already done, which they can compare with the original. Small things, when magnified, develop quite unexpected characters; for instance, you have handled a good many postage stamps, I suppose, but have you ever noticed the little white spots in the upper corner of a penny stamp, or even the difference in the foliage on the two sides of the wreath?"

Miss Gibson admitted that she had not.

"Very few people have, I suppose, excepting stamp collectors," continued Thorndyke; "but now just glance at this and you will find these unnoticed details forced upon your attention." As he spoke, he handed her a photograph, which he had taken from a drawer, showing a penny stamp enlarged to a length of eight inches.

While the ladies were marveling over this production, Polton proceeded with his work. The "Thumbograph" having been fixed in position, the light from a powerful incandescent gas lamp, fitted with a parabolic reflector, was concentrated on it, and the camera racked out to its proper distance.

"What are those figures intended to show?" inquired Miss Gibson, indicating the graduation on the side of one of the guides.

"They show the amount of magnification or reduction," Thorndyke explained. "When the pointer is opposite zero, the photograph is the same size as the object photographed; when it points to, say, times four, the photograph will be four times the width and length of the object, while if it should point to, say, divided by four, the photograph will be one-fourth the length of the object. It is now, you see, pointing to times eight, so the photograph will be eight times the diameter of the original thumb-mark."

By this time Polton had brought the camera to an accurate focus and, when we had all been gratified by a glimpse of the enlarged image on the focusing screen, we withdrew to a smaller room that was devoted to bacteriology and microscopical research, while the exposure was made and the plate developed. Here, after an interval, we were joined by Polton, who bore with infinite tenderness the dripping negative on which could be seen the grotesque transparency of a colossal thumb-mark.

This Thorndyke scrutinized eagerly, and having pronounced it satisfactory, informed Mrs. Hornby that the object of her visit was attained, and thanked her for the trouble she had taken.

"I am very glad we came," said Miss Gibson to me, as a little later we walked slowly up Mitre Court in the wake of Mrs. Hornby and Thorndyke; "and I am glad to have seen these wonderful instruments, too. It has made me realize that something is being done and that Dr. Thorndyke really has some object in view. It has really encouraged me immensely."

"And very properly so," I replied. "I, too, although I really know nothing of what my colleague is doing, feel very strongly that he would not take all this trouble and give up so much valuable time if he had not some very definite purpose and some substantial reasons for taking a hopeful view."

"Thank you for saying that," she rejoined warmly; "and you will let me have a crumb of comfort when you can, won't you?" She looked in my face so wistfully as she made this appeal that I was quite moved; and, indeed, I am not sure that my state of mind at that moment did not fully justify my colleague's reticence toward me.

However, I, fortunately, had nothing to tell, and so, when we emerged into Fleet Street to find Mrs. Hornby already ensconced in a hansom, I could only promise, as I grasped the hand that she offered to me, to see her again at the earliest opportunity—a promise that my inner consciousness assured me would be strictly fulfilled.

"You seem to be on quite confidential terms with our fair friend," Thorndyke remarked, as we strolled back toward his chambers. "You are an insinuating dog, Jervis."

"She is very frank and easy to get on with," I replied.

"Yes. A good girl and a clever girl, and comely to look upon withal. I suppose it would be superfluous for me to suggest that you mind your eye?"

"I shouldn't, in any case, try to cut out a man who is under a cloud," I replied sulkily.

"Of course you wouldn't; hence the need of attention to the oph-thalmic member. Have you ascertained what Miss Gibson's actual relation is to Reuben Hornby?"

"No," I answered.

"It might be worthwhile to find out," said Thorndyke; and then he relapsed into silence.

CHAPTER SIX

COMMITTED FOR TRIAL

Thorndyke's hint as to the possible danger foreshadowed by my growing intimacy with Juliet Gibson had come upon me as a complete surprise, and had, indeed, been resented by me as somewhat of an impertinence. Nevertheless, it gave me considerable food for meditation, and I presently began to suspect that the watchful eyes of my observant friend might have detected something in my manner toward Miss Gibson suggestive of sentiments that had been unsuspected by myself.

Of course it would be absurd to suppose that any real feeling could have been engendered by so ridiculously brief an acquaintance. I had only met the girl three times, and even now, excepting for business relations, was hardly entitled to more than a bow of recognition. But yet, when I considered the matter impartially and examined my own consciousness, I could not but recognize that she had aroused in me an interest which bore no relation to the part that she had played in the drama that was so slowly unfolding. She was undeniably a very handsome girl, and her beauty was of a type that specially appealed to me—full of dignity and character that gave promise of a splendid middle age. And her personality was in other ways not less attractive, for she was frank and open, sprightly and intelligent, and though evidently quite self-reliant, was in nowise lacking in that womanly softness that so strongly engages a man's sympathy.

In short, I realized that, had there been no such person as Reuben Hornby, I should have viewed Miss Gibson with uncommon interest.

But, unfortunately, Reuben Hornby was a most palpable reality, and, moreover, the extraordinary difficulties of his position entitled him to very special consideration by any man of honor. It was true that Miss Gibson had repudiated any feelings toward Reuben other than those of old-time friendship; but young ladies are not always impartial judges of their own feelings, and as a man of the world, I could not but have my own opinion on the matter—which opinion I believed to be shared by Thorndyke. The conclusions to which my cogitations at length brought me were: first, that I was an egotistical donkey, and, second, that my relations with Miss Gibson were of an exclusively business character and must in future be conducted on that basis, with the added consideration that I was the confidential agent, for the time being, of Reuben Hornby, and in honor bound to regard his interests as paramount.

"I am hoping," said Thorndyke, as he held out his hand for my teacup, "that these profound reflections of yours are connected with the Hornby affair; in which case I should expect to hear that the riddle is solved and the mystery made plain."

"Why should you expect that?" I demanded, reddening somewhat, I suspect, as I met his twinkling eye. There was something rather disturbing in the dry, quizzical smile that I encountered and the reflection that I had been under observation, and I felt as much embarrassed as I should suppose a self-conscious water-flea might feel on finding itself on the illuminated stage of a binocular microscope.

"My dear fellow," said Thorndyke, "you have not spoken a word for the last quarter of an hour; you have devoured your food with the relentless regularity of a sausage-machine, and you have, from time to time, made the most damnable faces at the coffeepot—though there I'll wager the coffeepot was even with you, if I may judge by the presentment that it offers of my own countenance."

I roused myself from my reverie with a laugh at Thorndyke's quaint conceit and a glance at the grotesquely distorted reflection of my face in the polished silver.

"I am afraid I *have* been a rather dull companion this morning," I admitted apologetically.

"By no means," replied Thorndyke with a grin. "On the contrary, I have found you both amusing and instructive, and I only spoke when I had exhausted your potentialities as a silent entertainer."

"You are pleased to be facetious at my expense," said I.

"Well, the expense was not a very heavy one," he retorted. "I have been merely consuming a by-product of your mental activity—Hallo! that's Anstey already."

A peculiar knock, apparently delivered with the handle of a walking-stick on the outer door, was the occasion of this exclamation, and as Thorndyke sprang up and flung the door open, a clear, musical voice was borne in, the measured cadences of which proclaimed at once the trained orator.

"Hail, learned brother!" it exclaimed. "Do I disturb you untimely at your studies?" Here our visitor entered the room and looked round critically. "'Tis even so," he declared. "Physiological chemistry and its practical applications appears to be the subject. A physico-chemical inquiry into the properties of streaky bacon and fried eggs. Do I see another learned brother?"

He peered keenly at me through his pince-nez, and I gazed at him in some embarrassment.

"This is my friend Jervis, of whom you have heard me speak," said Thorndyke. "He is with us in this case, you know."

"The echoes of your fame have reached me, sir," said Anstey, holding out his hand. "I am proud to know you. I should have recognized you instantly from the portrait of your lamented uncle in Greenwich Hospital."

"Anstey is a wag, you understand," explained Thorndyke, "but he has lucid intervals. He'll have one presently if we are patient."

"Patient!" snorted our eccentric visitor. "It is I who need to be patient when I am dragged into police courts and other sinks of iniquity to plead for common thieves and robbers like a Kennington Lane advocate."

"You've been talking to Lawley, I see," said Thorndyke.

"Yes, and he tells me that we haven't a leg to stand upon."

"No, we've got to stand on our heads, as men of intellect should. But Lawley knows nothing about the case."

"He thinks he knows it all," said Anstey.

"Most fools do," retorted Thorndyke. "They arrive at their knowledge by intuition—a deuced easy road and cheap traveling, too. We reserve our defense—I suppose you agree to that?"

"I suppose so. The magistrate is sure to commit unless you have an unquestionable *alibi*."

"We shall put in an *alibi*, but we are not depending on it."

"Then we had better reserve our defense," said Anstey; "and it is time that we wended on our pilgrimage, for we are due at Lawley's at half-past ten. Is Jervis coming with us?"

"Yes, you'd better come," said Thorndyke. "It's the adjourned hearing of poor Hornby's case, you know. There won't be anything done on our side, but we may be able to glean some hint from the prosecution."

"I should like to hear what takes place, at any rate," I said, and we accordingly sallied forth together in the direction of Lincoln's Inn, on the north side of which Mr. Lawley's office was situated.

"Ah!" said the solicitor, as we entered, "I am glad you've come; I was getting anxious—it doesn't do to be late on these occasions, you know. Let me see, do you know Mr. Walter Hornby? I don't think you do." He presented Thorndyke and me to our client's cousin, and as we shook hands, we viewed one another with a good deal of mutual interest.

"I have heard about you from my aunt," said he, addressing himself more particularly to me. "She appears to regard you as a kind of legal Maskelyne and Cooke. I hope, for my cousin's sake, that you will be able to work the wonders that she anticipates. Poor old fellow! He looks pretty bad, doesn't he?"

I glanced at Reuben, who was at the moment talking to Thorndyke, and as he caught my eye, he held out his hand with a warmth that I found very pathetic. He seemed to have aged since I had last seen him, and was pale and rather thinner, but he was composed in his manner and seemed to me to be taking his trouble very well on the whole.

"Cab's at the door, sir," a clerk announced.

"Cab," repeated Mr. Lawley, looking dubiously at me; "we want an omnibus."

"Dr. Jervis and I can walk," Walter Hornby suggested. "We shall probably get there as soon as you, and it doesn't matter if we don't."

"Yes, that will do," said Mr. Lawley; "you two walk down together. Now let us go."

We trooped out on to the pavement, beside which a four-wheeler was drawn up, and as the others were entering the cab, Thorndyke stood close beside me for a moment.

"Don't let him pump you," he said in a low voice, without looking at me; then he sprang into the cab and slammed the door.

"What an extraordinary affair this is," Walter Hornby remarked after we had been walking in silence for a minute or two; "a most ghastly business. I must confess that I can make neither head nor tail of it."

"How is that?" I asked.

"Why, do you see, there are apparently only two possible theories of the crime, and each of them seems to be unthinkable. On the one hand there is Reuben, a man of the most scrupulous honor, as far as my experience of him goes, committing a mean and sordid theft for which no motive can be discovered—for he is not poor, nor pecuniarily embarrassed, nor in the smallest degree avaricious. On the other hand, there is this thumb-print, which, in the opinion of the experts, is tantamount to the evidence of an eye witness that he did commit the theft. It is positively bewildering. Don't you think so?"

"As you put it," I answered, "the case is extraordinarily puzzling."

"But how else would you put it?" he demanded, with ill-concealed eagerness.

"I mean that, if Reuben is the man you believe him to be, the thing is incomprehensible."

"Quite so," he agreed, though he was evidently disappointed at my colorless answer.

He walked on silently for a few minutes and then said: "I suppose it would not be fair to ask if you see any way out of the difficulty? We are all naturally anxious about the upshot of the affair, seeing what poor old Reuben's position is."

"Naturally. But the fact is that I know no more than you do, and as to Thorndyke, you might as well cross-examine a Whitstable native as put questions to him."

"Yes, so I gathered from Juliet. But I thought you might have gleaned some notion of the line of defense from your work in the laboratory—the microscopical and photographic work I mean."

"I was never in the laboratory until last night, when Thorndyke took me there with your aunt and Miss Gibson; the work there is done by the laboratory assistant, and his knowledge of the case, I should say, is about as great as a type-founder's knowledge of the books that he is helping to produce. No; Thorndyke is a man who plays a single-handed game and no one knows what cards he holds until he lays them on the table."

My companion considered this statement in silence while I congratulated myself on having parried, with great adroitness, a rather inconvenient question. But the time was not far distant when I should have occasion to reproach myself bitterly for having been so explicit and emphatic.

"My uncle's condition," Walter resumed after a pause, "is a pretty miserable one at present, with this horrible affair added to his own personal worries."

"Has he any special trouble besides this, then?" I asked.

"Why, haven't you heard? I thought you knew about it, or I shouldn't have spoken—not that it is in any way a secret, seeing that it is public property in the city. The fact is that his financial affairs are a little entangled just now."

"Indeed!" I exclaimed, considerably startled by this new development.

"Yes, things have taken a rather awkward turn, though I think he will pull through all right. It is the usual thing, you know—investments, or perhaps one should say speculations. He appears to have sunk a lot of capital in mines—thought he was 'in the know,' not unnaturally; but it seems he wasn't after all, and the things have gone wrong, leaving him with a deal more money than he can afford locked up and the possibility of a dead loss if they don't revive. Then there are these infernal diamonds. He is not morally responsible, we know; but it is a question if he is not legally responsible, though the lawyers think he is not. Anyhow, there is going to be a meeting of the creditors tomorrow."

"And what do you think they will do?"

"Oh, they will, most probably, let him go on for the present; but, of course, if he is made accountable for the diamonds, there will be nothing for it but to 'go through the hoop,' as the sporting financier expresses it."

"The diamonds were of considerable value, then?"

"From twenty-five to thirty thousand pounds' worth vanished with that parcel."

I whistled. This was a much bigger affair than I had imagined, and I was wondering if Thorndyke had realized the magnitude of the robbery, when we arrived at the police court.

"I suppose our friends have gone inside," said Walter. "They must have got here before us."

This supposition was confirmed by a constable of whom we made inquiry, and who directed us to the entrance to the court. Passing down a passage and elbowing our way through the throng of idlers, we made for the solicitor's box, where we had barely taken our seats when the case was called.

Unspeakably dreary and depressing were the brief proceedings that followed, and dreadfully suggestive of the helplessness of even an innocent man on whom the law has laid its hand and in whose behalf its inexorable machinery has been set in motion.

The presiding magistrate, emotionless and dry, dipped his pen while Reuben, who had surrendered to his bail, was placed in the dock and the charge read over to him. The counsel representing the police gave an abstract of the case with the matter-of-fact air of a house-agent describing an eligible property. Then, when the plea of "not guilty" had been entered, the witnesses were called. There were only two, and when the name of the first, John Hornby, was called, I glanced toward the witness-box with no little curiosity.

I had not hitherto met Mr. Hornby, and as he now entered the box, I saw an elderly man, tall, florid, and well-preserved, but strained and wild in expression and displaying his uncontrollable agitation by continual nervous movements that contrasted curiously with the composed demeanor of the accused man. Nevertheless, he gave his evidence in a perfectly connected manner, recounting the events connected with the discovery of the crime in much the same words as I had heard Mr. Lawley use, though, indeed, he was a good deal more emphatic than that gentleman had been in regard to the excellent character borne by the prisoner.

After him came Mr. Singleton, of the finger-print department at Scotland Yard, to whose evidence I listened with close attention. He produced the paper which bore the thumb-print in blood (which had previously been identified by Mr. Hornby) and a paper bearing the print, taken by himself, of the prisoner's left thumb. These two thumb-prints, he stated, were identical in every respect.

"And you are of opinion that the mark on the paper that was found in Mr. Hornby's safe, was made by the prisoner's left thumb?" the magistrate asked in dry and businesslike tones.

"I am certain of it."

"You are of opinion that no mistake is possible?"

"No mistake is possible, your worship. It is a certainty."

The magistrate looked at Anstey inquiringly, whereupon the barrister rose.

"We reserve our defense, your worship."

The magistrate then, in the same placid, businesslike manner, committed the prisoner for trial at the Central Criminal Court, refusing to accept bail for his appearance, and as Reuben was led forth from the dock, the next case was called.

By special favor of the authorities, Reuben was to be allowed to make his journey to Holloway in a cab, thus escaping the horrors of the filthy and verminous prison van, and while this was being procured, his friends were permitted to wish him farewell.

"This is a hard experience, Hornby," said Thorndyke, when we three were, for a few moments, left apart from the others; and as he spoke the warmth of a really sympathetic nature broke through his habitual impassivity. "But be of good cheer; I have convinced myself of your innocence and have good hopes of convincing the world—though this is for your private ear, you understand, to be mentioned to no one."

Reuben wrung the hand of this "friend in need," but was unable, for the moment, to speak; and, as his self-control was evidently strained to the breaking point, Thorndyke, with a man's natural instinct, wished him a hasty good-bye, and passing his hand through my arm, turned away.

"I wish it had been possible to save the poor fellow from this delay, and especially from the degradation of being locked up in a jail," he exclaimed regretfully as we walked down the street.

"There is surely no degradation in being merely accused of a crime," I answered, without much conviction, however. "It may happen to the best of us; and he is still an innocent man in the eyes of the law."

"That, my dear Jervis, you know, as well as I do, to be mere casuistry," he rejoined. "The law professes to regard the unconvicted man as innocent; but how does it treat him? You heard how the magistrate addressed our friend; outside the court he would have called him

Mr. Hornby. You know what will happen to Reuben at Holloway. He will be ordered about by warders, will have a number label fastened on to his coat, he will be locked in a cell with a spy-hole in the door, through which any passing stranger may watch him; his food will be handed to him in a tin pan with a tin knife and spoon; and he will be periodically called out of his cell and driven round the exercise yard with a mob composed, for the most part, of the sweepings of the London slums. If he is acquitted, he will be turned loose without a suggestion of compensation or apology for these indignities or the losses he may have sustained through his detention."

"Still I suppose these evils are unavoidable," I said.

"That may or may not be," he retorted. "My point is that the presumption of innocence is a pure fiction; that the treatment of an accused man, from the moment of his arrest, is that of a criminal. However," he concluded, hailing a passing hansom, "this discussion must be adjourned or I shall be late at the hospital. What are you going to do?"

"I shall get some lunch and then call on Miss Gibson to let her know the real position."

"Yes, that will be kind, I think; baldly stated, the news may seem rather alarming. I was tempted to thrash the case out in the police court, but it would not have been safe. He would almost certainly have been committed for trial after all, and then we should have shown our hand to the prosecution."

He sprang into the hansom and was speedily swallowed up in the traffic, while I turned back toward the police court to make certain inquiries concerning the regulations as to visitors at Holloway prison. At the door I met the friendly inspector from Scotland Yard, who gave me the necessary information, whereupon with a certain homely little French restaurant in my mind, I bent my steps in the direction of Soho.

CHAPTER SEVEN

SHOALS AND QUICKSANDS

When I arrived at Endsley Gardens, Miss Gibson was at home, and to my unspeakable relief, Mrs. Hornby was not. My veneration for that lady's moral qualities was excessive, but her conversation drove me to the verge of insanity—an insanity not entirely free from homicidal tendencies.

"It is good of you to come—though I thought you would," Miss Gibson said impulsively, as we shook hands. "You have been so sympathetic and human—both you and Dr. Thorndyke—so free from professional stiffness. My aunt went off to see Mr. Lawley directly we got Walter's telegram."

"I am sorry for her," I said (and was on the point of adding "and him," but fortunately a glimmer of sense restrained me); "she will find him dry enough."

"Yes; I dislike him extremely. Do you know that he had the impudence to advise Reuben to plead 'guilty'?"

"He told us he had done so, and got a well-deserved snubbing from Thorndyke for his pains."

"I am so glad," exclaimed Miss Gibson viciously. "But tell me what has happened. Walter simply said, 'Transferred to higher court,' which we agreed was to mean, 'Committed for trial.' Has the defense failed? And where is Reuben?"

"The defense is reserved. Dr. Thorndyke considered it almost certain that the case would be sent for trial, and that being so, decided that it was essential to keep the prosecution in the dark as to the line of defense. You see, if the police knew what the defense was to be, they could revise their own plans accordingly."

"I see that," said she dejectedly, "but I am dreadfully disappointed. I had hoped that Dr. Thorndyke would get the case dismissed. What has happened to Reuben?"

This was the question that I had dreaded, and now that I had to answer it I cleared my throat and bent my gaze nervously on the floor.

"The magistrate refused bail," I said after an uncomfortable pause.

"Well?"

"Consequently Reuben has been—er—detained in custody."

"You don't mean to say that they have sent him to prison?" she exclaimed breathlessly.

"Not as a convicted prisoner, you know. He is merely detained pending his trial."

"But in prison?"

"Yes," I was forced to admit, "in Holloway prison."

She looked me stonily in the face for some seconds, pale and wide-eyed, but silent; then, with a sudden catch in her breath, she turned away, and, grasping the edge of the mantel-shelf, laid her head upon her arm and burst into a passion of sobbing.

Now I am not, in general, an emotional man, nor even especially impulsive; but neither am I a stock or a stone or an effigy of wood; which I most surely must have been if I could have looked without being deeply moved on the grief, so natural and unselfish, of this strong, brave, loyal-hearted woman. In effect, I moved to her side and, gently taking in mine the hand that hung down, murmured some incoherent words of consolation in a particularly husky voice.

Presently she recovered herself somewhat and softly withdrew her hand, as she turned toward me, drying her eyes.

"You must forgive me for distressing you, as I fear I have," she said; "for you are so kind, and I feel that you are really my friend and Reuben's."

"I am indeed, dear Miss Gibson," I replied, "and so, I assure you, is my colleague."

"I am sure of it," she rejoined. "But I was so unprepared for this—I cannot say why, excepting that I trusted so entirely in Dr. Thorndyke—and it is so horrible and, above all, so dreadfully suggestive of what may happen. Up to now the whole thing has seemed like a nightmare—terrifying, but yet unreal. But now that he is actually in prison, it has suddenly become a dreadful reality and I am overwhelmed with terror. Oh! Poor boy! What will become of him? For pity's sake, Dr. Jervis, tell me what is going to happen."

What could I do? I had heard Thorndyke's words of encouragement to Reuben and knew my colleague well enough to feel sure that he meant all he had said. Doubtless my proper course would have been to keep my own counsel and put Miss Gibson off with cautious ambiguities. But I could not; she was worthy of more confidence than that.

"You must not be unduly alarmed about the future," I said. "I have it from Dr. Thorndyke that he is convinced of Reuben's innocence, and is hopeful of being able to make it clear to the world. But I did not have this to repeat," I added, with a slight qualm of conscience.

"I know," she said softly, "and I thank you from my heart."

"And as to this present misfortune," I continued, "you must not let it distress you too much. Try to think of it as of a surgical operation, which is a dreadful thing in itself, but is accepted in lieu of something which is immeasurably more dreadful."

"I will try to do as you tell me," she answered meekly; "but it is so shocking to think of a cultivated gentleman like Reuben herded with common thieves and murderers and locked in a cage like some wild animal. Think of the ignominy and degradation!"

"There is no ignominy in being wrongfully accused," I said—a little guiltily, I must own, for Thorndyke's words came back to me with all their force. But regardless of this, I went on: "An acquittal will restore him to his position with an unstained character, and nothing but the recollection of a passing inconvenience to look back upon."

She gave her eyes a final wipe and resolutely put away her handkerchief.

"You have given me back my courage," she said, "and chased away my terror. I cannot tell you how I feel your goodness, nor have I any thank-offering to make, except the promise to be brave and patient henceforth, and trust in you entirely."

She said this with such a grateful smile, and looked withal so sweet and womanly, that I was seized with an overpowering impulse to take her in my arms. Instead of this I said with conscious feebleness: "I am more than thankful to have been able to give you any encouragement—which you must remember comes from me secondhand, after all. It is to Dr. Thorndyke that we all look for ultimate deliverance."

"I know. But it is you who came to comfort me in my trouble, so, you see, the honors are divided—and not divided quite equally, I fear, for women are unreasoning creatures, as, no doubt, your experience has informed you. I think I hear my aunt's voice, so you had better escape before your retreat is cut off. But before you go, you must tell me how and when I can see Reuben. I want to see him at the earliest possible moment. Poor fellow! He must not be allowed to feel that his friends have forgotten him even for a single instant."

"You can see him tomorrow, if you like," I said; and, casting my good resolutions to the winds, I added: "I shall be going to see him myself, and perhaps Dr. Thorndyke will go."

"Would you let me call at the Temple and go with you? Should I be much in the way? It is rather an alarming thing to go to a prison alone."

"It is not to be thought of," I answered. "If you will call at the Temple—it is on the way—we can drive to Holloway together. I suppose you are resolved to go? It will be rather unpleasant, as you are probably aware."

"I am quite resolved. What time shall I come to the Temple?"

"About two o'clock, if that will suit you."

"Very well. I will be punctual; and now you must go or you will be caught."

She pushed me gently toward the door and, holding out her hand, said—

"I haven't thanked you half enough, and I never can. Good-bye!"

She was gone, and I stood alone in the street, up which yellowish wreaths of fog were beginning to roll. It had been quite clear and bright when I entered the house, but now the sky was settling down into a colorless gray, the light was failing, and the houses dwindling into dim, unreal shapes that vanished at half their height. Nevertheless I stepped out briskly and strode along at a good pace, as a young man is apt to do when his mind is in somewhat of a ferment. In truth, I had a good deal to occupy my thoughts, and as will often happen both to young men and old, those matters that bore most directly upon my own life and prospects were the first to receive attention.

What sort of relations were growing up between Juliet Gibson and me? And what was my position? As to hers, it seemed plain enough; she was wrapped up in Reuben Hornby, and I was her very good friend because I was his. But for myself, there was no disguising the fact that I was beginning to take an interest in her that boded ill for my peace of mind.

Never had I met a woman who so entirely realized my conception of what a woman should be, nor one who exercised so great a charm over me. Her strength and dignity, her softness and dependency, to say nothing of her beauty, fitted her with the necessary weapons for my complete and utter subjugation. And utterly subjugated I was— there was no use in denying the fact, even though I realized already that the time would presently come when she would want me no more and there would remain no remedy for me but to go away and try to forget her.

But was I acting as a man of honor? To this I felt I could fairly answer yes for I was but doing my duty, and could hardly act differently if I wished to. Besides, I was jeopardizing no one's happiness but my own, and a man may do as he pleases with his own happiness. No; even Thorndyke could not accuse me of dishonorable conduct.

Presently my thoughts took a fresh turn, and I began to reflect upon what I had heard concerning Mr. Hornby. Here was a startling development, indeed, and I wondered what difference it would make in Thorndyke's hypothesis of the crime. What his theory was I had never been able to guess, but as I walked along through the thickening fog, I tried to fit this new fact into our collection of data and determine its bearings and significance.

In this, for a time, I failed utterly. The red thumb-mark filled my field of vision to the exclusion of all else. To me, as to everyone else but Thorndyke, this fact was final and pointed to a conclusion that was unanswerable. But as I turned the story of the crime over and over, there came to me presently an idea that set in motion a new and very startling train of thought.

Could Mr. Hornby himself be the thief? His failure appeared sudden to the outside world, but he must have seen difficulties coming. There, indeed, was the thumb-mark on the leaf which he had torn from his pocket-block. Yes! but who had seen him tear it off? No one. The fact rested on his bare statement.

But the thumb-mark? Well, it was possible (though unlikely)—still possible—that the mark might have been made accidentally on some previous occasion and forgotten by Reuben, or even unnoticed. Mr. Hornby had seen the "Thumbograph," in fact his own mark was in it, and so would have had his attention directed to the importance of finger-prints in identification. He might have kept the marked paper for future use, and, on the occasion of the robbery, penciled a dated inscription on it, and slipped it into the safe as a sure means of diverting suspicion. All this was improbable in the highest degree, but then so was every other explanation of the crime; and as to the unspeakable baseness of the deed, what action is too base for a gambler in difficulties?

I was so much excited and elated by my own ingenuity in having formed an intelligible and practicable theory of the crime that I was now impatient to reach home that I might impart my news to

Thorndyke and see how they affected him. But as I approached the center of the town, the fog grew so dense that all my attention was needed to enable me to thread my way safely through the traffic; while the strange, deceptive aspect that it lent to familiar objects and the obliteration of landmarks made my progress so slow that it was already past six o'clock when I felt my way down Middle Temple Lane and crept through Crown Office Row toward my colleague's chambers.

On the doorstep I found Polton peering with anxious face into the blank expanse of yellow vapor.

"The Doctor's late, sir," said he. "Detained by the fog, I expect. It must be pretty thick in the Borough."

(I may mention that, to Polton, Thorndyke was The Doctor. Other inferior creatures there were, indeed, to whom the title of "doctor" in a way, appertained; but they were of no account in Polton's eyes. Surnames were good enough for them.)

"Yes, it must be," I replied, "judging by the condition of the Strand."

I entered and ascended the stairs, glad enough of the prospect of a warm and well-lighted room after my comfortless groping in the murky streets, and Polton, with a final glance up and down the walk, reluctantly followed.

"You would like some tea, sir, I expect?" said he, as he let me in (though I had a key of my own now).

I thought I should, and he accordingly set about the preparations in his deft, methodical way, but with an air of abstraction that was unusual with him.

"The Doctor said he should be home by five," he remarked, as he laid the teapot on the tray.

"Then he is a defaulter," I answered. "We shall have to water his tea."

"A wonderful punctual man, sir, is the Doctor," pursued Polton. "Keeps his time to the minute, as a rule, he does."

"You can't keep your time to a minute in a 'London Particular,'" I said a little impatiently, for I wished to be alone that I might think over matters, and Polton's nervous flutterings irritated me somewhat. He was almost as bad as a female housekeeper.

The little man evidently perceived my state of mind, for he stole away silently, leaving me rather penitent and ashamed, and, as I presently discovered on looking out of the window, resumed his vigil on the doorstep. From this coign of vantage, he returned after a time to take away the tea things; and thereafter, though it was now dark as well as foggy, I could hear him softly flitting up and down the stairs with a gloomy stealthiness that at length reduced me to a condition as nervously apprehensive as his own.

CHAPTER EIGHT

A SUSPICIOUS ACCIDENT

The Temple clock had announced in soft and confidential tones that it was a quarter to seven, in which statement it was stoutly supported by its colleague on our mantelpiece, and still there was no sign of Thorndyke. It was really a little strange, for he was the soul of punctuality, and moreover, his engagements were of such a kind as rendered punctuality possible. I was burning with impatience to impart my news to him, and this fact, together with the ghostly proceedings of Polton, worked me up to a state of nervous tension that rendered either rest or thought equally impossible. I looked out of the window at the lamp below, glaring redly through the fog, and then, opening the door, went out on to the landing to listen.

At this moment Polton made a silent appearance on the stairs leading from the laboratory, giving me quite a start; and I was about to retire into the room when my ear caught the tinkle of a hansom approaching from Paper Buildings.

The vehicle drew nearer, and at length stopped opposite the house, on which Polton slid down the stairs with the agility of a harlequin. A few moments later, I heard his voice ascending from the hall—

"I do hope, sir, you're not much hurt?"

I ran down the stairs and met Thorndyke coming up slowly with his right hand on Polton's shoulder. His clothes were muddy, his left arm was in a sling, and a black handkerchief under his hat evidently concealed a bandage.

"I am not really hurt at all," Thorndyke replied cheerily, "though very disreputable to look at. Just came a cropper in the mud, Jervis," he added, as he noted my dismayed expression. "Dinner and a clothes-brush are what I chiefly need." Nevertheless, he looked very pale and shaken when he came into the light on the landing, and he sank into his easy chair in the limp manner of a man either very weak or very fatigued.

"How did it happen?" I asked when Polton had crept away on tiptoe to make ready for dinner.

Thorndyke looked round to make sure that his henchman had departed, and said—

"A queer affair, Jervis; a very odd affair indeed. I was coming up from the Borough, picking my way mighty carefully across the road on account of the greasy, slippery mud, and had just reached the foot of London Bridge when I heard a heavy lorry coming down the slope a good deal too fast, considering that it was impossible to see more than a dozen yards ahead, and I stopped on the curb to see it safely past. Just as the horses emerged from the fog, a man came up behind and lurched violently against me and, strangely enough, at the same moment passed his foot in front of mine. Of course I went sprawling into the road right in front of the lorry. The horses came stamping and sliding straight on to me, and, before I could wriggle out of the way, the hoof of one of them smashed in my hat—that was a new one that I came home in—and half-stunned me. Then the near wheel struck my head, making a dirty little scalp wound, and pinned down my sleeve so that I couldn't pull away my arm, which is consequently barked all the way down. It was a mighty near thing, Jervis; another inch or two and I should have been rolled out as flat as a starfish."

"What became of the man?" I asked, wishing I could have had a brief interview with him.

"Lost to sight though to memory dear: he was off like a lamp-lighter. An alcoholic apple-woman picked me up and escorted me back to the hospital. It must have been a touching spectacle," he added, with a dry smile at the recollection.

"And I suppose they kept you there for a time to recover?"

"Yes; I went into dry dock in the OP room, and then old Langdale insisted on my lying down for an hour or so in case any symptoms of concussion should appear. But I was only a trifle shaken and confused. Still, it was a queer affair."

"You mean the man pushing you down in that way?"

"Yes; I can't make out how his foot got in front of mine."

"You don't think it was intentional, surely?" I said.

"No, of course not," he replied, but without much conviction, as it seemed to me; and I was about to pursue the matter when Polton reappeared and my friend abruptly changed the subject.

After dinner I recounted my conversation with Walter Hornby, watching my colleague's face with some eagerness to see what effect this new information would produce on him. The result was, on the whole, disappointing. He was interested, keenly interested, but showed no symptoms of excitement.

"So John Hornby has been plunging in mines, eh?" he said, when I had finished. "He ought to know better at his age. Did you learn how long he had been in difficulties?"

"No. But it can hardly have been quite sudden and unforeseen."

"I should think not," Thorndyke agreed. "A sudden slump often proves disastrous to the regular Stock Exchange gambler who is paying differences on large quantities of unpaid-for stock. But it looks as if Hornby had actually bought and paid for these mines, treating them as investments rather than speculations, in which case the depreciation would not have affected him in the same way. It would be interesting to know for certain."

"It might have a considerable bearing on the present case, might it not?"

"Undoubtedly," said Thorndyke. "It might bear on the case in more ways than one. But you have some special point in your mind, I think."

"Yes. I was thinking that if these embarrassments had been growing up gradually for some time, they might have already assumed an acute form at the time of the robbery."

"That is well considered," said my colleague. "But what is the special bearing on the case supposing it was so?"

"On the supposition," I replied, "that Mr. Hornby was in actual pecuniary difficulties at the date of the robbery, it seems to me possible to construct a hypothesis as to the identity of the robber."

"I should like to hear that hypothesis stated," said Thorndyke, rousing himself and regarding me with lively interest.

"It is a highly improbable one," I began with some natural shyness at the idea of airing my wits before this master of inductive method; "in fact, it is almost fantastic."

"Never mind that," said he. "A sound thinker gives equal consideration to the probable and the improbable."

Thus encouraged, I proceeded to set forth the theory of the crime as it had occurred to me on my way home in the fog, and I was gratified to observe the close attention with which Thorndyke listened, and his little nods of approval at each point that I made.

When I had finished, he remained silent for some time, looking thoughtfully into the fire and evidently considering how my theory and the new facts on which it was based would fit in with the rest of the data. At length he spoke, without, however, removing his eyes from the red embers—

"This theory of yours, Jervis, does great credit to your ingenuity. We may disregard the improbability, seeing that the alternative theories are almost equally improbable, and the fact that emerges, and that gratifies me more than I can tell you, is that you are gifted with enough scientific imagination to construct a possible train of events. Indeed, the improbability—combined, of course, with possibility—really adds to the achievement, for the dullest mind can perceive the obvious—as, for instance, the importance of a finger-print. You have really done a great thing, and I congratulate you; for you have emancipated yourself, at least to some extent, from the great finger-print obsession, which has possessed the legal mind ever since Galton published his epoch-making monograph. In that work I remember he states that a finger-print affords evidence requiring no corroboration—a most dangerous and misleading statement which has been fastened upon eagerly by the police, who have naturally been delighted at obtaining a sort of magic touchstone by which they are saved the labor of investigation. But there is no such thing as a single fact that 'affords evidence requiring no corroboration.' As well might one expect to make a syllogism with a single premise."

"I suppose they would hardly go so far as that," I said, laughing.

"No," he admitted. "But the kind of syllogism that they do make is this—

"The crime was committed by the person who made this finger-print.

"But John Smith is the person who made the finger-print.

"Therefore the crime was committed by John Smith.'"

"Well, that is a perfectly good syllogism, isn't it?" I asked.

"Perfectly," he replied. "But, you see, it begs the whole question, which is, 'Was the crime committed by the person who made this finger-print?' That is where the corroboration is required."

"That practically leaves the case to be investigated without reference to the finger-print, which thus becomes of no importance."

"Not at all," rejoined Thorndyke; "the finger-print is a most valuable clue as long as its evidential value is not exaggerated. Take our present case, for instance. Without the thumb-print, the robbery might have been committed by anybody; there is no clue whatever. But the existence of the thumb-print narrows the inquiry down to Reuben or some person having access to his finger-prints."

"Yes, I see. Then you consider my theory of John Hornby as the perpetrator of the robbery as quite a tenable one?"

"Quite," replied Thorndyke. "I have entertained it from the first; and the new facts that you have gathered increase its probability. You remember I said that four hypotheses were possible: that the robbery was committed either by Reuben, by Walter, by John Hornby, or by some other person. Now, putting aside the 'some other person' for consideration only if the first three hypotheses fail, we have left, Reuben, Walter, and John. But if we leave the thumb-print out of the question, the probabilities evidently point to John Hornby, since he, admittedly, had access to the diamonds, whereas there is nothing to show that the others had. The thumb-print, however, transfers the suspicion to Reuben; but yet, as your theory makes evident, it does not completely clear John Hornby. As the case stands, the balance of probabilities may be stated thus: John Hornby undoubtedly had access to the diamonds, and therefore might have stolen them. But if the thumb-mark was made after he closed the safe and before he opened it again, some other person must have had access to them and was probably the thief.

"The thumb-mark is that of Reuben Hornby, a fact that establishes a *prima facie* probability that he stole the diamonds. But there is no evidence that he had access to them, and if he had not, he could not have made the thumb-mark in the manner and at the time stated.

"But John Hornby may have had access to the previously made thumb-mark of Reuben, and may possibly have obtained it; in which case he is almost certainly the thief.

"As to Walter Hornby, he may have had the means of obtaining Reuben's thumb-mark; but there is no evidence that he had access either to the diamonds or to Mr. Hornby's memorandum block. The *prima facie* probabilities in his case, therefore, are very slight."

"The actual points at issue, then," I said, "are whether Reuben had any means of opening the safe, and whether Mr. Hornby ever did actually have the opportunity of obtaining Reuben's thumb-mark in blood on his memorandum block."

"Yes," replied Thorndyke. "Those are the points—with some others—and they are likely to remain unsettled. Reuben's rooms have been searched by the police, who failed to find any skeleton or duplicate keys; but this proves nothing, as he would probably have made away with them when he heard of the thumb-mark being found. As to the other matter, I have asked Reuben, and he has no recollection of ever having made a thumb-mark in blood. So there the matter rests."

"And what about Mr. Hornby's liability for the diamonds?"

"I think we may dismiss that," answered Thorndyke. "He had undertaken no liability and there was no negligence. He would not be liable at law."

After my colleague retired, which he did quite early, I sat for a long time, pondering upon this singular case in which I found myself involved. And the more I thought about it, the more puzzled I became. If Thorndyke had no more satisfactory explanation to offer than that which he had given me this evening, the defense was hopeless, for the court was not likely to accept his estimate of the evidential value of finger-prints. Yet he had given Reuben something like a positive assurance that there would be an adequate defense, and had expressed his own positive conviction of the accused man's innocence. But Thorndyke was not a man to reach such a conviction through merely sentimental considerations. The inevitable conclusion was that he had something up his sleeve— that he had gained possession of some facts that had escaped my observation; and when I had reached this point, I knocked out my pipe and betook myself to bed.

CHAPTER NINE

THE PRISONER

On the following morning, as I emerged from my room, I met Polton coming up with a tray (our bedrooms were on the attic floor above the laboratory and workshop), and I accordingly followed him into my friend's chamber.

"I shan't go out today," said Thorndyke, "though I shall come down presently. It is very inconvenient, but one must accept the inevitable. I have had a knock on the head, and, although I feel none the worse, I must take the proper precautions—rest and a low diet—until I see that no results are going to follow. You can attend to the scalp wound and send round the necessary letters, can't you?"

I expressed my willingness to do all that was required and applauded my friend's self-control and good sense; indeed, I could not help contrasting the conduct of this busy, indefatigable man, cheerfully resigning himself to most distasteful inaction, with the fussy behavior of the ordinary patient who, with nothing of importance to do, can hardly be prevailed upon to rest, no matter how urgent the necessity. Accordingly, I breakfasted alone, and spent the morning in writing and dispatching letters to the various persons who were expecting visits from my colleague.

Shortly after lunch (a very spare one, by the way, for Polton appeared to include me in the scheme of reduced diet) my expectant ear caught the tinkle of a hansom approaching down Crown Office Row.

"Here comes your fair companion," said Thorndyke, whom I had acquainted with my arrangements. "Tell Hornby, from me, to keep up his courage, and, for yourself, bear my warning in mind. I should be sorry indeed if you ever had cause to regret that you had rendered me the very valuable services for which I am now indebted to you. Good-bye; don't keep her waiting."

I ran down the stairs and came out of the entry just as the cabman had pulled up and flung open the doors.

"Holloway Prison—main entrance," I said, as I stepped up on to the footboard.

"There ain't no back door there, sir," the man responded, with a grin; and I was glad that neither the answer nor the grin was conveyed to my fellow passenger.

"You are very punctual, Miss Gibson," I said. "It is not half-past one yet."

"Yes; I thought I should like to get there by two, so as to have as long a time with him as is possible without shortening your interview."

I looked at my companion critically. She was dressed with rather more than her usual care, and looked, in fact, a very fine lady indeed. This circumstance, which I noted at first with surprise and then with decided approbation, caused me some inward discomfort, for I had in my mind a very distinct and highly disagreeable picture of the visiting arrangements at a local prison in one of the provinces, at which I had acted temporarily as medical officer.

"I suppose," I said at length, "it is of no use for me to reopen the question of the advisability of this visit on your part?"

"Not the least," she replied resolutely, "though I understand and appreciate your motive in wishing to do so."

"Then," said I, "if you are really decided, it will be as well for me to prepare you for the ordeal. I am afraid it will give you a terrible shock."

"Indeed?" said she. "Is it so bad? Tell me what it will be like."

"In the first place," I replied, "you must keep in your mind the purpose of a prison like Holloway. We are going to see an innocent man—a cultivated and honorable gentleman. But the ordinary inmates of Holloway are not innocent men; for the most part, the remand cases on the male side are professional criminals, while the women are either petty offenders or chronic inebriates. Most of them are regular customers at the prison—such is the idiotic state of the law—who come into the reception room like travelers entering a familiar hostelry, address the prison officers by name, and demand the usual privileges and extra comforts—the 'drunks,' for instance, generally ask for a dose of bromide to steady their nerves and a light in the cell to keep away the horrors. And such being the character of the inmates, their friends who visit them are naturally of the same type—the lowest outpourings of the slums; and it is not surprising to find that the arrangements of the prison are made to fit its ordinary inmates. The innocent man is a negligible quantity, and no arrangements are made for him or his visitors."

"But shall we not be taken to Reuben's cell?" asked Miss Gibson.

"Bless you! no," I answered; and, determined to give her every inducement to change her mind, I continued: "I will describe the procedure as I have seen it—and a very dreadful and shocking sight I found it, I can tell you. It was while I was acting as a prison doctor in the Midlands that I had this experience. I was going my round one morning when, passing along a passage, I became aware of a strange, muffled roar from the other side of the wall.

"What is that noise?' I asked the warder who was with me.

"Prisoners seeing their friends,' he answered. 'Like to have a look at them, sir?'

"He unlocked a small door, and as he threw it open, the distant, muffled sound swelled into a deafening roar. I passed through the door and found myself in a narrow alley at one end of which a warder was sitting. The sides of the alley were formed by two immense cages with stout wire bars, one for the prisoners and the other for the visitors; and each cage was lined with faces and hands, all in incessant movement, the faces mouthing and grimacing, and the hands clawing restlessly at the bars. The uproar was so terrific that no single voice could be distinguished, though everyone present was shouting his loudest to make himself heard above the universal din. The result was a very strange and horrid illusion, for it seemed as if no one was speaking at all, but that the noise came from outside, and that each one of the faces—low, vicious faces, mostly—was silently grimacing and gibber-ing, snapping its jaws and glaring furiously at the occupants of the opposite cage. It was a frightful spectacle. I could think of nothing but the monkey-house at the Zoo. It seemed as if one ought to walk up the alley and offer nuts and pieces of paper to be torn to pieces."

"Horrible!" exclaimed Miss Gibson. "And do you mean to say that we shall be turned loose into one of these cages with a herd of other visitors?"

"No. You are not turned loose anywhere in a prison. The arrange-ment is this: each cage is divided by partitions into a number of small boxes or apartments, which are numbered. The prisoner is locked in one box and his visitor in the corresponding box opposite. They are thus confronted, with the width of the alley between them; they can see one another and talk but cannot pass any forbidden articles across—a very necessary precaution, I need hardly say."

"Yes, I suppose it is necessary, but it is horrible for decent people. Surely they ought to be able to discriminate."

"Why not give it up and let me take a message to Reuben? He would understand and be thankful to me for dissuading you."

"No, no," she said quickly; "the more repulsive it is, the greater the necessity for me to go. He must not be allowed to think that a trifling inconvenience or indignity is enough to scare his friends away. What building is that ahead?"

We had just swung round from Caledonian Road into a quiet and prosperous-looking suburban street, at the end of which rose the tower of a castellated building.

"That is the prison," I replied. "We are looking at it from the most advantageous point of view; seen from the back, and especially from the inside, it is a good deal less attractive."

Nothing more was said until the cab drove into the courtyard and set us down outside the great front gates. Having directed the cabman to wait for us, I rang the bell and we were speedily admitted through a wicket (which was immediately closed and locked) into a covered court closed in by a second gate, through the bars of which we could see across an inner courtyard to the actual entrance to the prison. Here, while the necessary formalities were gone through, we found ourselves part of a numerous and very motley company, for a considerable assemblage of the prisoners' friends was awaiting the moment of admission. I noticed that my companion was observing our fellow visitors with a kind of horrified curiosity, which she strove, however, and not unsuccessfully, to conceal; and certainly the appearance of the majority furnished eloquent testimony to the failure of crime as a means of worldly advancement. Their present position was productive of very varied emotions; some were silent and evidently stricken with grief; a larger number were voluble and excited, while a considerable proportion were quite cheerful and even inclined to be facetious.

At length the great iron gate was unlocked and our party taken in charge by a warder, who conducted us to that part of the building known as "the wing"; and, in the course of our progress, I could not help observing the profound impression made upon my companion by the circumstance that every door had to be unlocked to admit us and was locked again as soon as we had passed through.

"It seems to me," I said, as we neared our destination, "that you had better let me see Reuben first; I have not much to say to him and shall not keep you waiting long."

"Why do you think so?" she asked, with a shade of suspicion.

"Well," I answered, "I think you may be a little upset by the interview, and I should like to see you into your cab as soon as possible afterward."

"Yes," she said; "perhaps you are right, and it is kind of you to be so thoughtful on my account."

A minute later, accordingly, I found myself shut into a narrow box, like one of those that considerate pawnbrokers provide for their more diffident clients, and in a similar, but more intense, degree, pervaded by a subtle odor of uncleanness. The woodwork was polished to an unctuous smoothness by the friction of numberless dirty hands and soiled garments, and the general appearance—taken in at a glance as I entered—was such as to cause me to thrust my hands into my pockets and studiously avoid contact with any part of the structure but the floor. The end of the box opposite the door was closed in by a strong grating of wire—excepting the lower three feet, which was of wood—and looking through this, I perceived, behind a second grating, Reuben Hornby, standing in a similar attitude to my own. He was dressed in his usual clothes and with his customary neatness, but his face was unshaven and he wore, suspended from a buttonhole, a circular label bearing the characters "B.31"; and these two changes in his exterior carried with them a suggestiveness as subtle as it was unpleasant, making me more than ever regretful that Miss Gibson had insisted on coming.

"It is exceedingly good of you, Dr. Jervis, to come and see me," he said heartily, making himself heard quite easily, to my surprise, above the hubbub of the adjoining boxes; "but I didn't expect you here. I was told I could see my legal advisers in the solicitor's box."

"So you could," I answered. "But I came here by choice because I have brought Miss Gibson with me."

"I am sorry for that," he rejoined, with evident disapproval; "she oughtn't to have come among these riffraff."

"I told her so, and that you wouldn't like it, but she insisted."

"I know," said Reuben. "That's the worst of women—they will make a beastly fuss and sacrifice themselves when nobody wants them to. But I mustn't be ungrateful; she means it kindly, and she's a deuced good sort, is Juliet."

"She is indeed," I exclaimed, not a little disgusted at his cool, unappreciative tone; "a most noble-hearted girl, and her devotion to you is positively heroic."

The faintest suspicion of a smile appeared on the face seen through the double grating; on which I felt that I could have pulled his nose with pleasure—only that a pair of tongs of special construction would have been required for the purpose.

"Yes," he answered calmly, "we have always been very good friends."

A rejoinder of the most extreme acidity was on my lips. Damn the fellow! What did he mean by speaking in that supercilious tone of the loveliest and sweetest woman in the world? But, after all, one cannot trample on a poor devil locked up in a jail on a false charge, no matter how great may be the provocation. I drew a deep breath and, having recovered myself, outwardly at least, said—

"I hope you don't find the conditions here too intolerable?"

"Oh, no," he answered. "It's beastly unpleasant, of course, but it might easily be worse. I don't mind if it's only for a week or two; and I am really encouraged by what Dr. Thorndyke said. I hope he wasn't being merely soothing."

"You may take it that he was not. What he said, I am sure he meant. Of course, you know I am not in his confidence—nobody is—but I gather that he is satisfied with the defense he is preparing."

"If he is satisfied, I am," said Reuben, "and, in any case, I shall owe him an immense debt of gratitude for having stood by me and believed in me when all the world—except my aunt and Juliet—had condemned me."

He then went on to give me a few particulars of his prison life, and when he had chatted for a quarter of an hour or so, I took my leave to make way for Miss Gibson.

Her interview with him was not as long as I had expected, though, to be sure, the conditions were not very favorable either for the exchange of confidences or for utterances of a sentimental character. The consciousness that one's conversation could be overheard by the occupants of adjacent boxes destroyed all sense of privacy, to say nothing of the disturbing influence of the warder in the alley-way.

When she rejoined me, her manner was abstracted and very depressed, a circumstance that gave me considerable food for reflection as we made our way in silence toward the main entrance. Had she found Reuben as cool and matter-of-fact as I had? He was assuredly a very calm and self-possessed lover, and it was conceivable that his reception of the girl, strung up, as she was, to an acute pitch of emotion, might have been somewhat in the nature of an anticlimax. And then, was it possible that the feeling was on her side only? Could it be that the priceless pearl of her love was cast before—I was tempted to use the colloquial singular and call him an "unappreciative swine!" The thing was almost unthinkable to me, and yet I was tempted to dwell upon it; for when a man is in love—and I could no longer disguise my condition from myself—he is inclined to be humble and to gather up thankfully the treasure that is rejected of another.

I was brought up short in these reflections by the clank of the lock in the great iron gate. We entered together the gloomy vestibule, and a moment later were let out through the wicket into the courtyard; and as the lock clicked behind us, we gave a simultaneous sigh of relief to find ourselves outside the precincts of the prison, beyond the domain of bolts and bars.

I had settled Miss Gibson in the cab and given her address to the driver, when I noticed her looking at me, as I thought, somewhat wistfully.

"Can't I put you down somewhere?" she said, in response to a half-questioning glance from me.

I seized the opportunity with thankfulness and replied—

"You might set me down at King's Cross if it is not delaying you;" and giving the word to the cabman, I took my place by her side as the cab started and a black-painted prison van turned into the courtyard with its freight of squalid misery.

"I don't think Reuben was very pleased to see me," Miss Gibson remarked presently, "but I shall come again all the same. It is a duty I owe both to him and to myself."

I felt that I ought to endeavor to dissuade her, but the reflection that her visits must almost of necessity involve my companionship enfeebled my will. I was fast approaching a state of infatuation.

"I was so thankful," she continued, "that you prepared me. It was a horrible experience to see the poor fellow caged like a wild beast, with that dreadful label hanging from his coat; but it would have been overwhelming if I had not known what to expect."

As we proceeded, her spirits revived somewhat, a circumstance that she graciously ascribed to the enlivening influence of my society; and I then told her of the mishap that had befallen my colleague.

"What a terrible thing!" she exclaimed, with evidently unaffected concern. "It is the merest chance that he was not killed on the spot. Is he much hurt? And would he mind, do you think, if I called to inquire after him?"

I said that I was sure he would be delighted (being, as a matter of fact, entirely indifferent as to his sentiments on the subject in my delight at the proposal), and when I stepped down from the cab at King's Cross to pursue my way homeward, there already opened out before me the prospect of the renewal of this bittersweet and all too dangerous companionship on the morrow.

CHAPTER TEN

POLTON IS MYSTIFIED

A couple of days sufficed to prove that Thorndyke's mishap was not to be productive of any permanent ill consequences; his wounds progressed favorably and he was able to resume his ordinary avocations.

Miss Gibson's visit—but why should I speak of her in these formal terms? To me, when I thought of her, which I did only too often, she was Juliet, with perhaps an adjective thrown in; and as Juliet I shall henceforth speak of her (but without the adjective) in this narrative, wherein nothing has been kept back from the reader— Juliet's visit, then, had been a great success, for my colleague was really pleased by the attention, and displayed a quiet geniality that filled our visitor with delight.

He talked a good deal of Reuben, and I could see that he was endeavoring to settle in his own mind the vexed question of her relations with and sentiments toward our unfortunate client; but what conclusions he arrived at I was unable to discover, for he was by no means communicative after she had left. Nor was there any repetition of the visit—greatly to my regret—since, as I have said, he was able, in a day or two, to resume his ordinary mode of life.

The first evidence I had of his renewed activity appeared when I returned to the chambers at about eleven o'clock in the morning, to find Polton hovering dejectedly about the sitting room, apparently perpetrating as near an approach to a "spring clean" as could be permitted in a bachelor establishment.

"Hallo, Polton!" I exclaimed. "Have you contrived to tear yourself away from the laboratory for an hour or two?"

"No, sir," he answered gloomily. "The laboratory has torn itself away from me."

"What do you mean?" I asked.

"The Doctor has shut himself in and locked the door, and he says I am not to disturb him. It will be a cold lunch today."

"What is he doing in there?" I inquired.

"Ah!" said Polton. "That's just what I should like to know. I'm fair eaten up with curiosity. He is making some experiments in connection with some of his cases, and when the Doctor locks himself in to make experiments, something interesting generally follows. I should like to know what it is this time."

"I suppose there is a keyhole in the laboratory door?" I suggested, with a grin.

"Sir!" he exclaimed indignantly. "Dr. Jervis, I am surprised at you." Then, perceiving my facetious intent, he smiled also and added: "But there *is* a keyhole if you'd like to try it, though I'll wager the Doctor would see more of you than you would of him."

"You are mighty secret about your doings, you and the Doctor," I said.

"Yes," he answered. "You see, it's a queer trade this of the Doctor's, and there are some queer secrets in it. Now, for instance, what do you make of this?"

He produced from his pocket a leather case, whence he took a piece of paper that he handed to me. On it was a neatly executed drawing of what looked like one of a set of chessmen, with the dimensions written on the margin.

"It looks like a pawn—one of the Staunton pattern," I said.

"Just what I thought; but it isn't. I've got to make twenty-four of them, and what the Doctor is going to do with them fairly beats me."

"Perhaps he has invented some new game," I suggested facetiously.

"He is always inventing new games and playing them mostly in courts of law, and then the other players generally lose. But this is a puzzler, and no mistake. Twenty-four of these to be turned up in the best-seasoned boxwood! What can they be for? Something to do with the experiments he is carrying on upstairs at this very moment, I expect." He shook his head and, having carefully returned the drawing to his pocketbook, said, in a solemn tone—"Sir, there are times when the Doctor makes me fairly dance with curiosity. And this is one of them."

Although not afflicted with a curiosity so acute as that of Polton, I found myself speculating at intervals on the nature of my colleague's experiments and the purpose of the singular little objects that he had ordered to be made; but I was unacquainted with any of the cases on which he was engaged, excepting that of Reuben Hornby, and with the latter I was quite unable to connect a set of twenty-four boxwood chessmen. Moreover, on this day, I was to accompany

Juliet on her second visit to Holloway, and that circumstance gave me abundant mental occupation of another kind.

At lunch, Thorndyke was animated and talkative but not communicative. He "had some work in the laboratory that he must do himself," he said, but gave no hint as to its nature; and as soon as our meal was finished, he returned to his labors, leaving me to pace up and down the walk, listening with ridiculous eagerness for the sound of the hansom that was to transport me to the regions of the blessed, and—incidentally—to Holloway Prison.

When I returned to the Temple, the sitting room was empty and hideously neat, as the result of Polton's spring-cleaning efforts. My colleague was evidently still at work in the laboratory, and from the circumstance that the tea things were set out on the table and a kettle of water placed in readiness on the gas ring by the fireplace, I gathered that Polton also was full of business and anxious not to be disturbed.

Accordingly, I lit the gas and made my tea, enlivening my solitude by turning over in my mind the events of the afternoon.

Juliet had been charming—as she always was—frank, friendly, and unaffectedly pleased to have my companionship. She evidently liked me and did not disguise the fact—why should she indeed?—but treated me with a freedom, almost affectionate, as though I had been a favorite brother, which was very delightful, and would have been more so if I could have accepted the relationship. As to her feelings toward me, I had not the slightest misgiving, and so my conscience was clear; for Juliet was as innocent as a child, with the innocence that belongs to the direct, straightforward nature that neither does evil itself nor looks for evil motives in others. For myself, I was past praying for. The thing was done, and I must pay the price hereafter, content to reflect that I had trespassed against no one but myself. It was a miserable affair, and many a heartache did it promise me in the lonely days that were to come, when I should have said "good-bye" to the Temple and gone back to my old nomadic life; and yet I would not have had it changed if I could; would not have bartered the bittersweet memories for dull forgetfulness.

But other matters had transpired in the course of our drive than those that loomed so large to me in the egotism of my love. We had spoken of Mr. Hornby and his affairs, and from our talk, there had emerged certain facts of no little moment to the inquiry on which I was engaged.

"Misfortunes are proverbially sociable," Juliet had remarked, in reference to her adopted uncle. "As if this trouble about Reuben were not enough, there are worries in the city. Perhaps you have heard of them."

I replied that Walter had mentioned the matter to me.

"Yes," said Juliet rather viciously; "I am not quite clear as to what part that good gentleman has played in the matter. It has come out, quite accidentally, that he had a large holding in the mines himself, but he seems to have 'cut his loss,' as the phrase goes, and got out of them; though how he managed to pay such large differences is more than we can understand. We think he must have raised money somehow to do it."

"Do you know when the mines began to depreciate?" I asked.

"Yes, it was quite a sudden affair—what Walter calls 'a slump'—and it occurred only a few days before the robbery. Mr. Hornby was telling me about it only yesterday, and he recalled it to me by a ridiculous accident that happened on that day."

"What was that?" I inquired.

"Why, I cut my finger and nearly fainted," she answered, with a shamefaced little laugh. "It was rather a bad cut, you know, but I didn't notice it until I found my hand covered with blood. Then I turned suddenly faint and had to lie down on the hearthrug—it was in Mr. Hornby's study, which I was tidying up at the time. Here I was found by Reuben, and a dreadful fright it gave him at first; and then he tore up his handkerchief to tie up the wounded finger, and you never saw such an awful mess as he got his hands in. He might have been arrested as a murderer, poor boy, from the condition he was in. It will make your professional gorge rise to learn that he fastened up the extemporized bandage with red tape, which he got from the writing table after rooting about among the sacred papers in the most ruthless fashion.

"When he had gone, I tried to put the things on the table straight again, and really you might have thought some horrible crime had been committed; the envelopes and papers were all smeared with blood and marked with the print of gory fingers. I remembered it afterward, when Reuben's thumb-mark was identified, and thought that perhaps one of the papers might have got into the safe by accident; but Mr. Hornby told me that was impossible; he tore the leaf off his memorandum block at the time when he put away the diamonds."

Such was the gist of our conversation as the cab rattled through the streets on the way to the prison; and certainly it contained matter sufficiently important to draw away my thoughts from other subjects more agreeable, but less relevant to the case. With a sudden remembrance of my duty, I drew forth my notebook and was in the act of committing the statements to writing when Thorndyke entered the room.

"Don't let me interrupt you, Jervis," said he. "I will make myself a cup of tea while you finish your writing, and then you shall exhibit the day's catch and hang your nets out to dry."

I was not long in finishing my notes, for I was in a fever of impatience to hear Thorndyke's comments on my latest addition to our store of information. By the time the kettle was boiling, my entries were completed, and I proceeded forthwith to retail to my colleague those extracts from my conversation with Juliet that I have just recorded.

He listened, as usual, with deep and critical attention.

"This is very interesting and important," he said, when I had finished; "really, Jervis, you are a most invaluable coadjutor. It seems that information, which would be strictly withheld from the forbidding Jorkins, trickles freely and unasked into the ear of the genial Spenlow. Now, I suppose you regard your hypothesis as having received very substantial confirmation?"

"Certainly, I do."

"And very justifiably. You see now how completely you were in the right when you allowed yourself to entertain this theory of the crime in spite of its apparent improbability. By the light of these new facts it has become quite a probable explanation of the whole affair, and if it could only be shown that Mr. Hornby's memorandum block was among the papers on the table, it would rise to a high degree of probability. The obvious moral is, never disregard the improbable. By the way, it is odd that Reuben failed to recall this occurrence when I questioned him. Of course, the bloody finger-marks were not discovered until he had gone, but one would have expected him to recall the circumstance when I asked him, pointedly, if he had never left bloody finger-prints on any papers."

"I must try to find out if Mr. Hornby's memorandum block was on the table and among the marked papers," I said.

"Yes, that would be wise," he answered, "though I don't suppose the information will be forthcoming."

My colleague's manner rather disappointed me. He had heard my report with the greatest attention, he had discussed it with animation, but yet he seemed to attach to the new and—as they appeared to me—highly important facts an interest that was academic rather than practical. Of course, his calmness might be assumed; but this did not seem likely, for John Thorndyke was far too sincere and dignified a character to cultivate in private life the artifices of the actor. To strangers, indeed, he presented habitually a calm and impassive exterior; but this was natural to him, and was but the outward sign of his even and judicial habit of mind.

No; there was no doubt that my startling news had left him unmoved, and this must be for one of two reasons: either he already knew all that I had told him (which was perfectly possible), or he had some other and better means of explaining the crime. I was turning over these two alternatives, not unobserved by my watchful colleague, when Polton entered the room; a broad grin was on his face, and a drawing board, that he carried like a tray, bore twenty-four neatly turned boxwood pieces.

Thorndyke at once entered into the unspoken jest that beamed from the countenance of his subordinate.

"Here is Polton with a problem for you, Jervis," he said. "He assumes that I have invented a new parlor game, and has been trying to work out the moves. Have you succeeded yet, Polton?"

"No, sir, I haven't; but I suspect that one of the players will be a man in a wig and gown."

"Perhaps you are right," said Thorndyke; "but that doesn't take you very far. Let us hear what Dr. Jervis has to say."

"I can make nothing of them," I answered. "Polton showed me the drawing this morning, and then was terrified lest he had committed a breach of confidence, and I have been trying ever since, without a glimmer of success, to guess what they can be for."

"H'm," grunted Thorndyke, as he sauntered up and down the room, teacup in hand, "to guess, eh? I like not that word 'guess' in the mouth of a man of science. What do you mean by a 'guess'?"

His manner was wholly facetious, but I professed to take his question seriously, and replied—

"By a guess, I mean a conclusion arrived at without data."

"Impossible!" he exclaimed, with mock sternness. "Nobody but an utter fool arrives at a conclusion without data."

"Then I must revise my definition instantly," I rejoined. "Let us say that a guess is a conclusion drawn from insufficient facts."

"That is better," said he; "but perhaps it would be better still to say that a guess is a particular and definite conclusion deduced from facts which properly yield only a general and indefinite one. Let us take an instance," he continued. "Looking out of the window, I see a man walking round Paper Buildings. Now suppose I say, after the fashion of the inspired detective of the romances, 'That man is a stationmaster or inspector,' that would be a guess. The observed facts do not yield the conclusion, though they do warrant a conclusion less definite and more general."

"You'd have been right though, sir!" exclaimed Polton, who had stepped forward with me to examine the unconscious subject of the demonstration. "That gent used to be the stationmaster at Camberwell. I remember him well."

The little man was evidently greatly impressed.

"I happen to be right, you see," said Thorndyke; "but I might as easily have been wrong."

"You weren't though, sir," said Polton. "You spotted him at a glance."

In his admiration of the result, he cared not a fig for the correctness of the means by which it had been attained.

"Now why do I suggest that he is a stationmaster?" pursued Thorndyke, disregarding his assistant's comment.

"I suppose you were looking at his feet," I answered. "I seem to have noticed that peculiar, splay-footed gait in stationmasters, now that you mention it."

"Quite so. The arch of the foot has given way; the plantar ligaments have become stretched and the deep calf muscles weakened. Then, since bending of the weakened arch causes discomfort, the feet have become turned outward, by which the bending of the foot is reduced to a minimum; and as the left foot is the more flattened, so it is turned out more than the right. Then the turning out of the toes causes the legs to splay outward from the knees downward—a very conspicuous condition in a tall man like this one—and you notice that the left leg splays out more than the other.

"But we know that depression of the arch of the foot is brought about by standing for long periods. Continuous pressure on a living structure weakens it, while intermittent pressure strengthens it; so the man who stands on his feet continuously develops a flat instep and a weak calf, while the professional dancer or runner acquires a high instep and a strong calf. Now there are many occupations which involve prolonged standing and so induce the condition of flat foot: waiters, hall-porters, hawkers, policemen, shop-walkers, salesmen, and station officials are examples. But the waiter's gait is characteristic—a quick, shuffling walk which enables him to carry liquids without spilling them. This man walks with a long, swinging stride; he is obviously not a waiter. His dress and appearance in general exclude the idea of a hawker or even a hall-porter; he is a man of poor physique and so cannot be a policeman. The shop-walker or salesman is accustomed to move in relatively confined spaces, and so acquires a short, brisk step, and his dress tends to rather exuberant smartness;

the station official patrols long platforms, often at a rapid pace, and so tends to take long strides, while his dress is dignified and neat rather than florid. The last-mentioned characteristics, you see, appear in the subject of our analysis; he agrees with the general description of a stationmaster. But if we therefore conclude that he *is* a stationmaster, we fall into the time-honored fallacy of the undistributed middle term—the fallacy that haunts all brilliant guessers, including the detective, not only of romance, but too often also of real life. All that the observed facts justify us in inferring is that this man is engaged in some mode of life that necessitates a good deal of standing; the rest is mere guesswork."

"It's wonderful," said Polton, gazing at the now distant figure; "perfectly wonderful. I should never have known he was a station-master." With this and a glance of deep admiration at his employer, he took his departure.

"You will also observe," said Thorndyke, with a smile, "that a fortunate guess often brings more credit than a piece of sound reasoning with a less striking result."

"Yes, that is unfortunately the case, and it is certainly true in the present instance. Your reputation, as far as Polton is concerned, is now firmly established even if it was not before. In his eyes you are a wizard from whom nothing is hidden. But to return to these little pieces, as I must call them, for the lack of a better name. I can form no hypothesis as to their use. I seem to have no 'departure,' as the nautical phrase goes, from which to start an inquiry. I haven't even the material for guesswork. Ought I to be able to arrive at any opinion on the subject?"

Thorndyke picked up one of the pieces, fingering it delicately and inspecting with a critical eye the flat base on which it stood, and reflected for a few moments.

"It is easy to trace a connection when one knows all the facts," he said at length, "but it seems to me that you have the materials from which to form a conjecture. Perhaps I am wrong, but I think, when you have had more experience, you will find yourself able to work out a problem of this kind. What is required is constructive imagination and a rigorous exactness in reasoning. Now, you are a good reasoner, and you have recently shown me that you have the necessary imagination; you merely lack experience in the use of your faculties. When you learn my purpose in having these things made—as you will before long—you will probably be surprised that their use did not occur to you. And now let us go forth and take a brisk walk to refresh ourselves (or perhaps I should say myself) after the day's labor."

CHAPTER ELEVEN

THE AMBUSH

"I am going to ask for your collaboration in another case," said Thorndyke, a day or two later. "It appears to be one of suicide, but the solicitors to the 'Griffin' office have asked me to go down to the place, which is in the neighborhood of Barnet, and be present at the *post-mortem* and the inquest. They have managed to arrange that the inquest shall take place directly after the *post-mortem*, so that we shall be able to do the whole business in a single visit."

"Is the case one of any intricacy?" I asked.

"I don't think so," he answered. "It looks like a common suicide; but you can never tell. The importance of the case at present arises entirely from the heavy insurance; a verdict of suicide will mean a gain of ten thousand pounds to the 'Griffin,' so, naturally, the directors are anxious to get the case settled and not inclined to boggle over a little expense."

"Naturally. And when will the expedition take place?" I asked.

"The inquest is fixed for tomorrow—what is the matter? Does that fall foul of any arrangement of yours?"

"Oh, nothing of any importance," I replied hastily, deeply ashamed of the momentary change of countenance that my friend had been so quick to observe.

"Well, what is it?" persisted Thorndyke. "You have got something on."

"It is nothing, I tell you, but what can be quite easily arranged to suit your plans."

"*Cherchez la*—h'm?" queried Thorndyke, with an exasperating grin.

"Yes," I answered, turning as red as a pickled cabbage; "since you are so beastly inquisitive. Miss Gibson wrote, on behalf of Mrs. Hornby, asking me to dine with them *en famille* tomorrow evening, and I sent off an acceptance an hour ago."

"And you call that 'nothing of any importance'!" exclaimed Thorndyke. "Alas! and likewise alackaday (which is an approximately synonymous expression)! The age of chivalry is past, indeed. Of course you must keep your appointment; I can manage quite well alone."

"We shouldn't be back early enough for me to go to Kensington from the station, I suppose?"

"No; certainly not. I find that the trains are very awkward; we should not reach King's Cross until nearly one in the morning."

"Then, in that case, I shall write to Miss Gibson and excuse myself."

"Oh, I wouldn't do that," said Thorndyke; "it will disappoint them, and really it is not necessary."

"I shall write forthwith," I said firmly, "so please don't try to dissuade me. I have been feeling quite uncomfortable at the thought that, all the time I have been in your employ, I seem to have done nothing but idle about and amuse myself. The opportunity of doing something tangible for my wage is too precious to be allowed to slip."

Thorndyke chuckled indulgently. "You shall do as you please, my dear boy," he said; "but don't imagine that you have been eating the bread of idleness. When you see this Hornby case worked out in detail, you will be surprised to find how large a part you have taken in unravelling it. Your worth to me has been far beyond your poor little salary, I can assure you."

"It is very handsome of you to say that," I said, highly gratified to learn that I was really of use, and not, as I had begun to suspect, a mere object of charity.

"It is perfectly true," he answered; "and now, since you are going to help me in this case, I will set you your task. The case, as I have said, appears to be quite simple, but it never does to take the simplicity for granted. Here is the letter from the solicitors giving the facts as far as they are known at present. On the shelves there you will find Casper, Taylor, Guy, and Ferrier, and the other authorities on medical jurisprudence, and I will put out one or two other books that you may find useful. I want you to extract and make classified notes of everything that may bear on such a case as the present one may turn out to be. We must go prepared to meet any contingency that may arise. This is my invariable practice, and even if the case turns out to be quite simple, the labor is never wasted, for it represents so much experience gained."

"Casper and Taylor are pretty old, aren't they?" I objected.

"So is suicide," he retorted drily. "It is a capital mistake to neglect the old authorities. 'There were strong men before Agamemnon,' and some of them were uncommonly strong, let me tell you. Give your best attention to the venerable Casper and the obsolete Taylor and you will not be without your reward."

As a result of these injunctions, I devoted the remainder of the day to the consideration of the various methods by which a man might contrive to effect his exit from the stage of human activities. And a very engrossing study I found it, and the more interesting in view of the problem that awaited solution on the morrow; but yet not so engrossing but that I was able to find time to write a long, rather intimate and minutely explanatory letter to Miss Gibson, in which I even mentioned the hour of our return as showing the impossibility of my keeping my engagement. Not that I had the smallest fear of her taking offence, for it is an evidence of my respect and regard for her that I cancelled the appointment without a momentary doubt that she would approve of my action; but it was pleasant to write to her at length and to feel the intimacy of keeping her informed of the details of my life.

The case, when we came to inquire into it on the spot, turned out to be a suicide of the most transparent type; whereat both Thorndyke and I were, I think, a little disappointed—he at having apparently done so little for a very substantial fee, and I at having no opportunity for applying my recently augmented knowledge.

"Yes," said my colleague, as we rolled ourselves up in our rugs in adjacent corners of the railway carriage, "it has been a flat affair, and the whole thing could have been managed by the local solicitor. But it is not a waste of time after all, for, you see, I have to do many a day's work for which I get not a farthing of payment, nor even any recognition, so that I do not complain if I occasionally find myself receiving more payment than my actual services merit. And as to you, I take it that you have acquired a good deal of valuable knowledge on the subject of suicide, and knowledge, as the late Lord Bacon remarked with more truth than originality, is power."

To this I made no reply, having just lit my pipe and feeling uncommonly drowsy; and, my companion having followed my example, we smoked in silence, becoming more and more somnolent, until the train drew up in the terminus and we turned out, yawning and shivering, on to the platform.

"Bah!" exclaimed Thorndyke, drawing his rug round his shoulders; "this is a cheerless hour—a quarter past one. See how chilly and miserable all these poor devils of passengers look. Shall we cab it or walk?"

"I think a sharp walk would rouse our circulation after sitting huddled up in the carriage for so long," I answered.

"So do I," said Thorndyke, "so let us away; hark forward! And also tallyho! In fact one might go so far as to say Yoicks! That gentleman appears to favor the strenuous life, if one may judge by the size of his sprocket-wheel."

He pointed to a bicycle that was drawn up by the curb in the approach—a machine of the road-racer type, with an enormous sprocket-wheel, indicating a gear of, at least, ninety.

"Some scorcher or amateur racer, probably," I said, "who takes the opportunity of getting a spin on the wood pavement when the streets are empty." I looked round to see if I could identify the owner, but the machine appeared to be, for the moment, taking care of itself.

King's Cross is one of those districts of which the inhabitants are slow in settling down for the night, and even at a quarter past one in the morning, its streets are not entirely deserted. Here and there the glimmer of a streetlamp or the far-reaching ray from a tall electric light reveals the form of some nocturnal prowler creeping along with catlike stealthiness, or bursting, catlike, into unmelodious song. Not greatly desirous of the society of these roysterers, we crossed quickly from the station into the Gray's Inn Road, now silent and excessively dismal in aspect, and took our way along the western side. We had turned the curve and were crossing Manchester Street, when a series of yelps from ahead announced the presence of a party of merrymakers, whom we were not yet able to see, however, for the night was an exceptionally dark one; but the sounds of revelry continued to increase in volume as we proceeded, until, as we passed Sidmouth Street, we came in sight of the revelers. They were some half-dozen in number, all of them roughs of the hooligan type, and they were evidently in boisterous spirits, for, as they passed the entrance to the Royal Free Hospital, they halted and battered furiously at the gate. Shortly after this exploit, they crossed the road on to our side, whereupon Thorndyke caught my arm and slackened his pace.

"Let them draw ahead," said he. "It is a wise precaution to give all hooligan gangs a very wide berth at this time of night. We had better turn down Heathcote Street and cross Mecklenburgh Square."

We continued to walk on at reduced speed until we reached Heathcote Street, into which we turned and so entered Mecklenburgh Square, where we mended our pace once more.

"The hooligan," pursued Thorndyke, as we walked briskly across the silent square, "covers a multitude of sins, ranging from highway robbery with violence and paid assassination (technically known as 'bashing') down to the criminal folly of the philanthropic magistrate, who seems to think that his function in the economy of nature is to secure the survival of the unfittest. There goes a cyclist along Guildford Street. I wonder if that is our strenuous friend from the station. If so, he has slipped past the hooligans."

We were just entering Doughty Street, and as Thorndyke spoke, a man on a bicycle was visible for an instant at the crossing of the two streets. When we reached Guildford Street, we both looked down the long, lamp-lighted vista, but the cyclist had vanished.

"We had better go straight on into Theobald's Road," said Thorndyke, and we accordingly pursued our way up the fine old-world street, from whose tall houses our footfalls echoed, so that we seemed to be accompanied by an invisible multitude, until we reached that part where it unaccountably changes its name and becomes John Street.

"There always seems to me something very pathetic about these old Bloomsbury streets," said Thorndyke, "with their faded grandeur and dignified seediness. They remind me of some prim and aged gentlewoman in reduced circumstances who—Hallo! What was that?"

A faint, sharp thud from behind had been followed instantly by the shattering of a ground-floor window in front.

We both stopped dead and remained, for a couple of seconds, staring into the gloom, from whence the first sound had come; then Thorndyke darted diagonally across the road at a swift run and I immediately followed.

At the moment when the affair happened, we had gone about forty yards up John Street, that is, from the place where it is crossed by Henry Street, and we now raced across the road to the further corner of the latter street. When we reached it, however, the little thoroughfare was empty, and as we paused for a moment, no sound of retreating footsteps broke the silence.

"The shot certainly came from here!" said Thorndyke; "come on." And he again broke into a run. A few yards up the street, a mews turns off to the left, and into this my companion plunged, motioning me to go straight on, which I accordingly did, and in a few paces reached the top of the street. Here a narrow thoroughfare, with a broad, smooth pavement, bears off to the left, parallel with the mews, and, as I arrived at the corner and glanced up the little street, I saw a man on a bicycle gliding swiftly and silently toward Little James' Street.

With a mighty shout of "Stop thief!" I started in hot pursuit, but, though the man's feet were moving in an apparently leisurely

manner, he drew ahead at an astonishing pace, in spite of my efforts to overtake him; and it then dawned upon me that the slow
revolutions of his feet were due, in reality, to the unusually high
gear of the machine that he was riding. As I realized this, and at
the same moment recalled the bicycle that we had seen in the
station, the fugitive swung round into Little James' Street and
vanished.

The speed at which the man was traveling made further pursuit
utterly futile, so I turned and walked back, panting and perspiring
from the unwonted exertion. As I reentered Henry Street, Thorndyke
emerged from the mews and halted on seeing me.

"Cyclist?" he asked laconically, as I came up.

"Yes," I answered; "riding a machine geared up to about ninety."

"Ah! he must have followed us from the station," said Thorndyke.
"Did you notice if he was carrying anything?"

"He had a walking-stick in his hand. I didn't see anything else."

"What sort of walking-stick?"

"I couldn't see very distinctly. It was a stoutish stick—I should
say a Malacca, probably—and it had what looked like a horn handle.
I could see that as he passed a streetlamp."

"What kind of lamp had he?"

"I couldn't see; but, as he turned the corner, I noticed that it
seemed to burn very dimly."

"A little vaseline, or even oil, smeared on the outside of the glass
will reduce the glare of a lamp very appreciably," my companion remarked, "especially on a dusty road. Ha! here is the proprietor of the
broken window. He wants to know, you know."

We had once more turned into John Street and now perceived a
man, standing on the wide doorstep of the house with the shattered
window, looking anxiously up and down the street.

"Do either of you gents know anything about this here?" he asked, pointing to the broken pane.

"Yes," said Thorndyke, "we happened to be passing when it was done; in fact," he added, "I rather suspect that the missile, whatever it was, was intended for our benefit."

"Oh!" said the man. "Who done it?"

"That I can't say," replied Thorndyke. "Whoever he was, he made off on a bicycle and we were unable to catch him."

"Oh!" said the man once more, regarding us with growing suspicion. "On a bicycle, hay! Dam funny, ain't it? What did he do it with?"

"That is what I should like to find out," said Thorndyke. "I see this house is empty."

"Yes, it's empty—leastways it's to let. I'm the caretaker. But what's that got to do with it?"

"Merely this," answered Thorndyke, "that the object—stone, bullet, or whatever it may have been—was aimed, I believe, at me, and I should like to ascertain its nature. Would you do me the favor of permitting me to look for it?"

The caretaker was evidently inclined to refuse this request, for he glanced suspiciously from my companion to me once or twice before replying, but at length, he turned toward the open door and gruffly invited us to enter.

A paraffin lamp was on the floor in a recess of the hall, and this our conductor took up when he had closed the street door.

"This is the room," he said, turning the key and thrusting the door open; "the library they call it, but it's the front parlor in plain English." He entered and, holding the lamp above his head, stared balefully at the broken window.

Thorndyke glanced quickly along the floor in the direction that the missile would have taken, and then said—

"Do you see any mark on the wall there?"

As he spoke, he indicated the wall opposite the window, which obviously could not have been struck by a projectile entering with such extreme obliquity; and I was about to point out this fact when I fortunately remembered the great virtue of silence.

Our friend approached the wall, still holding up the lamp, and scrutinized the surface with close attention; and while he was thus engaged, I observed Thorndyke stoop quickly and pick up something, which he deposited carefully, and without remark, in his waistcoat pocket.

"I don't see no bruise anywhere," said the caretaker, sweeping his hand over the wall.

"Perhaps the thing struck this wall," suggested Thorndyke, pointing to the one that was actually in the line of fire. "Yes, of course," he added, "it would be this one—the shot came from Henry Street."

The caretaker crossed the room and threw the light of his lamp on the wall thus indicated.

"Ah! Here we are!" he exclaimed, with gloomy satisfaction, pointing to a small dent in which the wallpaper was turned back and the plaster exposed; "looks almost like a bullet mark, but you say you didn't hear no report."

"No," said Thorndyke, "there was no report; it must have been a catapult."

The caretaker set the lamp down on the floor and proceeded to grope about for the projectile, in which operation we both assisted; and I could not suppress a faint smile as I noted the earnestness with which Thorndyke peered about the floor in search of the missile that was quietly reposing in his waistcoat pocket.

We were deep in our investigations when there was heard an uncompromising double knock at the street door, followed by the loud pealing of a bell in the basement.

"Bobby, I suppose," growled the caretaker. "Here's a blooming fuss about nothing." He caught up the lamp and went out, leaving us in the dark.

"I picked it up, you know," said Thorndyke, when we were alone.

"I saw you," I answered.

"Good; I applaud your discretion," he rejoined. The caretaker's supposition was correct. When he returned, he was accompanied by a burly constable, who saluted us with a cheerful smile and glanced facetiously round the empty room.

"Our boys," said he, nodding toward the broken window; "they're playful lads, that they are. You were passing when it happened, sir, I hear."

"Yes," answered Thorndyke; and he gave the constable a brief account of the occurrence, which the latter listened to, notebook in hand.

"Well," said he when the narrative was concluded, "if those hooligan boys are going to take to catapults, they'll make things lively all round."

"You ought to run some of 'em in," said the caretaker.

"Run 'em in!" exclaimed the constable in a tone of disgust; "yes! And then the magistrate will tell 'em to be good boys and give 'em five shillings out of the poor box to buy illustrated Testaments. I'd Testament them, the worthless varmints!"

He rammed his notebook fiercely into his pocket and stalked out of the room into the street, whither we followed.

"You'll find that bullet or stone when you sweep up the room," he said, as he turned on to his beat; "and you'd better let us have it. Good night, sir."

He strolled off toward Henry Street, while Thorndyke and I resumed our journey southward.

"Why were you so secret about that projectile?" I asked my friend as we walked up the street.

"Partly to avoid discussion with the caretaker," he replied; "but principally because I thought it likely that a constable would pass the house and, seeing the light, come in to make inquiries."

"And then?"

"Then I should have had to hand over the object to him."

"And why not? Is the object a specially interesting one?"

"It is highly interesting to me at the present moment," replied Thorndyke, with a chuckle, "because I have not examined it. I have a theory as to its nature, which theory I should like to test before taking the police into my confidence."

"Are you going to take me into your confidence?" I asked.

"When we get home, if you are not too sleepy," he replied.

On our arrival at his chambers, Thorndyke desired me to light up and clear one end of the table while he went up to the workshop to fetch some tools. I turned back the table cover and, having adjusted the gas so as to light this part of the table, waited in some impatience for my colleague's return. In a few minutes he reentered, bearing a small vise, a metal saw, and a wide-mouthed bottle.

"What have you got in that bottle?" I asked, perceiving a metal object inside it.

"That is the projectile, which I have thought fit to rinse in distilled water, for reasons that will presently appear."

He agitated the bottle gently for a minute or so, and then, with a pair of dissecting forceps, lifted out the object and held it above the surface of the water to drain, after which he laid it carefully on a piece of blotting paper.

I stooped over the projectile and examined it with great curiosity, while Thorndyke stood by regarding me with almost equal interest.

"Well," he said, after watching me in silence for some time, "what do you see?"

"I see a small brass cylinder," I answered, "about two inches long and rather thicker than an ordinary lead pencil. One end is conical, and there is a small hole at the apex which seems to contain a steel point; the other end is flat, but has in the center a small square projection such as might fit a watch-key. I notice also a small hole in the side of the cylinder close to the flat end. The thing looks like a miniature shell, and appears to be hollow."

"It is hollow," said Thorndyke. "You must have observed that, when I held it up to drain, the water trickled out through the hole at the pointed end."

"Yes, I noticed that."

"Now take it up and shake it."

I did so and felt some heavy object rattle inside it.

"There is some loose body inside it," I said, "which fits it pretty closely, as it moves only in the long diameter."

"Quite so; your description is excellent. And now, what is the nature of this projectile?"

"I should say it is a miniature shell or explosive bullet."

"Wrong!" said Thorndyke. "A very natural inference, but a wrong one."

"Then what is the thing?" I demanded, my curiosity still further aroused.

"I will show you," he replied. "It is something much more subtle than an explosive bullet—which would really be a rather crude appliance—admirably thought out and thoroughly well executed. We have to deal with a most ingenious and capable man."

I was fain to laugh at his enthusiastic appreciation of the methods of his would-be assassin, and the humor of the situation then appeared to dawn on him, for he said, with an apologetic smile—

"I am not expressing approval, you must understand, but merely professional admiration. It is this class of criminal that creates the necessity for my services. He is my patron, so to speak; my ultimate employer. For the common crook can be dealt with quite efficiently by the common policeman!"

While he was speaking he had been fitting the little cylinder between two pads of tissue-paper in the vice, which he now screwed up tight. Then, with the fine metal saw, he began to cut the projectile, lengthwise, into two slightly unequal parts. This operation took some time, especially since he was careful not to cut the loose body inside, but at length the section was completed and the interior of the cylinder exposed, when he released it from the vice and held it up before me with an expression of triumph.

"Now, what do you make it?" he demanded.

I took the object in my fingers and looked at it closely, but was at first more puzzled than before. The loose body I now saw to be a cylinder of lead about half an inch long, accurately fitting the inside of the cylinder but capable of slipping freely backward and forward. The steel point I had noticed in the hole at the apex of the conical end was now seen to be the pointed termination of a slender steel rod that projected fully an inch into the cavity of the cylinder, and the conical end itself was a solid mass of lead.

"Well?" queried Thorndyke, seeing that I was still silent.

"You tell me it is not an explosive bullet," I replied, "otherwise I should have been confirmed in that opinion. I should have said that the percussion cap was carried by this lead plunger and struck on the end of that steel rod when the flight of the bullet was suddenly arrested."

"Very good indeed," said Thorndyke. "You are right so far that this is, in fact, the mechanism of a percussion shell.

"But look at this. You see this little rod was driven inside the bullet when the latter struck the wall. Let us replace it in its original position."

He laid the end of a small flat file against the end of the rod and pressed it firmly, when the rod slid through the hole until it projected an inch beyond the apex of the cone. Then he handed the projectile back to me.

A single glance at the point of the steel rod made the whole thing clear, and I gave a whistle of consternation; for the "rod" was a fine tube with a sharply pointed end.

"The infernal scoundrel!" I exclaimed; "it is a hypodermic needle."

"Yes. A veterinary hypodermic, of extra large bore. Now you see the subtlety and ingenuity of the whole thing. If he had had a reasonable chance he would certainly have succeeded."

"You speak quite regretfully," I said, laughing again at the oddity of his attitude toward the assassin.

"Not at all," he replied. "I have the character of a single-handed player, but even the most self-reliant man can hardly make a *post-mortem* on himself. I am merely appreciating an admirable piece of mechanical design most efficiently carried out. Observe the completeness of the thing, and the way in which all the necessities of the case are foreseen and met. This projectile was discharged from a powerful air gun—the walking-stick form—provided with a force-pump and key. The barrel of that gun was rifled."

"How do you know that?" I asked.

"Well, to begin with, it would be useless to fit a needle to the projectile unless the latter was made to travel with the point forward; but there is direct evidence that the barrel was rifled. You notice the little square projection on the back surface of the cylinder. That was evidently made to fit a washer or wad—probably a thin plate of soft metal, which would be driven by the pressure from behind into the grooves of the rifling and thus give a spinning motion to the bullet. When the latter left the barrel, the wad would drop off, leaving it free."

"I see. I was wondering what the square projection was for. It is, as you say, extremely ingenious."

"Highly ingenious," said Thorndyke, enthusiastically, "and so is the whole device. See how perfectly it would have worked but for a mere fluke and for the complication of your presence. Supposing that I had been alone, so that he could have approached to a shorter distance. In that case he would not have missed, and the thing would have been done. You see how it was intended to be done, I suppose?"

"I think so," I answered; "but I should like to hear your account of the process."

"Well, you see, he first finds out that I am returning by a late train—which he seems to have done—and he waits for me at the terminus. Meanwhile he fills the cylinder with a solution of a powerful alkaloidal poison, which is easily done by dipping the needle into the liquid and sucking at the small hole near the back end, when the piston will be drawn up and the liquid will follow it. You notice that the upper side of the piston is covered with vaseline—introduced through the hole, no doubt—which would prevent the poison from coming out into the mouth, and make the cylinder secure from leakage. On my arrival, he follows me on his bicycle until I pass through a sufficiently secluded neighborhood. Then he approaches me, or passes me and waits round a corner, and shoots at pretty close range. It doesn't matter where he hits me; all parts are equally vital, so he can aim at the middle of my back. Then the bullet comes spinning through the air point foremost; the needle passes through the clothing and enters the flesh, and as the bullet is suddenly stopped, the heavy piston flies down by its own great momentum and squirts out a jet of the poison into the tissues. The bullet then disengages itself and drops on to the ground.

"Meanwhile, our friend has mounted his bicycle and is off, and when I feel the prick of the needle, I turn and, without stopping to look for the bullet, immediately give chase. I am, of course, not able to overtake a man on a racing machine, but still I follow him some distance. Then the poison begins to take effect—the more rapidly from the violent exercise—and presently I drop insensible. Later on, my body is found. There are no marks of violence, and probably the needle-puncture escapes observation at the *post-mortem,* in which case the verdict will be death from heart failure. Even if the poison and the puncture are discovered, there is no clue. The bullet lies some streets away, and is probably picked up by some boy or passing stranger, who cannot conjecture its use, and who would never connect it with the man who was found dead. You will admit that the whole plan has been worked out with surprising completeness and foresight."

"Yes," I answered; "there is no doubt that the fellow is a most infernally clever scoundrel. May I ask if you have any idea who he is?"

"Well," Thorndyke replied, "seeing that, as Carlyle has unkindly pointed out, clever people are not in an overwhelming majority, and that, of the clever people whom I know, only a very few are interested in my immediate demise, I am able to form a fairly probable conjecture."

"And what do you mean to do?"

"For the present I shall maintain an attitude of masterly inactivity and avoid the night air."

"But, surely," I exclaimed, "you will take some measures to protect yourself against attempts of this kind. You can hardly doubt now that your accident in the fog was really an attempted murder."

"I never did doubt it, as a matter of fact, although I prevaricated at the time. But I have not enough evidence against this man at present and, consequently, can do nothing but show that I suspect him, which would be foolish. Whereas, if I lie low, one of two things will happen; either the occasion for my removal (which is only a temporary one) will pass, or he will commit himself—will put a definite clue into my hands. Then we shall find the air-cane, the bicycle, perhaps a little stock of poison, and certain other trifles that I have in my mind, which will be good confirmatory evidence, though insufficient in themselves. And now, I think, I must really adjourn this meeting, or we shall be good for nothing tomorrow."

CHAPTER TWELVE

IT MIGHT HAVE BEEN

It was now only a week from the date on which the trial was to open. In eight days the mystery would almost certainly be solved (if it was capable of solution), for the trial promised to be quite a short one, and then Reuben Hornby would be either a convicted felon or a free man, clear of the stigma of the crime.

For several days past, Thorndyke had been in almost constant possession of the laboratory, while his own small room, devoted ordinarily to bacteriology and microscopical work was kept continually locked; a state of things that reduced Polton to a condition of the most extreme nervous irritation, especially when, as he told me indignantly, he met Mr. Anstey emerging from the holy of holies, grinning and rubbing his hands and giving utterance to genial but unparliamentary expressions of amused satisfaction.

I had met Anstey on several occasions lately, and each time liked him better than the last; for his whimsical, facetious manner covered a nature (as it often does) that was serious and thoughtful; and I found him not only a man of considerable learning, but one also of a lofty standard of conduct. His admiration for Thorndyke was unbounded, and I could see that the two men collaborated with the utmost sympathy and mutual satisfaction.

But although I regarded Mr. Anstey with feelings of the liveliest friendship, I was far from gratified when, on the morning of which I am writing, I observed him from our sitting room window crossing the graveled space from Crown Office Row and evidently bearing down on our chambers. For the fact is that I was awaiting the arrival of Juliet, and should greatly have preferred to be alone at the moment, seeing that Thorndyke had already gone out. It is true that my fair enslaver was not due for nearly half an hour, but then, who could say how long Anstey would stay, or what embarrassments might arise from my efforts to escape? By all of which it may be perceived that my disease had reached a very advanced stage, and that I was unequal to those tactics of concealment that are commonly attributed to the ostrich.

A sharp rap of the knocker announced the arrival of the disturber of my peace, and when I opened the door, Anstey walked in with the air of a man to whom an hour more or less is of no consequence whatever. He shook my hand with mock solemnity and, seating himself upon the edge of the table, proceeded to roll a cigarette with exasperating deliberation.

"I infer," said he, "that our learned brother is practicing parlor magic upstairs, or peradventure he has gone on a journey?"

"He has a consultation this morning," I answered. "Was he expecting you?"

"Evidently not, or he would have been here. No, I just looked in to ask a question about the case of your friend Hornby. You know it comes on for trial next week?"

"Yes; Thorndyke told me. What do you think of Hornby's prospects? Is he going to be convicted, or will he get an acquittal?"

"*He* will be entirely passive," replied Anstey, "but *we*"—here he slapped his chest impressively—"are going to secure an acquittal. You will be highly entertained, my learned friend, and Mr. The Enemy will be excessively surprised." He inspected the newly made cigarette with a critical air and chuckled softly.

"You seem pretty confident," I remarked.

"I am," he answered, "though Thorndyke considers failure possible—which, of course, it is if the jury-box should chance to be filled with microcephalic idiots and the judge should prove incapable of understanding simple technical evidence. But we hope that neither of these things will happen, and if they do not, we feel pretty safe. By the way, I hope I am not divulging your principal's secrets?"

"Well," I replied, with a smile, "you have been more explicit than Thorndyke ever has."

"Have I?" he exclaimed, with mock anxiety; "then I must swear you to secrecy. Thorndyke is so very close—and he is quite right, too. I never cease admiring his tactics of allowing the enemy to fortify and barricade the entrance that he does *not* mean to attack. But I see you are wishing me at the devil, so give me a cigar and I will go—though not to that particular destination."

"Will you have one of Thorndyke's special brand?" I asked malignantly.

"What! those foul Trichinopolies? Not while brown paper is to be obtained at every stationer's; I'd sooner smoke my own wig."

I tendered my own case, from which he selected a cigar with anxious care and much sniffing; then he bade me a ceremonious adieu and departed down the stairs, blithely humming a melody from the latest comic opera.

He had not left more than five minutes when a soft and elaborate rat-tat from the little brass knocker brought my heart into my mouth. I ran to the door and flung it open, revealing Juliet standing on the threshold.

"May I come in?" she asked. "I want to have a few words with you before we start."

I looked at her with some anxiety, for she was manifestly agitated, and the hand that she held out to me trembled.

"I am greatly upset, Dr. Jervis," she said, ignoring the chair that I had placed for her. "Mr. Lawley has been giving us his views of poor Reuben's case, and his attitude fills me with dismay."

"Hang Mr. Lawley!" I muttered, and then apologized hastily. "What made you go to him, Miss Gibson?"

"I didn't go to him; he came to us. He dined with us last night—he and Walter—and his manner was gloomy in the extreme. After dinner Walter took him apart with me and asked him what he really thought of the case. He was most pessimistic. 'My dear sir,' he said, 'the only advice I can give you is that you prepare yourself to contemplate disaster as philosophically as you can. In my opinion your cousin is almost certain to be convicted.' 'But,' said Walter, 'what about the defense? I understood that there was at least a plausible case.' Mr. Lawley shrugged his shoulders. 'I have a sort of *alibi* that will go for nothing, but I have no evidence to offer in answer to that of the prosecution, and no case; and I may say, speaking in confidence, that I do not believe there is any case. I do not see how there can be any case, and I have heard nothing from Dr. Thorndyke to lead me to suppose that he has really done anything in the matter.' Is this true, Dr. Jervis? Oh! do tell me the real truth about it! I have been so miserable and terrified since I heard this, and I was so full of hope before. Tell me, is it true? Will Reuben be sent to prison after all?"

In her agitation she laid her hands on my arm and looked up into my face with her gray eyes swimming with tears, and was so piteous, so trustful, and, withal, so bewitching that my reserve melted like snow before a July sun.

"It is not true," I answered, taking her hands in mine and speaking perforce in a low tone that I might not betray my emotion. "If it were, it would mean that I have willfully deceived you, that I have been false to our friendship; and how much that friendship has been to me, no one but myself will ever know."

She crept a little closer to me with a manner at once penitent and wheedling.

"You are not going to be angry with me, are you? It was foolish of me to listen to Mr. Lawley after all you have told me, and it did look like a want of trust in you, I know. But you, who are so strong and wise, must make allowance for a woman who is neither. It is all so terrible that I am quite unstrung; but say you are not really displeased with me, for that would hurt me most of all."

Oh! Delilah! That concluding stroke of the shears severed the very last lock, and left me—morally speaking—as bald as a billiard ball. Henceforth I was at her mercy and would have divulged, without a scruple, the uttermost secrets of my principal, but that that astute gentleman had placed me beyond the reach of temptation.

"As to being angry with you," I answered, "I am not, like Thorndyke, one to essay the impossible, and if I could be angry, it would hurt me more than it would you. But, in fact, you are not to blame at all, and I am an egotistical brute. Of course you were alarmed and distressed; nothing could be more natural. So now let me try to chase away your fears and restore your confidence.

"I have told you what Thorndyke said to Reuben: that he had good hopes of making his innocence clear to everybody. That alone should have been enough."

"I know it should," murmured Juliet remorsefully; "please forgive me for my want of faith."

"But," I continued, "I can quote you the words of one to whose opinions you will attach more weight. Mr. Anstey was here less than half an hour ago—"

"Do you mean Reuben's counsel?"

"Yes."

"And what did he say? Oh, do tell me what he said."

"He said, in brief, that he was quite confident of obtaining an acquittal, and that the prosecution would receive a great surprise. He seemed highly pleased with his brief, and spoke with great admiration of Thorndyke."

"Did he really say that—that he was confident of an acquittal?" Her voice was breathless and unsteady, and she was clearly, as she had said, quite unstrung. "What a relief it is," she murmured incoherently; "and so very, very kind of you!" She wiped her eyes and laughed a queer, shaky little laugh; then, quite suddenly, she burst into a passion of sobbing.

Hardly conscious of what I did, I drew her gently toward me, and rested her head on my shoulder whilst I whispered into her ear I know not what words of consolation; but I am sure that I called her "dear Juliet," and probably used other expressions equally improper and reprehensible. Presently she recovered herself and, having dried her eyes, regarded me somewhat shamefacedly, blushing hotly, but smiling very sweetly nevertheless.

"I am ashamed of myself," she said, "coming here and weeping on your bosom like a great baby. It is to be hoped that your other clients do not behave in this way."

Whereat we both laughed heartily, and our emotional equilibrium being thus restored, we began to think of the object of our meeting.

"I am afraid I have wasted a great deal of time," said Juliet, looking at her watch. "Shall we be too late, do you think?"

"I hope not," I replied, "for Reuben will be looking for us; but we must hurry."

I caught up my hat, and we went forth, closing the oak behind us, and took our way up King's Bench Walk in silence, but with a new and delightful sense of intimate comradeship. I glanced from time to time at my companion, and noted that her cheek still bore a rosy flush, and when she looked at me, there was a sparkle in her eye, and a smiling softness in her glance, that stirred my heart until I trembled with the intensity of the passion that I must needs conceal. And even while I was feeling that I must tell her all, and have done with it, tell her that I was her abject slave, and she my goddess, my queen; that in the face of such a love as mine, no man could have any claim upon her; even then, there arose the still, small voice that began to call me an unfaithful steward and to remind me of a duty and trust that were sacred even beyond love.

In Fleet Street I hailed a cab, and as I took my seat beside my fair companion, the voice began to wax and speak in bolder and sterner accents.

"Christopher Jervis," it said, "what is this that you are doing? Are you a man of honor or nought but a mean, pitiful blackguard?

You, the trusted agent of this poor, misused gentleman, are you not planning in your black heart how you shall rob him of that which, if he is a man at all, must be more to him than his liberty, or even his honor? Shame on you for a miserable weakling! Have done with these philanderings and keep your covenants like a gentleman—or, at least, an honest man!"

At this point in my meditations, Juliet turned toward me with a coaxing smile.

"My legal adviser seems to be revolving some deep and weighty matter," she said.

I pulled myself together and looked at her—at her sparkling eyes and rosy, dimpling cheeks, so winsome and lovely and lovable.

"Come," I thought, "I must put an end to this at once, or I am lost." But it cost me a very agony of effort to do it—which agony, I trust, may be duly set to my account by those who may sit in judgement on me.

"Your legal adviser, Miss Gibson," I said (and at that "Miss Gibson," I thought she looked at me a little queerly), "has been reflecting that he has acted considerably beyond his jurisdiction."

"In what respect?" she asked.

"In passing on to you information which was given to him in very strict confidence and, in fact, with an implied promise of secrecy on his part."

"But the information was not of a very secret character, was it?"

"More so than it appeared. You see, Thorndyke thinks it so important not to let the prosecution suspect that he has anything up his sleeve that he has kept even Mr. Lawley in the dark, and he has never said as much to me as Anstey did this morning."

"And now you are sorry you told me; you think I have led you into a breach of trust. Is it not so?" She spoke without a trace of petulance, and her tone of dignified self-accusation made me feel a veritable worm.

"My dear Miss Gibson," I expostulated, "you entirely misunderstand me. I am not in the least sorry that I told you. How could I have done otherwise under the circumstances? But I want you to understand that I have taken the responsibility of communicating to you what is really a professional secret, and that you are to consider it as such."

"That was how I understood it," replied Juliet; "and you may rely upon me not to utter a syllable on the subject to anyone."

I thanked her for this promise, and then, by way of making conversation, gave her an account in detail of Anstey's visit, not even omitting the incident of the cigar.

"And are Dr. Thorndyke's cigars so extraordinarily bad?" she asked.

"Not at all," I replied; "only they are not to every man's taste. The Trichinopoly cheroot is Thorndyke's one dissipation, and I must say, he takes it very temperately. Under ordinary circumstances he smokes a pipe; but after a specially heavy day's work, or on any occasion of festivity or rejoicing, he indulges in a Trichinopoly, and he smokes the very best that can be got."

"So even the greatest men have their weaknesses," Juliet moralized; "but I wish I had known Dr. Thorndyke's sooner, for Mr. Hornby had a large box of Trichinopoly cheroots given to him, and I believe they were exceptionally fine ones. However, he tried one and didn't like it, so he transferred the whole consignment to Walter, who smokes all sorts and conditions of cigars."

So we talked on from one commonplace to another, and each more conventional than the last. In my nervousness, I overdid my part, and having broken the ice, proceeded to smash it to impalpable fragments. Endeavoring merely to be unemotional and to avoid undue intimacy of manner, I swung to the opposite extreme and became almost stiff; and perhaps the more so since I was writhing with the agony of repression.

Meanwhile a corresponding change took place in my companion. At first her manner seemed doubtful and bewildered; then she, too, grew more distant and polite and less disposed for conversation. Perhaps her conscience began to rebuke her, or it may be that my coolness suggested to her that her conduct had not been quite of the kind that would have commended itself to Reuben. But however that may have been, we continued to draw further and further apart; and in that short half hour we retraced the steps of our growing friendship to such purpose that, when we descended from the cab at the prison gate, we seemed more like strangers than on the first day that we met. It was a miserable ending to all our delightful comradeship, and yet what other end could one expect in this world of cross purposes and things that might have been? In the extremity of my wretchedness, I could have wept on the bosom of the portly warder who opened the wicket, even as Juliet had wept upon mine; and it was almost a relief to me, when our brief visit was over, to find that we should not return together to King's Cross as was our wont, but that Juliet would go back by omnibus that she might do some shopping in Oxford Street, leaving me to walk home alone.

I saw her into her omnibus and stood on the pavement, looking wistfully at the lumbering vehicle as it dwindled in the distance. At last, with a sigh of deepest despondency, I turned my face homeward and, walking like one in a dream, retraced the route over which I had journeyed so often of late and with such different sensations.

CHAPTER THIRTEEN

MURDER BY POST

The next few days were perhaps the most unhappy that I have known. My life, indeed, since I had left the hospital had been one of many disappointments and much privation. Unfulfilled desires and ambitions unrealized had combined with distaste for the daily drudgery that had fallen to my lot to embitter my poverty and cause me to look with gloomy distrust upon the unpromising future. But no sorrow that I had hitherto experienced could compare with the grief that I now felt in contemplating the irretrievable ruin of what I knew to be the great passion of my life. For to a man like myself, of few friends and deep affections, one great emotional upheaval exhausts the possibilities of nature; leaving only the capacity for feeble and ineffective echoes. The edifice of love that is raised upon the ruins of a great passion can compare with the original no more than can the paltry mosque that perches upon the mound of Jonah with the glories of the palace that lies entombed beneath.

I had made a pretext to write to Juliet and had received a reply quite frank and friendly in tone, by which I knew that she had not—as some women would have done—set the blame upon me for our temporary outburst of emotion. And yet there was a subtle difference from her previous manner of writing that only emphasized the finality of our separation.

I think Thorndyke perceived that something had gone awry, though I was at great pains to maintain a cheerful exterior and keep myself occupied, and he probably formed a pretty shrewd guess at the nature of the trouble; but he said nothing, and I only judged that he had observed some change in my manner by the fact that there was blended with his usual quiet geniality an almost insensible note of sympathy and affection.

A couple of days after my last interview with Juliet, an event occurred which served, certainly, to relieve the tension and distract my thoughts, though not in a very agreeable manner.

It was the pleasant, reposeful hour after dinner when it was our custom to sit in our respective easy chairs and, as we smoked our pipes, discuss some of the many topics in which we had a common interest. The postman had just discharged into the capacious letterbox an avalanche of letters and circulars, and as I sat glancing through the solitary letter that had fallen to my share, I looked from time to time at Thorndyke and noticed, as I had often done before, with some surprise, a curious habit that he had of turning over and closely scrutinizing every letter and package before he opened it.

"I observe, Thorndyke," I now ventured to remark, "that you always examine the outside of a letter before looking at the inside. I have seen other people do the same, and it has always appeared to me a singularly foolish proceeding. Why speculate over an un-opened letter when a glance at the contents will tell you all there is to know?"

"You are perfectly right," he answered, "if the object of the in-spection is to discover who is the sender of the letter. But that is not my object. In my case the habit is one that has been deliberately cultivated—not in reference to letters only, but to everything that comes into my hands—the habit of allowing nothing to pass with-out a certain amount of conscious attention. The observant man is, in reality, the attentive man, and the so-called power of observation is simply the capacity for continuous attention. As a matter of fact, I have found in practice, that the habit is a useful one even in refer-ence to letters; more than once I have gleaned a hint from the outside of a letter that has proved valuable when applied to the contents. Here, for instance, is a letter which has been opened after being fas-tened up—apparently by the aid of steam. The envelope is soiled and rubbed, and smells faintly of stale tobacco, and has evidently been carried in a pocket along with a well-used pipe. Why should it have been opened? On reading it I perceive that it should have reached me two days ago, and that the date has been skillfully altered from the thirteenth to the fifteenth. The inference is that my correspondent has a highly untrustworthy clerk."

"But the correspondent may have carried the letter in his own pocket," I objected.

"Hardly," replied Thorndyke. "He would not have troubled to steam his own letter open and close it again; he would have cut the envelope and addressed a fresh one. This the clerk could not do, be-cause the letter was confidential and was addressed in the principal's handwriting. And the principal would have almost certainly added a postscript; and, moreover, he does not smoke. This, however, is all very obvious; but here is something rather more subtle which I have put aside for more detailed examination. What do you make of it?"

He handed me a small parcel to which was attached by string a typewritten address label, the back of which bore the printed inscription, "James Bartlett and Sons, Cigar Manufacturers, London and Havana."

"I am afraid," said I, after turning the little packet over and examining every part of it minutely, "that this is rather too subtle for me. The only thing that I observe is that the typewriter has bungled the address considerably. Otherwise this seems to me a very ordinary packet indeed."

"Well, you have observed one point of interest, at any rate," said Thorndyke, taking the packet from me. "But let us examine the thing systematically and note down what we see. In the first place, you will notice that the label is an ordinary luggage label such as you may buy at any stationer's, with its own string attached. Now, manufacturers commonly use a different and more substantial pattern, which is attached by the string of the parcel. But that is a small matter. What is much more striking is the address on the label. It is typewritten and, as you say, typed very badly. Do you know anything about typewriters?"

"Very little."

"Then you do not recognize the machine? Well, this label was typed with a Blickensderfer—an excellent machine, but not the form most commonly selected for the rough work of a manufacturer's office; but we will let that pass. The important point is this: the Blickensderfer Company make several forms of machine, the smallest and lightest of which is the literary, specially designed for the use of journalists and men of letters. Now this label was typed with the literary machine, or, at least, with the literary typewheel; which is really a very remarkable circumstance indeed."

"How do you know that?" I asked.

"By this asterisk, which has been written by mistake, the inexpert operator having pressed down the figure lever instead of the one for capitals. The literary typewheel is the only one that has an asterisk, as I noticed when I was thinking of purchasing a machine. Here, then, we have a very striking fact, for even if a manufacturer chose to use a 'Blick' in his factory, it is inconceivable that he should select the literary form in preference to the more suitable 'commercial' machine."

"Yes," I agreed; "it is certainly very singular."

"And now," pursued Thorndyke, "to consider the writing itself. It has been done by an absolute beginner. He has failed to space in two places, he has written five wrong letters, and he has written figures instead of capitals in two instances."

"Yes; he has made a shocking muddle of it. I wonder he didn't throw the label away and type another."

"Precisely," said Thorndyke. "And if we wish to find out why he did not, we have only to look at the back of the label. You see that the name of the firm, instead of being printed on the label itself in the usual manner, is printed on a separate slip of paper, which is pasted on the label—a most foolish and clumsy arrangement, involving an immense waste of time. But if we look closely at the printed slip itself, we perceive something still more remarkable; for that slip has been cut down to fit the label, and has been cut with a pair of scissors. The edges are not quite straight, and in one place the 'overlap,' which is so characteristic of the cut made with scissors, can be seen quite plainly."

He handed the packet to me with a reading-lens, through which I could distinctly make out the points he had mentioned.

"Now I need not point out to you," he continued, "that these slips would, ordinarily, have been trimmed by the printer to the correct size in his machine, which would leave an absolutely true edge; nor need I say that no sane businessman would adopt such a device as this. The slip of paper has been cut with scissors to fit the label, and it has then been pasted on to the surface that it has been made to fit, when all this waste of time and trouble—which, in practice, means money—could have been saved by printing the name on the label itself."

"Yes, that is so; but I still do not see why the fellow should not have thrown away this label and typed another."

"Look at the slip again," said Thorndyke. "It is faintly but evenly discolored and, to me, has the appearance of having been soaked in water. Let us, for the moment, assume that it has been. That would look as if it had been removed from some other package, which again would suggest that the person using it had only the one slip, which he had soaked off the original package, dried, cut down, and pasted on the present label. If he pasted it on before typing the address—which he would most probably have done—he might well be unwilling to risk destroying it by soaking it a second time."

"You think, then, there is a suspicion that the package may have been tampered with?"

"There is no need to jump to conclusions," replied Thorndyke. "I merely gave this case as an instance showing that careful examination of the outside of a package or letter may lead us to bestow a little extra attention on the contents. Now let us open it and see what those contents are."

With a sharp knife he divided the outside cover, revealing a stout cardboard box wrapped in a number of advertisement sheets. The box, when the lid was raised, was seen to contain a single cigar—a large cheroot—packed in cotton wool.

"A 'Trichy,' by Jove!" I exclaimed. "Your own special fancy, Thorndyke."

"Yes; and another anomaly, at once, you see, which might have escaped our notice if we had not been on the *qui vive*."

"As a matter of fact, I *don't* see," said I. "You will think me an awful blockhead, but I don't perceive anything singular in a cigar manufacturer sending a sample cigar."

"You read the label, I think?" replied Thorndyke. "However, let us look at one of these leaflets and see what they say. Ah! here we are: 'Messrs. Bartlett and Sons, who own extensive plantations on the island of Cuba, manufacture their cigars exclusively from selected leaves grown by themselves.' They would hardly make a Trichinopoly cheroot from leaf grown in the West Indies, so we have here a striking anomaly of an East Indian cigar sent to us by a West Indian grower."

"And what do you infer from that?"

"Principally that this cigar—which, by the way, is an uncommonly fine specimen and which I would not smoke for ten thousand pounds—is deserving of very attentive examination." He produced from his pocket a powerful doublet lens, with the aid of which he examined every part of the surface of the cigar, and finally, both ends.

"Look at the small end," he said, handing me the cigar and the lens, "and tell me if you notice anything."

I focused the lens on the flush-cut surface of closely rolled leaf, and explored every part of it minutely.

"It seems to me," I said, "that the leaf is opened slightly in the center, as if a fine wire had been passed up it."

"So it appeared to me," replied Thorndyke; "and, as we are in agreement so far, we will carry our investigations a step further."

He laid the cigar down on the table and, with the keen, thin-bladed penknife, neatly divided it lengthwise into two halves.

"*Ecce signum!*" exclaimed Thorndyke, as the two parts fell asunder; and for a few moments, we stood silently regarding the dismembered cheroot. For, about half an inch from the small end, there appeared a little circular patch of white, chalky material which, by the even manner in which it was diffused among the leaf, had evidently been deposited from a solution.

"Our ingenious friend again, I surmise," said Thorndyke at length, taking up one of the halves and examining the white patch through his lens. "A thoughtful soul, Jervis, and original, too. I wish his talents could be applied in some other direction. I shall have to remonstrate with him if he becomes troublesome."

"It is your duty to society, Thorndyke," I exclaimed passionately, "to have this infernal, cold-blooded scoundrel arrested instantly. Such a man is a standing menace to the community. Do you really know who sent this thing?"

"I can form a pretty shrewd guess, which, however, is not quite the same thing. But, you see, he has not been quite so clever this time, for he has left one or two traces by which his identity might be ascertained."

"Indeed! What traces has he left?"

"Ah! now there is a nice little problem for us to consider." He settled himself in his easy chair and proceeded to fill his pipe with the air of a man who is about to discuss a matter of merely general interest.

"Let us consider what information this ingenious person has given us about himself. In the first place, he evidently has a strong interest in my immediate decease. Now, why should he feel so urgent a desire for my death? Can it be a question of property? Hardly; for I am far from a rich man, and the provisions of my will are known to me alone. Can it then be a question of private enmity or revenge? I think not. To the best of my belief, I have no private enemies whatever. There remains only my vocation as an investigator in the fields of legal and criminal research. His interest in my death must, therefore, be connected with my professional activities. Now, I am at present conducting an exhumation which may lead to a charge of murder; but if I were to die tonight, the inquiry would be carried out with equal efficiency by Professor Spicer or some other toxicologist. My death would not affect the prospects of the accused. And so in one or two other cases that I have in hand; they could be equally well conducted by someone else. The inference is that our friend is not connected with any of these cases, but that he believes me to possess some exclusive information concerning him—believes me to be the one person in the world who suspects and can convict him. Let us assume the existence of such a person—a person of whose guilt I alone have evidence. Now this person, being unaware that I have communicated my knowledge to a third party, would reasonably suppose that by making away with me, he had put himself in a position of security.

"Here, then, is our first point. The sender of this offering is probably a person concerning whom I hold certain exclusive information.

"But see, now, the interesting corollary that follows from this. I, alone, suspect this person; therefore I have not published my suspicions, or others would suspect him, too. Why, then, does he suspect me of suspecting him, since I have not spoken? Evidently, he, too, must be in possession of exclusive information. In other words, my suspicions are correct; for if they were not, he could not be aware of their existence.

"The next point is the selection of this rather unusual type of cigar. Why should he have sent a Trichinopoly instead of an ordinary Havana such as Bartletts actually manufacture? It looks as if he were aware of my peculiar predilection and, by thus consulting my personal tastes, had guarded against the chance of my giving the cigar to some other person. We may, therefore, infer that our friend probably has some knowledge of my habits.

"The third point is, what is the social standing of this gentle stranger, whom we will call X? Now, Bartletts do not send their advertisements and samples to Thomas, Richard, and Henry. They send, chiefly, to members of the professions and men of means and position. It is true that the original package might have been annexed by a clerk, office boy, or domestic servant; but the probabilities are that X received the package himself, and this is borne out by the fact that he was able to obtain access to a powerful alkaloidal poison—such as this undoubtedly is."

"In that case he would probably be a medical man or a chemist," I suggested.

"Not necessarily," replied Thorndyke. "The laws relating to poisons are so badly framed and administered that any well-to-do person, who has the necessary knowledge, can obtain almost any poison that he wants. But social position is an important factor, whence we may conclude that X belongs, at least, to the middle class.

"The fourth point relates to the personal qualities of X. Now it is evident, from this instance alone, that he is a man of exceptional intelligence, of considerable general information, and both ingenious and resourceful. This cigar device is not only clever and original, but it has been adapted to the special circumstances with remarkable forethought. Thus the cheroot was selected, apparently, for two excellent reasons: first, that it was the most likely form to be smoked by the person intended, and second, that it did not require to have the end cut off—which might have led to a discovery of the poison. The plan also shows a certain knowledge of chemistry; the poison was not intended merely to be dissolved in the moisture of the mouth. The idea evidently was that the steam generated by the combustion of the leaf at the distal end, would condense in the cooler part of the cigar and dissolve the poison, and the solution would then be drawn into the mouth. Then the nature of the poison and certain similarities of procedure seem to identify X with the cyclist who used that ingenious bullet. The poison in this case is a white, noncrystalline solid; the poison contained in the bullet was a solution of a white, noncrystalline solid, which analysis showed to be the most poisonous of all akaloids.

"The bullet was virtually a hypodermic syringe; the poison in this cigar has been introduced, in the form of an alcoholic or ethereal solution, by a hypodermic syringe. We shall thus be justified in assuming that the bullet and the cigar came from the same person; and, if this be so, we may say that X is a person of considerable knowledge, of great ingenuity, and no mean skill as a mechanician—as shown by the manufacture of the bullet.

"These are our principal facts—to which we may add the surmise that he has recently purchased a secondhand Blickensderfer of the literary form or, at least, fitted with a literary typewheel."

"I don't quite see how you arrive at that," I said, in some surprise.

"It is merely a guess, you know," he replied, "though a probable one. In the first place, he is obviously unused to typing, as the numerous mistakes show; therefore he has not had the machine very long. The type is that which is peculiar to the Blickensderfer, and in one of the mistakes, an asterisk has been printed in place of a letter. But the literary typewheel is the only one that has the asterisk. As to the age of the machine, there are evident signs of wear, for some of the letters have lost their sharpness, and this is most evident in the case of those letters which are the most used—the 'e,' you will notice, for instance, is much worn; and 'e' occurs more frequently than any other letter of the alphabet. Hence the machine, if recently purchased, was bought secondhand."

"But," I objected, "it may not have been his own machine at all."

"That is quite possible," answered Thorndyke, "though, considering the secrecy that would be necessary, the probabilities are in favor of his having bought it. But, in any case, we have here a means of identifying the machine, should we ever meet with it."

He picked up the label and handed it to me, together with his pocket lens.

"Look closely at the 'e' that we have been discussing; it occurs five times; in 'Thorndyke,' in 'Bench,' in 'Inner,' and in 'Temple.' Now in each case you will notice a minute break in the loop, just at the summit. That break corresponds to a tiny dent in the type—caused, probably, by its striking some small, hard object."

"I can make it out quite distinctly," I said, "and it should be a most valuable point for identification."

"It should be almost conclusive," Thorndyke replied, "especially when joined to other facts that would be elicited by a search of his premises. And now let us just recapitulate the facts which our friend X has placed at our disposal.

"First: X is a person concerning whom I possess certain exclusive information.

"Second: He has some knowledge of my personal habits.

"Third: He is a man of some means and social position.

"Fourth: He is a man of considerable knowledge, ingenuity, and mechanical skill.

"Fifth: He has probably purchased, quite recently, a secondhand 'Blick' fitted with a literary typewheel.

"Sixth: That machine, whether his own or some other person's property, can be identified by a characteristic mark on the small 'e.'

"If you will note down those six points and add that X is probably an expert cyclist and a fairly good shot with a rifle, you may possibly be able, presently, to complete the equation, X equals . . . ?"

"I am afraid," I said, "I do not possess the necessary data; but I suspect you do, and if it is so, I repeat that it is your duty to society—to say nothing of your clients, whose interests would suffer by your death—to have this fellow laid by the heels before he does any mischief."

"Yes; I shall have to interfere if he becomes really troublesome, but I have reasons for wishing to leave him alone at present."

"You do really know who he is, then?"

"Well, I think I can solve the equation that I have just offered to you for solution. You see, I have certain data, as you suggest, which you do not possess. There is, for instance, a certain ingenious gentleman concerning whom I hold what I believe to be exclusive information, and my knowledge of him does not make it appear unlikely that he might be the author of these neat little plans."

"I am much impressed," I said as I put away my notebook, after having jotted down the points that Thorndyke had advised me to consider—"I am much impressed by your powers of observation and your capacity for reasoning from apparently trivial data; but I do not see, even now, why you viewed that cigar with such immediate and decided suspicion. There was nothing actually to suggest the existence of poison in it, and yet you seemed to form the suspicion at once and to search for it as though you expected to find it."

"Yes," replied Thorndyke; "to a certain extent you are right. The idea of a poisoned cigar was not new to me—and thereby hangs a tale."

He laughed softly and gazed into the fire with eyes that twinkled with quiet amusement. "You have heard me say," he resumed, after a short pause, "that when I first took these chambers, I had practically nothing to do. I had invented a new variety of medico-legal practice and had to build it up by slow degrees, and the natural consequence was that, for a long time, it yielded nothing but almost unlimited leisure. Now, that leisure was by no means wasted, for I employed it in considering the class of cases in which I was likely to be employed, and in working out theoretical examples; and seeing that crimes against the person have nearly always a strong medical interest, I gave them special attention. For instance, I planned a series of murders, selecting royal personages and great ministers as the victims, and on each murder I brought to bear all the special knowledge, skill, and ingenuity at my command. I inquired minutely into the habits of my hypothetical victims; ascertained who were their associates, friends, enemies, and servants; considered their diet, their residences, their modes of conveyance, the source of their clothing, and, in fact, everything it was necessary to know in order to achieve their deaths with certainty and with absolute safety to the murderer."

"How deeply gratified and flattered those great personages would have felt," I remarked, "if they had known how much attention they were receiving."

"Yes; I suppose it would have been somewhat startling, to the prime minister, for instance, to have learned that he was being watched and studied by an attentive observer and that the arrangements for his decease had been completed down to the minutest detail. But, of course, the application of the method to a particular case was the essential thing, for it brought into view all the incidental difficulties, in meeting which all the really interesting and instructive details were involved. Well, the particulars of these crimes I wrote out at length, in my private shorthand, in a journal which I kept for the purpose—and which, I need not say, I locked up securely in my safe when I was not using it. After completing each case, it was my custom to change sides and play the game over again from the opposite side of the board; that is to say, I added, as an appendix to each case, an analysis with a complete scheme for the detection of the crime. I have in my safe at the present moment six volumes of cases, fully indexed; and I can assure you that they are not only highly instructive reading, but are really valuable as works of reference."

"That I can readily believe," I replied, laughing heartily, nevertheless, at the grotesqueness of the whole proceeding, "though they might have proved rather incriminating documents if they had passed out of your possession."

"They would never have been read," rejoined Thorndyke. "My shorthand is, I think, quite undecipherable; it has been so made intentionally with a view to secrecy."

"And have any of your theoretical cases ever turned up in real life?"

"Several of them have, though very imperfectly planned and carried out as a rule. The poisoned cigar is one of them, though, of course I should never have adopted such a conspicuous device for presenting it; and the incident of the other night is a modification—for the worse—of another. In fact, most of the intricate and artistic crimes with which I have had to deal professionally have had their more complete and elaborate prototypes in my journals."

I was silent for some time, reflecting on the strange personality of my gifted friend and the singular fitness that he presented for the part he had chosen to play in the drama of social life; but presently my thoughts returned to the peril that overshadowed him, and I came back, once more, to my original question.

"And now, Thorndyke," I said, "that you have penetrated both the motives and the disguise of this villain, what are you going to do? Is he to be put safely under lock and key, or is he to be left in peace and security to plan some other, and perhaps more successful, scheme for your destruction?"

"For the present," replied Thorndyke, "I am going to put these things in a place of safety. Tomorrow you shall come with me to the hospital and see me place the ends of the cigar in the custody of Dr. Chandler, who will make an analysis and report on the nature of the poison. After that we shall act in whatever way seems best."

Unsatisfactory as this conclusion appeared, I knew it was useless to raise further objections, and accordingly, when the cigar with its accompanying papers and wrappings had been deposited in a drawer, we dismissed it, if not from our thoughts, at least from our conversation.

CHAPTER FOURTEEN

A STARTLING DISCOVERY

The morning of the trial, so long looked forward to, had at length arrived, and the train of events which it has been my business to chronicle in this narrative was now fast drawing to an end. To me those events had been in many ways of the deepest moment. Not only had they transported me from a life of monotonous drudgery into one charged with novelty and dramatic interest; not only had they introduced me to a renascence of scientific culture and revived under new conditions my intimacy with the comrade of my student days; but, far more momentous than any of these, they had given me the vision—all too fleeting—of happiness untold, with the reality of sorrow and bitter regret that promised to be all too enduring.

Whence it happened that on this morning my thoughts were tinged with a certain grayness. A chapter in my life that had been both bitter and sweet was closing, and already I saw myself once more an Ishmaelite and a wanderer among strangers.

This rather egotistical frame of mind, however, was soon dispelled when I encountered Polton, for the little man was in a veritable twitter of excitement at the prospect of witnessing the clearing up of the mysteries that had so severely tried his curiosity; and even Thorndyke, beneath his habitual calm, showed a trace of expectancy and pleasurable anticipation.

"I have taken the liberty of making certain little arrangements on your behalf," he said, as we sat at breakfast, "of which I hope you will not disapprove. I have written to Mrs. Hornby, who is one of the witnesses, to say that you will meet her at Mr. Lawley's office and escort her and Miss Gibson to the court. Walter Hornby may be with them, and, if he is, you had better leave him, if possible, to come on with Lawley."

"You will not come to the office, then?"

"No. I shall go straight to the court with Anstey. Besides, I am expecting Superintendent Miller from Scotland Yard, who will probably walk down with us."

"I am glad to hear that," I said; "for I have been rather uneasy at the thought of your mixing in the crowd without some kind of protection."

"Well, you see that I am taking precautions against the assaults of the too-ingenious X, and to tell the truth—and also to commit a flagrant bull—I should never forgive myself if I allowed him to kill me before I had completed Reuben Hornby's defense. Ah, here is Polton—that man is on wires this morning; he has been wandering in and out of the rooms ever since he came, like a cat in a new house."

"It's quite true, sir," said Polton, smiling and unabashed, "so it's no use denying it. I have come to ask what we are going to take with us to the court."

"You will find a box and a portfolio on the table in my room," replied Thorndyke. "We had better also take a microscope and the micrometers, though we are not likely to want them; that is all, I think."

"A box and a portfolio," repeated Polton in a speculative tone. "Yes, sir, I will take them with me." He opened the door and was about to pass out, when, perceiving a visitor ascending the stairs, he turned back.

"Here's Mr. Miller, from Scotland Yard, sir; shall I show him in?"

"Yes, do." He rose from his chair as a tall, military-looking man entered the room and saluted, casting, at the same time, an inquiring glance in my direction.

"Good morning, Doctor," he said briskly. "I got your letter and couldn't make such of it, but I have brought down a couple of plain-clothes men and a uniform man, as you suggested. I understand you want a house watched?"

"Yes, and a man, too. I will give you the particulars presently—that is, if you think you can agree to my conditions."

"That I act entirely on my own account and make no communication to anybody? Well, of course, I would rather you gave me all the facts and let me proceed in the regular way; but if you make conditions, I have no choice but to accept them, seeing that you hold the cards."

Perceiving that the matter in hand was of a confidential nature, I thought it best to take my departure, which I accordingly did, as soon as I had ascertained that it wanted yet half an hour to the time at which Mrs. Hornby and Juliet were due at the lawyer's office.

Mr. Lawley received me with stiffness that bordered on hostility. He was evidently deeply offended at the subordinate part that he had been compelled to play in the case, and was at no great pains to conceal the fact.

"I am informed," said he, in a frosty tone, when I had explained my mission, "that Mrs. Hornby and Miss Gibson are to meet you here. The arrangement is none of my making; none of the arrangements in this case are of my making. I have been treated throughout with a lack of ceremony and confidence that is positively scandalous. Even now, I—the solicitor for the defense—am completely in the dark as to what defense is contemplated, though I fully expect to be involved in some ridiculous fiasco. I only trust that I may never again be associated with any of your hybrid practitioners. *Ne sutor ultra crepidam*, sir, is an excellent motto; let the medical cobbler stick to his medical last."

"It remains to be seen what kind of boot he can turn out on the legal last," I retorted.

"That is so," he rejoined; "but I hear Mrs. Hornby's voice in the outer office, and as neither you nor I have any time to waste in idle talk, I suggest that you make your way to the court without delay. I wish you good morning!"

Acting on this very plain hint, I retired to the clerks' office, where I found Mrs. Hornby and Juliet, the former undisguisedly tearful and terrified, and the latter calm, though pale and agitated.

"We had better start at once," I said, when we had exchanged greetings. "Shall we take a cab or walk?"

"I think we will walk, if you don't mind," said Juliet. "Mrs. Hornby wants to have a few words with you before we go into court. You see, she is one of the witnesses, and she is terrified lest she should say something damaging to Reuben."

"By whom was the subpoena served?" I asked.

"Mr. Lawley sent it," replied Mrs. Hornby, "and I went to see him about it the very next day, but he wouldn't tell me anything— he didn't seem to know what I was wanted for, and he wasn't at all nice—not at all."

"I expect your evidence will relate to the 'Thumbograph,'" I said. "There is really nothing else in connection with the case that you have any knowledge of."

"That is just what Walter said," exclaimed Mrs. Hornby. "I went to his rooms to talk the matter over with him. He is very upset about the whole affair, and I am afraid he thinks very badly of poor Reuben's prospects. I only trust he may be wrong! Oh dear! What a dreadful thing it is, to be sure!" Here the poor lady halted to mop her eyes elaborately, to the surprise and manifest scorn of a passing errand boy.

"He was very thoughtful and sympathetic—Walter, I mean, you know," pursued Mrs. Hornby, "and most helpful. He asked me all I knew about that horrid little book, and took down my answers in writing. Then he wrote out the questions I was likely to be asked, with my answers, so that I could read them over and get them well into my head. Wasn't it good of him! And I made him print them with his machine so that I could read them without my glasses, and he did it beautifully. I have the paper in my pocket now."

"I didn't know Mr. Walter went in for printing," I said. "Has he a regular printing press?"

"It isn't a printing press exactly," replied Mrs. Hornby; "it is a small thing with a lot of round keys that you press down—Dickensblerfer, I think it is called—ridiculous name, isn't it? Walter bought it from one of his literary friends about a week ago; but he is getting quite clever with it already, though he does make a few mistakes still, as you can see."

She halted again, and began to search for the opening of a pocket which was hidden away in some occult recess of her clothing, all unconscious of the effect that her explanation had produced on me. For, instantly, as she spoke, there flashed into my mind one of the points that Thorndyke had given me for the identification of the mysterious X. "He has probably purchased, quite recently, a secondhand Blickensderfer, fitted with a literary typewheel." The coincidence was striking and even startling, though a moment's reflection convinced me that it was nothing more than a coincidence; for there must be hundreds of secondhand "Blicks" on the market, and as to Walter Hornby, he certainly could have no quarrel with Thorndyke, but would rather be interested in his preservation on Reuben's account.

These thoughts passed through my mind so rapidly that by the time Mrs. Hornby had run her pocket to earth, I had quite recovered from the momentary shock.

"Ah! here it is," she exclaimed triumphantly, producing an obese Morocco purse. "I put it in here for safety, knowing how liable one is to get one's pocket picked in these crowded London streets." She opened the bulky receptacle and drew it out after the manner of a concertina, exhibiting multitudinous partitions, all stuffed with pieces of paper, coils of tape and sewing silk, buttons, samples of dress materials, and miscellaneous rubbish, mingled indiscriminately with gold, silver, and copper coins.

"Now just run your eye through that, Dr. Jervis," she said, handing me a folded paper, "and give me your advice on my answers."

I opened the paper and read: "The Committee of the Society for the Protection of Paralyzed Idiots, in submitting this—"

"Oh! that isn't it; I have given you the wrong paper. How silly of me! That is the appeal of—you remember, Juliet, dear, that troublesome person—I had, really, to be quite rude, you know, Dr. Jervis; I had to tell him that charity begins at home, although, thank Heaven! none of us are paralyzed, but we must consider our own, mustn't we? And then—"

"Do you think this is the one, dear?" interposed Juliet, in whose pale cheek the ghost of a dimple had appeared. "It looks cleaner than most of the others."

She selected a folded paper from the purse which Mrs. Hornby was holding with both hands extended to its utmost, as though she were about to produce a burst of music, and, opening it, glanced at its contents.

"Yes, this is your evidence," she said, and passed the paper to me.

I took the document from her hand and, in spite of the conclusion at which I had arrived, examined it with eager curiosity. And at the very first glance I felt my head swim and my heart throb violently. For the paper was headed: "Evidence respecting the Thumbograph," and in every one of the five small "e's" that occurred in that sentence I could see plainly by the strong outdoor light a small break or interval in the summit of the loop.

I was thunderstruck.

One coincidence was quite possible and even probable; but the two together, and the second one of so remarkable a character, were beyond all reasonable limits of probability. The identification did not seem to admit of a doubt, and yet—

"Our legal adviser appears to be somewhat preoccupied," remarked Juliet, with something of her old gaiety of manner; and, in fact, though I held the paper in my hand, my gaze was fixed unmeaningly on an adjacent lamppost. As she spoke, I pulled myself together and, scanning the paper hastily, was fortunate enough to find in the first paragraph matter requiring comment.

"I observe, Mrs. Hornby," I said, "that in answer to the first question, 'Whence did you obtain the "Thumbograph"?' you say, 'I do not remember clearly; I think I must have bought it at a railway bookstall.' Now I understood that it was brought home and given to you by Walter himself."

"That was what I thought," replied Mrs. Hornby, "but Walter tells me that it was not so, and of course, he would remember better than I should."

"But, my dear aunt, I am sure he gave it to you," interposed Juliet. "Don't you remember? It was the night the Colleys came to dinner, and we were so hard-pressed to find amusement for them, when Walter came in and produced the 'Thumbograph.'"

"Yes, I remember quite well now," said Mrs. Hornby. "How fortunate that you reminded me. We must alter that answer at once."

"If I were you, Mrs. Hornby," I said, "I would disregard this paper altogether. It will only confuse you and get you into difficulties. Answer the questions that are put, as well as you can, and if you don't remember, say so."

"Yes, that will be much the wisest plan," said Juliet. "Let Dr. Jervis take charge of the paper and rely on your own memory."

"Very well, my dear," replied Mrs. Hornby, "I will do what you think best, and you can keep the paper, Dr. Jervis, or throw it away."

I slipped the document into my pocket without remark, and we proceeded on our way, Mrs. Hornby babbling inconsequently, with occasional outbursts of emotion, and Juliet silent and abstracted. I struggled to concentrate my attention on the elder lady's conversation, but my thoughts continually reverted to the paper in my pocket, and the startling solution that it seemed to offer of the mystery of the poisoned cigar.

Could it be that Walter Hornby was in reality the miscreant X? The thing seemed incredible, for, hitherto, no shadow of suspicion had appeared to fall on him. And yet there was no denying that his description tallied in a very remarkable manner with that of the hypothetical X. He was a man of some means and social position; he was a man of considerable knowledge and mechanical skill, though as to his ingenuity I could not judge. He had recently bought a secondhand Blickensderfer which probably had a literary typewheel, since it was purchased from a literary man; and that machine showed the characteristic mark on the small "e." The two remaining points, indeed, were not so clear. Obviously I could form no opinion as to whether or not Thorndyke held any exclusive information concerning him, and with reference to his knowledge of my friend's habits, I was at first inclined to be doubtful until I suddenly recalled, with a pang of remorse and self-accusation, the various details that I had communicated to Juliet and that she might easily, in all innocence, have handed on to Walter. I had, for instance, told her of Thorndyke's preference for the Trichinopoly cheroot, and of this she might very naturally have spoken to Walter, who possessed a supply of them. Again, with regard to the time of our arrival at King's Cross, I had informed her of this in a letter that was in no way confidential, and again there was no reason why the information should not have been passed on to Walter, who was to have been one of the party at the family dinner. The coincidence seemed complete enough, in all truth; yet it was incredible that Reuben's cousin could be so black-hearted a villain or could have any motive for these dastardly crimes.

Suddenly a new idea struck me. Mrs. Hornby had obtained access to this typewriting machine; and if Mrs. Hornby could do so, why not John Hornby? The description would, for the most part, fit the elder man as well as the younger, though I had no evidence of his possessing any special mechanical skill; but my suspicions had already fastened upon him, and I remembered that Thorndyke had by no means rejected my theory which connected him with the crime.

At this point, my reflections were broken in upon by Mrs. Hornby, who grasped my arm and uttered a deep groan. We had reached the corner of the Old Bailey, and before us were the frowning walls of Newgate. Within those walls, I knew—though I did not mention the fact—that Reuben Hornby was confined with the other prisoners who were awaiting their trial; and a glance at the massive masonry, stained to a dingy gray by the grime of the city, put an end to my speculations and brought me back to the drama that was so nearly approaching its climax.

Down the old thoroughfare, crowded with so many memories of hideous tragedy; by the side of the gloomy prison; past the debtors' door with its forbidding spiked wicket; past the gallows gate with its festoons of fetters; we walked in silence until we reached the entrance to the Sessions House.

Here I was not a little relieved to find Thorndyke on the lookout for us, for Mrs. Hornby, in spite of really heroic efforts to control her emotion, was in a state of impending hysteria, while Juliet, though outwardly calm and composed, showed by the waxen pallor of her cheeks and a certain wildness of her eyes that all her terror was reviving; and I was glad that they were spared the unpleasantness of contact with the policemen who guarded the various entrances.

"We must be brave," said Thorndyke gently, as he took Mrs. Hornby's hand, "and show a cheerful face to our friend who has so much to bear and who bears it so patiently. A few more hours, and I hope we shall see restored, not only his liberty, but his honor. Here is Mr. Anstey, who, we trust, will be able to make his innocence apparent."

Anstey, who, unlike Thorndyke, had already donned his wig and gown, bowed gravely, and together, we passed through the mean and grimy portals into a dark hall. Policemen in uniform and unmistakable detectives stood about the various entries, and little knots of people, evil-looking and unclean for the most part, lurked in the background or sat on benches and diffused through the stale, musty air that distinctive but indescribable odor that clings to police vans and prison reception rooms; an odor that, in the present case, was pleasantly mingled with the suggestive aroma of disinfectants. Through the unsavory throng we hurried, and up a staircase to a landing from which several passages diverged. Into one of these passages—a sort of "dark entry," furnished with a cage-like gate of iron bars—we passed to a black door, on which was painted the inscription, "Old Court. Counsel and clerks."

Anstey held the door open for us, and we passed through into the court, which at once struck me with a sense of disappointment. It was smaller than I had expected, and plain and mean to the point of sordidness. The woodwork was poor, thinly disguised by yellow graining, and slimy with dirt wherever a dirty hand could reach it. The walls were distempered a pale, greenish gray; the floor was of bare and dirty planking, and the only suggestions of dignity or display were those offered by the canopy over the judge's seat—lined with scarlet baize and surmounted by the royal arms—the scarlet cushions of the bench, and the large, circular clock in the gallery, which was embellished with a gilded border and asserted its importance by a loud, aggressive tick.

Following Anstey and Thorndyke into the well of the court, we were ushered into one of the seats reserved for counsel—the third from the front—where we sat down and looked about us, while our two friends seated themselves in the front bench next to the central table. Here, at the extreme right, a barrister—presumably the counsel for the prosecution—was already in his place and absorbed in the brief that lay on the desk before him. Straight before us were the seats for the jury, rising one above the other, and at their side the witness-box. Above us on the right was the judge's seat, and immediately below it a structure somewhat resembling a large pew or a counting-house desk, surmounted by a brass rail, in which a person in a gray wig—the clerk of the court—was mending a quill pen. On our left rose the dock—suggestively large and roomy—enclosed at the sides with high glazed frames; and above it, near the ceiling, was the spectators' gallery.

"What a hideous place!" exclaimed Juliet, who separated me from Mrs. Hornby. "And how sordid and dirty everything looks!"

"Yes," I answered. "The uncleanness of the criminal is not confined to his moral being; wherever he goes, he leaves a trail of actual, physical dirt. It is not so long ago that the dock and the bench alike used to be strewn with medicinal herbs, and I believe the custom still survives of furnishing the judge with a nosegay as a preventive of jail-fever."

"And to think that Reuben should be brought to a place like this!" Juliet continued bitterly; "to be herded with such people as we saw downstairs!"

She sighed and looked round at the benches that rose behind us, where a half-dozen reporters were already seated and apparently in high spirits at the prospect of a sensational case.

Our conversation was now interrupted by the clatter of feet on the gallery stairs, and heads began to appear over the wooden parapet. Several junior counsel filed into the seats in front of us; Mr. Lawley and his clerk entered the attorney's bench; the ushers took their stand below the jury-box; a police officer seated himself at a desk in the dock; and inspectors, detectives and miscellaneous officers began to gather in the entries or peer into the court through the small, glazed openings in the doors.

CHAPTER FIFTEEN

THE FINGER-PRINT EXPERTS

The hum of conversation that had been gradually increasing as the court filled suddenly ceased. A door at the back of the dais was flung open; counsel, solicitors, and spectators alike rose to their feet; and the judge entered, closely followed by the Lord Mayor, the sheriff, and various civic magnates, all picturesque and gorgeous in their robes and chains of office. The Clerk of Arraigns took his place behind his table under the dais; the counsel suspended their conversation and fingered their briefs; and, as the judge took his seat, lawyers, officials, and spectators took their seats, and all eyes were turned toward the dock.

A few moments later Reuben Hornby appeared in the enclosure in company with a warder, the two rising, apparently, from the bowels of the earth, and, stepping forward to the bar, stood with a calm and self-possessed demeanor, glancing somewhat curiously around the court. For an instant his eye rested upon the group of friends and well-wishers seated behind the counsel, and the faintest trace of a smile appeared on his face; but immediately he turned his eyes away and never again throughout the trial looked in our direction.

The Clerk of Arraigns now rose and, reading from the indictment which lay before him on the table, addressed the prisoner—

"Reuben Hornby, you stand indicted for that you did, on the ninth or tenth day of March, feloniously steal a parcel of diamonds of the goods and chattels of John Hornby. Are you guilty or not guilty?"

"Not guilty," replied Reuben.

The Clerk of Arraigns, having noted the prisoner's reply, then proceeded—

"The gentlemen whose names are about to be called will form the jury who are to try you. If you wish to object to any of them, you must do so as each comes to the book to be sworn, and before he is sworn. You will then be heard."

In acknowledgment of this address, which was delivered in clear, ringing tones, and with remarkable distinctness, Reuben bowed to the clerk, and the process of swearing in the jury was commenced, while the counsel opened their briefs and the judge conversed facetiously with an official in a fur robe and a massive neck chain.

Very strange, to unaccustomed eyes and ears, was the effect of this function—half-solemn and half-grotesque, with an effect intermediate between that of a religious rite and that of a comic opera. Above the half-suppressed hum of conversation the clerk's voice arose at regular intervals, calling out the name of one of the jurymen, and as its owner stood up, the court usher, black-gowned and sacerdotal of aspect, advanced and proffered the book. Then, as the juryman took the volume in his hand, the voice of the usher resounded through the court like that of a priest intoning some refrain or antiphon—an effect that was increased by the rhythmical and archaic character of the formula—

"Samuel Seppings!"

A stolid-looking working man rose and, taking the Testament in his hand, stood regarding the usher while that official sang out in a solemn monotone—

"You shall well and truly try and true deliverance make between our Sovereign Lord the King and the prisoner at the bar, whom you shall have in charge, and a true verdict give according to the evidence. So help you God!"

"James Piper!" Another juryman rose and was given the Book to hold; and again the monotonous singsong arose—

"You shall well and truly try and true deliverance make, etc."

"I shall scream aloud if that horrible chant goes on much longer," Juliet whispered. "Why don't they all swear at once and have done with it?"

"That would not meet the requirements," I answered. "However, there are only two more, so you must have patience."

"And you will have patience with me, too, won't you? I am horribly frightened. It is all so solemn and dreadful."

"You must try to keep up your courage until Dr. Thorndyke has given his evidence," I said. "Remember that, until he has spoken, everything is against Reuben; so be prepared."

"I will try," she answered meekly; "but I can't help being terrified."

The last of the jurymen was at length sworn, and when the clerk had once more called out the names one by one, the usher counting loudly as each man answered to his name, the latter officer turned to the Court and spectators, and proclaimed in solemn tones—

"If anyone can inform my Lords the King's justices, the King's attorney-general, or the King's sergeant, ere this inquest be now taken between our Sovereign Lord the King and the prisoner at the bar, of any treason, murder, felony, or misdemeanor, committed or done by him, let him come forth and he shall be heard; for the prisoner stands at the bar upon his deliverance."

This proclamation was followed by a profound silence, and after a brief interval, the Clerk of Arraigns turned toward the jury and addressed them collectively—

"Gentlemen of the jury, the prisoner at the bar stands indicted by the name of Reuben Hornby, for that he, on the ninth or tenth of March, feloniously did steal, take, and carry away a parcel of diamonds of the goods of John Hornby. To this indictment he has pleaded that he is not guilty, and your charge is to inquire whether he be guilty or not and to hearken to the evidence."

When he had finished his address, the clerk sat down, and the judge, a thin-faced, hollow-eyed elderly man, with bushy gray eyebrows and a very large nose, looked attentively at Reuben for some moments over the tops of his gold-rimmed pince-nez. Then he turned toward the counsel nearest the bench and bowed slightly.

The barrister bowed in return and rose, and for the first time, I obtained a complete view of Sir Hector Trumpler, KC, the counsel for the prosecution. His appearance was not prepossessing nor—though he was a large man and somewhat florid as to his countenance—particularly striking, except for a general air of untidiness. His gown was slipping off one shoulder, his wig was perceptibly awry, and his pince-nez threatened every moment to drop from his nose.

"The case that I have to present to you, my lord and gentlemen of the jury," he began in a clear, though unmusical voice, "is one the like of which is but too often met with in this court. It is one in which we shall see unbounded trust met by treacherous deceit, in which we shall see countless benefactions rewarded by the basest ingratitude, and in which we shall witness the deliberate renunciation of a life of honorable effort in favor of the tortuous and precarious ways of the criminal. The facts of the case are briefly as follows: The prosecutor in this case—most unwilling prosecutor, gentlemen—is Mr. John Hornby, who is a metallurgist and dealer in precious metals. Mr. Hornby has two nephews, the orphan sons of his two elder brothers, and I may tell you that since the decease of their parents, he has acted the part of a father to both of them. One of these nephews is Mr. Walter Hornby, and the other is Reuben Hornby, the prisoner at the bar. Both of these nephews were received by Mr. Hornby into his business with a view to their succeeding him when he should retire, and both, I need not say, occupied positions of trust and responsibility.

"Now, on the evening of the ninth of March there was delivered to Mr. Hornby a parcel of rough diamonds of which one of his clients asked him to take charge pending their transfer to the brokers. I need not burden you with irrelevant details concerning this transaction. It will suffice to say that the diamonds, which were of the aggregate value of about thirty thousand pounds, were delivered to him, and the unopened package deposited by him in his safe, together with a slip of paper on which he had written in pencil a memorandum of the circumstances. This was on the evening of the ninth of March, as I have said. Having deposited the parcel, Mr. Hornby locked the safe, and shortly afterward left the premises and went home, taking the keys with him.

"On the following morning, when he unlocked the safe, he perceived with astonishment and dismay that the parcel of diamonds had vanished. The slip of paper, however, lay at the bottom of the safe, and on picking it up, Mr. Hornby perceived that it bore a smear of blood, and in addition, the distinct impression of a human thumb.

On this he closed and locked the safe and sent a note to the police station, in response to which a very intelligent officer—Inspector Sanderson—came and made a preliminary examination. I need not follow the case further, since the details will appear in the evidence, but I may tell you that, in effect, it has been made clear, beyond all doubt, that the thumb-print on that paper was the thumb-print of the prisoner, Reuben Hornby."

He paused to adjust his glasses, which were in the very act of falling from his nose, and hitch up his gown, while he took a leisurely survey of the jury, as though he were estimating their impression-ability. At this moment I observed Walter Hornby enter the court and take up a position at the end of our bench nearest the door; and, immediately after, Superintendent Miller came in and seated himself on one of the benches opposite.

"The first witness whom I shall call," said Sir Hector Trumpler, "is John Hornby."

Mr. Hornby, looking wild and agitated, stepped into the witness-box, and the usher, having handed him the Testament, sang out—

"The evidence you shall give to the court and jury sworn, between our Sovereign Lord the King and the prisoner at the bar shall be the truth, the whole truth, and nothing but the truth; so help you God!"

Mr. Hornby kissed the Book and, casting a glance of unutterable misery at his nephew, turned toward the counsel.

"Your name is John Hornby, is it not?" asked Sir Hector.

"It is."

"And you occupy premises in St. Mary Axe?"

"Yes. I am a dealer in precious metals, but my business consists principally in the assaying of samples of ore and quartz and bars of silver and gold."

"Do you remember what happened on the ninth of March last?"

"Perfectly. My nephew Reuben—the prisoner—delivered to me a parcel of diamonds which he had received from the purser of the *Elmina Castle*, to whom I had sent him as my confidential agent. I had intended to deposit the diamonds with my banker, but when the prisoner arrived at my office, the banks were already closed, so I had to put the parcel, for the night, in my own safe. I may say that the prisoner was not in any way responsible for the delay."

"You are not here to defend the prisoner," said Sir Hector. "Answer my questions and make no comments, if you please. Was anyone present when you placed the diamonds in the safe?"

"No one was present but myself."

"I did not ask if you were present when you put them in," said Sir Hector (whereupon the spectators sniggered and the judge smiled indulgently). "What else did you do?"

"I wrote in pencil on a leaf of my pocket memorandum block, 'Handed in by Reuben at 7.3 p.m., 9.3.01,' and initialed it. Then I tore the leaf from the block and laid it on the parcel, after which I closed the safe and locked it."

"How soon did you leave the premises after this?"

"Almost immediately. The prisoner was waiting for me in the outer office—"

"Never mind where the prisoner was; confine your answers to what is asked. Did you take the keys with you?"

"Yes."

"When did you next open the safe?"

"On the following morning at ten o'clock."

"Was the safe locked or unlocked when you arrived?"

"It was locked. I unlocked it."

"Did you notice anything unusual about the safe?"

"No."

"Had the keys left your custody in the interval?"

"No. They were attached to a keychain, which I always wear."

"Are there any duplicates of those keys?—the keys of the safe, I mean."

"No, there are no duplicates."

"Have the keys ever gone out of your possession?"

"Yes. If I have had to be absent from the office for a considerable time, it has been my custom to hand the keys to one of my nephews, whichever has happened to be in charge at the time."

"And never to any other person?"

"Never to any other person."

"What did you observe when you opened the safe?"

"I observed that the parcel of diamonds had disappeared."

"Did you notice anything else?"

"Yes. I found the leaf from my memorandum block lying at the bottom of the safe. I picked it up and turned it over, and then saw that there were smears of blood on it and what looked like the print of a thumb in blood. The thumb-mark was on the under-surface, as the paper lay at the bottom of the safe."

"What did you do next?"

"I closed and locked the safe, and sent a note to the police station saying that a robbery had been committed on my premises."

"You have known the prisoner several years, I believe?"

"Yes; I have known him all his life. He is my eldest brother's son."

"Then you can tell us, no doubt, whether he is left-handed or right-handed?"

"I should say he was ambidextrous, but he uses his left hand by preference."

"A fine distinction, Mr. Hornby; a very fine distinction. Now tell me, did you ascertain beyond all doubt that the diamonds were really gone?"

"Yes; I examined the safe thoroughly, first by myself and afterward with the police. There was no doubt that the diamonds had really gone."

"When the detective suggested that you should have the thumb-prints of your two nephews taken, did you refuse?"

"I refused."

"Why did you refuse?"

"Because I did not choose to subject my nephews to the indignity. Besides, I had no power to make them submit to the proceeding."

"Had you any suspicions of either of them?"

"I had no suspicions of anyone."

"Kindly examine this piece of paper, Mr. Hornby," said Sir Hector, passing across a small, oblong slip, "and tell us if you recognize it."

Mr. Hornby glanced at the paper for a moment, and then said—

"This is the memorandum slip that I found lying at the bottom of the safe."

"How do you identify it?"

"By the writing on it, which is in my own hand, and bears my initials."

"Is it the memorandum that you placed on the parcel of diamonds?"

"Yes."

"Was there any thumb-mark or blood-smear on it when you placed it in the safe?"

"No."

"Was it possible that there could have been any such marks?"

"Quite impossible. I tore it from my memorandum block at the time I wrote upon it."

"Very well." Sir Hector Trumpler sat down, and Mr. Anstey stood up to cross-examine the witness.

"You have told us, Mr. Hornby," said he, "that you have known the prisoner all his life. Now what estimate have you formed of his character?"

"I have always regarded him as a young man of the highest character—honorable, truthful, and in every way trustworthy. I have never, in all my experience of him, known him to deviate a hair's-breadth from the strictest honor and honesty of conduct."

"You regarded him as a man of irreproachable character. Is that so?"

"That is so; and my opinion of him is unchanged."

"Has he, to your knowledge, any expensive or extravagant habits?"

"No. His habits are simple and rather thrifty."

"Have you ever known him to bet, gamble, or speculate?"

"Never."

"Has he ever seemed to be in want of money?"

"No. He has a small private income, apart from his salary, which I know he does not spend, since I have occasionally employed my broker to invest his savings."

"Apart from the thumb-print which was found in the safe, are you aware of any circumstances that would lead you to suspect the prisoner of having stolen the diamonds?"

"None whatever."

Mr. Anstey sat down, and as Mr. Hornby left the witness-box, mopping the perspiration from his forehead, the next witness was called.

"Inspector Sanderson!"

The dapper police officer stepped briskly into the box, and having been duly sworn, faced the prosecuting counsel with the air of a man who was prepared for any contingency.

"Do you remember," said Sir Hector, after the usual preliminaries had been gone through, "what occurred on the morning of the tenth of March?"

"Yes. A note was handed to me at the station at 10.23 a.m. It was from Mr. John Hornby, and stated that a robbery had occurred at his premises in St. Mary Axe. I went to the premises and arrived there at 10.31 a.m. There I saw the prosecutor, Mr. John Hornby, who told me that a parcel of diamonds had been stolen from the safe. At his request I examined the safe. There were no signs of its having been forced open; the locks seemed to be quite uninjured and in good order. Inside the safe, on the bottom, I found two good-sized drops of blood, and a slip of paper with pencil-writing on it. The paper bore two blood smears and a print of a human thumb in blood."

"Is this the paper?" asked the counsel, passing a small slip across to the witness.

"Yes," replied the inspector, after a brief glance at the document.

"What did you do next?"

"I sent a message to Scotland Yard acquainting the Chief of the Criminal Investigation Department with the facts, and then went back to the station. I had no further connection with the case."

Sir Hector sat down, and the judge glanced at Anstey.

"You tell us," said the latter, rising, "that you observed two good-sized drops of blood on the bottom of the safe. Did you notice the condition of the blood, whether moist or dry?"

"The blood looked moist, but I did not touch it. I left it undisturbed for the detective officers to examine."

The next witness called was Sergeant Bates, of the Criminal Investigation Department. He stepped into the box with the same ready, businesslike air as the other officer and, having been sworn, proceeded to give his evidence with a fluency that suggested careful preparation, holding an open notebook in his hand but making no references to it.

"On the tenth of March, at 12.08 p.m., I received instructions to proceed to St. Mary Axe to inquire into a robbery that had taken place there. Inspector Sanderson's report was handed to me, and I read it in the cab on my way to the premises. On arriving at the premises at 12.30 p.m., I examined the safe carefully. It was quite uninjured, and there were no marks of any kind upon it. I tested the locks and found them perfect; there were no marks or indications of any picklock having been used. On the bottom of the inside, I observed two rather large drops of a dark fluid. I took up some of the fluid on a piece of paper and found it to be blood. I also found, in the bottom of the safe, the burnt head of a wax match, and on searching the floor of the office, I found, close by the safe, a used wax match from which the head had fallen. I also found a slip of paper which appeared to have been torn from a perforated block. On it was written in pencil, 'Handed in by Reuben at 7.3 p.m. 9.3.01. J. H.' There were two smears of blood on the paper and the impression of a human thumb in blood. I took possession of the paper in order that it might be examined by the experts. I inspected the office doors and the outer door of the premises, but found no signs of forcible entrance on any of them. I questioned the housekeeper, but obtained no information from him. I then returned to headquarters, made my report, and handed the paper with the marks on it to the Superintendent."

"Is this the paper that you found in the safe?" asked the counsel, once more handing the leaflet across.

"Yes; this is the paper."

"What happened next?"

"The following afternoon I was sent for by Mr. Singleton, of the Finger-print Department. He informed me that he had gone through the files and had not been able to find any thumb-print resembling the one on the paper, and recommended me to endeavor to obtain prints of the thumbs of any persons who might have been concerned in the robbery. He also gave me an enlarged photograph of the thumb-print for reference if necessary. I accordingly went to St. Mary Axe and had an interview with Mr. Hornby, when I requested him to allow me to take prints of the thumbs of all the persons employed on the premises, including his two nephews. This he refused, saying that he distrusted finger-prints and that there was no suspicion of anyone on the premises. I asked if he would allow his nephews to furnish their thumb-prints privately, to which he replied, 'Certainly not.'"

"Had you then any suspicion of either of the nephews?"

"I thought they were both open to some suspicion. The safe had certainly been opened with false keys, and as they had both had the real keys in their possession, it was possible that one of them might have taken impressions in wax and made counterfeit keys."

"Yes."

"I called on Mr. Hornby several times and urged him, for the sake of his nephews' reputations, to sanction the taking of the thumb-prints; but he refused very positively and forbade them to submit, although I understood that they were both willing. It then occurred to me to try if I could get any help from Mrs. Hornby, and on the fifteenth of March I called at Mr. Hornby's private house and saw her. I explained to her what was wanted to clear her nephews from the suspicion that rested on them, and she then said that she could dispose of those suspicions at once, for she could show me the thumb-prints of the whole family: she had them all in a 'Thumbograph.'"

"A 'Thumbograph'?" repeated the judge. "What is a 'Thumbograph'?"

Anstey rose with the little red-covered volume in his hand.

"A 'Thumbograph,' my lord," said he, "is a book, like this, in which foolish people collect the thumb-prints of their more foolish acquaintances."

He passed the volume up to the judge, who turned over the leaves curiously and then nodded to the witness.

"Yes. She said she had them all in a 'Thumbograph.'"

"Then she fetched from a drawer a small red-covered book, which she showed to me. It contained the thumb-prints of all the family and some of her friends."

"Is this the book?" asked the judge, passing the volume down to the witness.

The sergeant turned over the leaves until he came to one which he apparently recognized, and said—

"Yes, m'lord; this is the book. Mrs. Hornby showed me the thumb-prints of various members of the family, and then found those of the two nephews. I compared them with the photograph that I had with me and discovered that the print of the left thumb of Reuben Hornby was in every respect identical with the thumb-print shown in the photograph."

"What did you do then?"

"I asked Mrs. Hornby to lend me the 'Thumbograph' so that I might show it to the Chief of the Finger-print Department, to which she consented. I had not intended to tell her of my discovery, but as I was leaving, Mr. Hornby arrived home, and when he heard of what had taken place, he asked me why I wanted the book, and then I told him. He was greatly astonished and horrified, and wished me to return the book at once. He proposed to let the whole matter drop and take the loss of the diamonds on himself; but I pointed out that this was impossible as it would practically amount to compounding a felony. Seeing that Mrs. Hornby was so distressed at the idea of her book being used in evidence against her nephew, I promised her that I would return it to her if I could obtain a thumb-print in any other way.

"I then took the 'Thumbograph' to Scotland Yard and showed it to Mr. Singleton, who agreed that the print of the left thumb of Reuben Hornby was in every respect identical with the thumb-print on the paper found in the safe. On this I applied for a warrant for the arrest of Reuben Hornby, which I executed on the following morning. I told the prisoner what I had promised Mrs. Hornby, and he then offered to allow me to take a print of his left thumb so that his aunt's book should not have to be used in evidence."

"How is it, then," asked the judge, "that it has been put in evidence?"

"It has been put in by the defense, my lord," said Sir Hector Trumpler.

"I see," said the judge. "A hair of the dog that bit him.' The 'Thumbograph' is to be applied as a remedy on the principle that *similia similibus curantur*. Well?"

"When I arrested him, I administered the usual caution, and the prisoner then said, 'I am innocent. I know nothing about the robbery.'"

The counsel for the prosecution sat down, and Anstey rose to cross-examine.

"You have told us," said he, in his clear, musical voice, "that you found at the bottom of the safe two rather large drops of a dark fluid which you considered to be blood. Now, what led you to believe that fluid to be blood?"

"I took some of the fluid up on a piece of white paper, and it had the appearance and color of blood."

"Was it examined microscopically or otherwise?"

"Not to my knowledge."

"Was it quite liquid?"

"Yes, I should say quite liquid."

"What appearance had it on paper?"

"It looked like a clear red liquid of the color of blood, and was rather thick and sticky."

Anstey sat down, and the next witness, an elderly man, answering to the name of Francis Simmons, was called.

"You are the housekeeper at Mr. Hornby's premises in St. Mary Axe?" asked Sir Hector Trumpler.

"I am."

"Did you notice anything unusual on the night of the ninth of March?"

"I did not."

"Did you make your usual rounds on that occasion?"

"Yes. I went all over the premises several times during the night, and the rest of the time, I was in a room over the private office."

"Who arrived first on the morning of the tenth?"

"Mr. Reuben. He arrived about twenty minutes before anybody else."

"What part of the building did he go to?"

"He went into the private office, which I opened for him. He remained there until a few minutes before Mr. Hornby arrived, when he went up to the laboratory."

"Who came next?"

"Mr. Hornby, and Mr. Walter came in just after him."

The counsel sat down, and Anstey proceeded to cross-examine the witness.

"Who was the last to leave the premises on the evening of the ninth?"

"I am not sure."

"Why are you not sure?"

"I had to take a note and a parcel to a firm in Shoreditch. When I started, a clerk named Thomas Holker was in the outer office and Mr. Walter Hornby was in the private office. When I returned they had both gone."

"Was the outer door locked?"

"Yes."

"Had Holker a key of the outer door?"

"No. Mr. Hornby and his two nephews had each a key, and I have one. No one else had a key."

"How long were you absent?"

"About three-quarters of an hour."

"Who gave you the note and the parcel?"

"Mr. Walter Hornby."

"When did he give them to you?"

"He gave them to me just before I started, and told me to go at once for fear the place should be closed before I got there."

"And was the place closed?"

"Yes. It was all shut up, and everybody had gone."

Anstey resumed his seat, the witness shuffled out of the box with an air of evident relief, and the usher called out, "Henry James Singleton."

Mr. Singleton rose from his seat at the table by the solicitors for the prosecution and entered the box. Sir Hector adjusted his glasses, turned over a page of his brief, and cast a steady and impressive glance at the jury.

"I believe, Mr. Singleton," he said at length, "that you are connected with the Finger-print Department at Scotland Yard?"

"Yes. I am one of the chief assistants in that department."

"What are your official duties?"

"My principal occupation consists in the examination and comparison of the finger-prints of criminals and suspected persons. These finger-prints are classified by me according to their characters and arranged in files for reference."

"I take it that you have examined a great number of finger-prints?"

"I have examined many thousands of finger-prints, and have studied them closely for purposes of identification."

"Kindly examine this paper, Mr. Singleton"—here the fatal leaflet was handed to him by the usher—"have you ever seen it before?"

"Yes. It was handed to me for examination at my office on the tenth of March."

"There is a mark upon it—the print of a finger or thumb. Can you tell us anything about that mark?"

"It is the print of the left thumb of Reuben Hornby, the prisoner at the bar."

"You are quite sure of that?"

"I am quite sure."

"Do you swear that the mark upon that paper was made by the thumb of the prisoner?"

"I do."

"Could it not have been made by the thumb of some other person?"

"No; it is impossible that it could have been made by any other person."

At this moment I felt Juliet lay a trembling hand on mine, and glancing at her, I saw that she was deathly pale. I took her hand in mine and, pressing it gently, whispered to her, "Have courage; there is nothing unexpected in this."

"Thank you," she whispered in reply, with a faint smile; "I will try; but it is all so horribly unnerving."

"You consider," Sir Hector proceeded, "that the identity of this thumb-print admits of no doubt?"

"It admits of no doubt whatever," replied Mr. Singleton.

"Can you explain to us, without being too technical, how you have arrived at such complete certainty?"

"I myself took a print of the prisoner's thumb—having first obtained the prisoner's consent after warning him that the print would be used in evidence against him—and I compared that print with the mark on this paper. The comparison was made with the greatest care and by the most approved method, point by point and detail by detail, and the two prints were found to be identical in every respect.

"Now it has been proved by exact calculations—which calculations I have personally verified—-that the chance that the print of a single finger of any given person will be exactly like the print of the same finger of any other given person is as one to sixty-four thousand millions. That is to say that, since the number of the entire human race is about sixteen thousand millions, the chance is about one to four that the print of a single finger of any one person will be identical with that of the same finger of any other member of the human race.

"It has been said by a great authority—and I entirely agree with the statement—that a complete, or nearly complete, accordance between two prints of a single finger affords evidence requiring no corroboration that the persons from whom they were made are the same.

"Now, these calculations apply to the prints of ordinary and normal fingers or thumbs. But the thumb from which these prints were taken is not ordinary or normal. There is upon it a deep but clean linear scar—the scar of an old incised wound—and this scar passes across the pattern of the ridges, intersecting the latter at certain places and disturbing their continuity at others. Now this very characteristic scar is an additional feature, having a set of chances of its own. So that we have to consider not only the chance that the print of the prisoner's left thumb should be identical with the print of some other person's left thumb—which is as one to sixty-four thousand millions—but the further chance that these two identical thumb-prints should be traversed by the impression of a scar identical in size and appearance, and intersecting the ridges at exactly the same places and producing failures of continuity in the ridges of exactly the same character. But these two chances, multiplied into one another, yield an ultimate chance of about one to four thousand trillions that the prisoner's left thumb will exactly resemble the print of some other person's thumb, both as to the pattern and the scar which crosses the pattern; in other words such a coincidence is an utter impossibility."

Sir Hector Trumpler took off his glasses and looked long and steadily at the jury as though he should say, "Come, my friends; what do you think of that?" Then he sat down with a jerk and turned toward Anstey and Thorndyke with a look of triumph.

"Do you propose to cross-examine the witness?" inquired the judge, seeing that the counsel for the defense made no sign.

"No, my lord," replied Anstey.

Thereupon Sir Hector Trumpler turned once more toward the defending counsel, and his broad, red face was illumined by a smile of deep satisfaction. That smile was reflected on the face of Mr. Singleton as he stepped from the box, and as I glanced at Thorndyke, I seemed to detect, for a single instant, on his calm and immovable countenance, the faintest shadow of a smile.

"Herbert John Nash!"

A plump, middle-aged man, of keen, though studious, aspect, stepped into the box, and Sir Hector rose once more.

"You are one of the chief assistants in the Finger-print Department, I believe, Mr. Nash?"

"I am."

"Have you heard the evidence of the last witness?"

"I have."

"Do you agree with the statements made by that witness?"

"Entirely. I am prepared to swear that the print on the paper found in the safe is that of the left thumb of the prisoner, Reuben Hornby."

"And you are certain that no mistake is possible?"

"I am certain that no mistake is possible."

Again Sir Hector glanced significantly at the jury as he resumed his seat, and again Anstey made no sign beyond the entry of a few notes on the margin of his brief.

"Are you calling any more witnesses?" asked the judge, dipping his pen in the ink.

"No, my lord," replied Sir Hector. "That is our case."

Upon this Anstey rose and, addressing the judge, said—

"I call witnesses, my lord."

The judge nodded and made an entry in his notes while Anstey delivered his brief introductory speech—

"My lord and gentlemen of the jury, I shall not occupy the time of the Court with unnecessary appeals at this stage, but shall proceed to take the evidence of my witnesses without delay."

There was a pause of a minute or more, during which the silence was broken only by the rustle of papers and the squeaking of the judge's quill pen. Juliet turned a white, scared face to me and said in a hushed whisper—

"This is terrible. That last man's evidence is perfectly crushing. What can possibly be said in reply? I am in despair; oh! poor Reuben! He is lost, Dr. Jervis! He hasn't a chance now."

"Do you believe that he is guilty?" I asked.

"Certainly not!" she replied indignantly. "I am as certain of his innocence as ever."

"Then," said I, "if he is innocent, there must be some means of proving his innocence."

"Yes. I suppose so," she rejoined in a dejected whisper. "At any rate we shall soon know now."

At this moment the usher's voice was heard calling out the name of the first witness for the defense.

"Edmund Horford Rowe!"

A keen-looking, gray-haired man, with a shaven face and close-cut side-whiskers, stepped into the box and was sworn in due form.

"You are a doctor of medicine, I believe," said Anstey, addressing the witness, "and lecturer on Medical Jurisprudence at the South London Hospital?"

"I am."

"Have you had occasion to study the properties of blood?"

"Yes. The properties of blood are of great importance from a medico-legal point of view."

"Can you tell us what happens when a drop of blood—say from a cut finger—falls upon a surface such as the bottom of an iron safe?"

"A drop of blood from a living body falling upon any nonabsorbent surface will, in the course of a few minutes, solidify into a jelly which will, at first, have the same bulk and color as the liquid blood."

"Will it undergo any further change?"

"Yes. In a few minutes more the jelly will begin to shrink and become more solid so that the blood will become separated into two parts, the solid and the liquid. The solid part will consist of a firm, tough jelly of a deep red color, and the liquid part will consist of a pale yellow, clear, watery liquid."

"At the end, say, of two hours, what will be the condition of the drop of blood?"

"It will consist of a drop of clear, nearly colorless liquid, in the middle of which will be a small, tough, red clot."

"Supposing such a drop to be taken up on a piece of white paper, what would be its appearance?"

"The paper would be wetted by the colorless liquid, and the solid clot would probably adhere to the paper in a mass."

"Would the blood on the paper appear as a clear, red liquid?"

"Certainly not. The liquid would appear like water, and the clot would appear as a solid mass sticking to the paper."

"Does blood always behave in the way you have described?"

"Always, unless some artificial means are taken to prevent it from clotting."

"By what means can blood be prevented from clotting or solidifying?"

"There are two principal methods. One is to stir or whip the fresh blood rapidly with a bundle of fine twigs. When this is done, the fibrin—the part of the blood that causes solidification—adheres to the twigs, and the blood that remains, though it is unchanged in appearance, will remain liquid for an indefinite time. The other method is to dissolve a certain proportion of some alkaline salt in the fresh blood, after which it no longer has any tendency to solidify."

"You have heard the evidence of Inspector Sanderson and Sergeant Bates?"

"Yes."

"Inspector Sanderson has told us that he examined the safe at 10.31 a.m. and found two good-sized drops of blood on the bottom. Sergeant Bates has told us that he examined the safe two hours later, and that he took up one of the drops of blood on a piece of white paper. The blood was then quite liquid, and on the paper, it looked like a clear, red liquid of the color of blood. What should you consider the condition and nature of that blood to have been?"

"If it was really blood at all, I should say that it was either defibrinated blood—that is, blood from which the fibrin has been extracted by whipping—or that it had been treated with an alkaline salt."

"You are of opinion that the blood found in the safe could not have been ordinary blood shed from a cut or wound?"

"I am sure it could not have been."

"Now, Dr. Rowe, I am going to ask you a few questions on another subject. Have you given any attention to finger-prints made by bloody fingers?"

"Yes. I have recently made some experiments on the subject."

"Will you give us the results of those experiments?"

"My object was to ascertain whether fingers wet with fresh blood would yield distinct and characteristic prints. I made a great number of trials, and as a result found that it is extremely difficult to obtain a clear print when the finger is wetted with fresh blood. The usual result is a mere red blot showing no ridge pattern at all, owing to the blood filling the furrows between the ridges. But if the blood is allowed to dry almost completely on the finger, a very clear print is obtained."

"Is it possible to recognize a print that has been made by a nearly dry finger?"

"Yes; quite easily. The half-dried blood is nearly solid and adheres to the paper in a different way from the liquid, and it shows minute details, such as the mouths of the sweat glands, which are always obliterated by the liquid."

"Look carefully at this paper, which was found in the safe, and tell me what you see."

The witness took the paper and examined it attentively, first with the naked eye and then with a pocket-lens.

"I see," said he, "two blood-marks and a print, apparently of a thumb. Of the two marks, one is a blot, smeared slightly by a finger or thumb; the other is a smear only. Both were evidently produced with quite liquid blood. The thumb-print was also made with liquid blood."

"You are quite sure that the thumb-print was made with liquid blood?"

"Quite sure."

"Is there anything unusual about the thumb-print?"

"Yes. It is extraordinarily clear and distinct. I have made a great number of trials and have endeavored to obtain the clearest prints possible with fresh blood; but none of my prints are nearly as distinct as this one."

Here the witness produced a number of sheets of paper, each of which was covered with the prints of bloody fingers, and compared them with the memorandum slip.

The papers were handed to the judge for his inspection, and Anstey sat down, when Sir Hector Trumpler rose, with a somewhat puzzled expression on his face, to cross-examine.

"You say that the blood found in the safe was defibrinated or artificially treated. What inference do you draw from that fact?"

"I infer that it was not dropped from a bleeding wound."

"Can you form any idea how such blood should have got into the safe?"

"None whatever."

"You say that the thumb-print is a remarkably distinct one. What conclusion do you draw from that?"

"I do not draw any conclusion. I cannot account for its distinctness at all."

The learned counsel sat down with rather a baffled air, and I observed a faint smile spread over the countenance of my colleague.

"Arabella Hornby."

A muffled whimpering from my neighbor on the left hand was accompanied by a wild rustling of silk. Glancing at Mrs. Hornby, I saw her stagger from the bench, shaking like a jelly, mopping her eyes with her handkerchief and grasping her open purse. She entered the witness-box and, having gazed wildly round the court, began to search the multitudinous compartments of her purse.

"The evidence you shall give," sang out the usher—whereat Mrs. Hornby paused in her search and stared at him apprehensively—"to the court and jury sworn, between our Sovereign Lord the King and the prisoner at the bar shall be the truth,—"

"Certainly," said Mrs. Hornby stiffly, "I—"

"—the whole truth, and nothing but the truth; so help you God!"

He held out the Testament, which she took from him with a trembling hand and forthwith dropped with a resounding bang on to the floor of the witness-box, diving after it with such precipitancy that her bonnet jammed violently against the rail of the box.

She disappeared from view for a moment, and then rose from the depths with a purple face and her bonnet flattened and cocked over one ear like an artillery-man's forage cap.

"Kiss the Book, if you please," said the usher, suppressing a grin by an heroic effort, as Mrs. Hornby, encumbered by her purse, her handkerchief and the Testament, struggled to unfasten her bonnet-strings. She clawed frantically at her bonnet and, having dusted the Testament with her handkerchief, kissed it tenderly and laid it on the rail of the box, whence it fell instantly on to the floor of the court.

"I am really very sorry!" exclaimed Mrs. Hornby, leaning over the rail to address the usher as he stooped to pick up the Book, and discharging on to his back a stream of coins, buttons, and folded bills from her open purse; "you will think me very awkward, I'm afraid."

She mopped her face and replaced her bonnet rakishly on one side, as Anstey rose and passed a small red book across to her.

"Kindly look at that book, Mrs. Hornby."

"I'd rather not," said she, with a gesture of repugnance. "It is associated with matters of so extremely disagreeable a character—"

"Do you recognize it?"

"Do I recognize it! How can you ask me such a question when you must know—"

"Answer the question," interposed the judge. "Do you or do you not recognize the book in your hand?"

"Of course I recognize it. How could I fail to—"

"Then say so," said the judge.

"I have said so," retorted Mrs. Hornby indignantly.

The judge nodded to Anstey, who then continued—"It is called a 'Thumbograph,' I believe."

"Yes: the name 'Thumbograph' is printed on the cover, so I suppose that is what it is called."

"Will you tell us, Mrs. Hornby, how the 'Thumbograph' came into your possession?"

For one moment Mrs. Hornby stared wildly at her interrogator; then she snatched a paper from her purse, unfolded it, gazed at it with an expression of dismay, and crumpled it up in the palm of her hand.

"You are asked a question," said the judge.

"Oh! yes," said Mrs. Hornby. "The Committee of the Society—no, that is the wrong one—I mean Walter, you know—at least—"

"I beg your pardon," said Anstey, with polite gravity.

"You were speaking of the committee of some society," interposed the judge. "What society were you referring to?"

Mrs. Hornby spread out the paper and, after a glance at it, replied—

"The Society of Paralyzed Idiots, your worship," whereat a rumble of suppressed laughter arose from the gallery.

"But what has that society to do with the 'Thumbograph'?" inquired the judge.

"Nothing, your worship. Nothing at all."

"Then why did you refer to it?"

"I am sure I don't know," said Mrs. Hornby, wiping her eyes with the paper and then hastily exchanging it for her handkerchief.

The judge took off his glasses and gazed at Mrs. Hornby with an expression of bewilderment. Then he turned to the counsel and said in a weary voice—"Proceed, if you please, Mr. Anstey."

"Can you tell us, Mrs. Hornby, how the 'Thumbograph' came into your possession?" said the latter in persuasive accents.

"I thought it was Walter, and so did my niece, but Walter says it was not, and he ought to know, being young and having a most excellent memory, as I had myself when I was his age, and really, you know, it can't possibly matter where I got the thing—"

"But it does matter," interrupted Anstey. "We wish particularly to know."

"If you mean that you wish to get one like it—"

"We do not," said Anstey. "We wish to know how that particular 'Thumbograph' came into your possession. Did you, for instance, buy it yourself, or was it given to you by someone?"

"Walter says I bought it myself, but I thought he gave it to me, but he says he did not, and you see—"

"Never mind what Walter says. What is your own impression?"

"Why I still think that he gave it to me, though, of course, seeing that my memory is not what it was—"

"You think that Walter gave it to you?"

"Yes, in fact I feel sure he did, and so does my niece."

"Walter is your nephew, Walter Hornby?"

"Yes, of course. I thought you knew."

"Can you recall the occasion on which the 'Thumbograph' was given to you?"

"Oh yes, quite distinctly. We had some people to dinner—some people named Colley—not the Dorsetshire Colleys, you know, although they are exceedingly nice people, as I have no doubt the other Colleys are, too, when you know them, but we don't. Well, after dinner we were a little dull and rather at a loss, because Juliet, my niece, you know, had cut her finger and couldn't play the piano excepting with the left hand, and that is so monotonous as well as fatiguing, and the Colleys are not musical, excepting Adolphus, who plays the trombone, but he hadn't got it with him, and then, fortunately, Walter came in and brought the 'Thumbograph' and took all our thumb-prints and his own as well, and we were very much amused, and Matilda Colley—that is the eldest daughter but one—said that Reuben jogged her elbow, but that was only an excuse—"

"Exactly," interrupted Anstey. "And you recollect quite clearly that your nephew Walter gave you the 'Thumbograph' on that occasion?"

"Oh, distinctly; though, you know, he is really my husband's nephew—"

"Yes. And you are sure that he took the thumb-prints?"

"Quite sure."

"And you are sure that you never saw the 'Thumbograph' before that?"

"Never. How could I? He hadn't brought it."

"Have you ever lent the 'Thumbograph' to anyone?"

"No, never. No one has ever wanted to borrow it, because, you see—"

"Has it never, at any time, gone out of your possession?"

"Oh, I wouldn't say that; in fact, I have often thought, though I hate suspecting people, and I really don't suspect anybody in particular, you know, but it certainly was very peculiar and I can't explain it in any other way. You see, I kept the 'Thumbograph' in a drawer in my writing table, and in the same drawer I used to keep my handkerchief-bag—in fact I do still, and it is there at this very moment, for in my hurry and agitation, I forgot about it until we were in the cab, and then it was too late, because Mr. Lawley—"

"Yes. You kept it in a drawer with your handkerchief-bag."

"That was what I said. Well, when Mr. Hornby was staying at Brighton, he wrote to ask me to go down for a week and bring Juliet—Miss Gibson, you know—with me. So we went, and, just as we were starting, I sent Juliet to fetch my handkerchief-bag from the drawer, and I said to her, 'Perhaps we might take the thumb-book with us; it might come in useful on a wet day.' So she went, and presently she came back and said that the 'Thumbograph' was not in the drawer. Well, I was so surprised that I went back with her and looked myself, and sure enough the drawer was empty. Well, I didn't think much of it at the time, but when we came home again, as soon as we got out of the cab, I gave Juliet my handkerchief-bag to put away, and presently she came running to me in a great state of excitement. 'Why, Auntie,' she said,' the "Thumbograph" is in the drawer; somebody must have been meddling with your writing table.' I went with her to the drawer, and there, sure enough, was the 'Thumbograph.' Somebody must have taken it out and put it back while we were away."

"Who could have had access to your writing table?"

"Oh, anybody, because, you see, the drawers were never locked. We thought it must have been one of the servants."

"Had anyone been to the house during your absence?"

"No. Nobody, except, of course, my two nephews; and neither of them had touched it, because we asked them, and they both said they had not."

"Thank you." Anstey sat down, and Mrs. Hornby having given another correcting twist to her bonnet, was about to step down from the box when Sir Hector rose and bestowed upon her an intimidating stare.

"You made some reference," said he, "to a society—the Society of Paralyzed Idiots, I think, whatever that may be. Now what caused you to make that reference?"

"It was a mistake; I was thinking of something else."

"I know it was a mistake. You referred to a paper that was in your hand."

"I did not refer to it, I merely looked at it. It is a letter from the Society of Paralyzed Idiots. It is nothing to do with me really, you know; I don't belong to the society, or anything of that sort."

"Did you mistake that paper for some other paper?"

"Yes, I took it for a paper with some notes on it to assist my memory."

"What kind of notes?"

"Oh, just the questions I was likely to be asked."

"Were the answers that you were to give to those questions also written on the paper?"

"Of course they were. The questions would not have been any use without the answers."

"Have you been asked the questions that were written on the paper?"

"Yes; at least, some of them."

"Have you given the answers that were written down?"

"I don't think I have—in fact, I am sure I haven't, because, you see—"

"Ah! you don't think you have." Sir Hector Trumpler smiled significantly at the jury, and continued—

"Now who wrote down those questions and answers?"

"My nephew, Walter Hornby. He thought, you know—"

"Never mind what he thought. Who advised or instructed him to write them down?"

"Nobody. It was entirely his own idea, and very thoughtful of him, too, though Dr. Jervis took the paper away from me and said I must rely on my memory."

Sir Hector was evidently rather taken aback by this answer, and sat down suddenly, with a distinctly chapfallen air.

"Where is this paper on which the questions and answers are written?" asked the judge. In anticipation of this inquiry, I had already handed it to Thorndyke, and had noted by the significant glance that he bestowed on me that he had not failed to observe the peculiarity in the type. Indeed the matter was presently put beyond all doubt, for he hastily passed to me a scrap of paper, on which I found, when I opened it out, that he had written "X = W.H."

As Anstey handed the rather questionable document up to the judge, I glanced at Walter Hornby and observed him to flush angrily, though he strove to appear calm and unconcerned, and the look that he directed at his aunt was very much the reverse of benevolent.

"Is this the paper?" asked the judge, passing it down to the witness.

"Yes, your worship," answered Mrs. Hornby, in a tremulous voice; whereupon the document was returned to the judge, who proceeded to compare it with his notes.

"I shall order this document to be impounded," said he sternly, after making a brief comparison. "There has been a distinct attempt to tamper with witnesses. Proceed with your case, Mr. Anstey."

There was a brief pause, during which Mrs. Hornby tottered across the court and resumed her seat, gasping with excitement and relief; then the usher called out—

"John Evelyn Thorndyke!"

"Thank God!" exclaimed Juliet, clasping her hands. "Oh! will he be able to save Reuben? Do you think he will, Dr. Jervis?"

"There is someone who thinks he will," I replied, glancing toward Polton, who, clasping in his arms the mysterious box and holding on to the microscope case, gazed at his master with a smile of ecstasy. "Polton has more faith than you have, Miss Gibson."

"Yes, the dear, faithful little man!" she rejoined. "Well, we shall know the worst very soon now, at any rate."

"The worst or the best," I said. "We are now going to hear what the defense really is."

"God grant that it may be a good defense," she exclaimed in a low voice; and I—though not ordinarily a religious man—murmured "Amen!"

CHAPTER SIXTEEN

THORNDYKE PLAYS HIS CARD

As Thorndyke took his place in the box, I looked at him with a sense of unreasonable surprise, feeling that I had never before fully realized what manner of man my friend was as to his externals. I had often noted the quiet strength of his face, its infinite intelligence, its attractiveness and magnetism; but I had never before appreciated what now impressed me most: that Thorndyke was actually the handsomest man I had ever seen. He was dressed simply, his appearance unaided by the flowing gown or awe-inspiring wig, and yet his presence dominated the court. Even the judge, despite his scarlet robe and trappings of office, looked commonplace by comparison, while the jurymen, who turned to look at him, seemed like beings of an inferior order. It was not alone the distinction of the tall figure, erect and dignified, nor the power and massive composure of his face, but the actual symmetry and comeliness of the face itself that now arrested my attention; a comeliness that made it akin rather to some classic mask, wrought in the ivory-toned marble of Pentelicus, than to the eager faces that move around us in the hurry and bustle of a life at once strenuous and trivial.

"You are attached to the medical school at St. Margaret's Hospital, I believe, Dr. Thorndyke?" said Anstey.

"Yes. I am the lecturer on Medical Jurisprudence and Toxicology."

"Have you had much experience of medico-legal inquiries?"

"A great deal. I am engaged exclusively in medico-legal work."

"You heard the evidence relating to the two drops of blood found in the safe?"

"I did."

"What is your opinion as to the condition of that blood?"

"I should say there is no doubt that it had been artificially treated—probably by defibrination."

"Can you suggest any explanation of the condition of that blood?"

"I can."

"Is your explanation connected with any peculiarities in the thumb-print on the paper that was found in the safe?"

"It is."

"Have you given any attention to the subject of finger-prints?"

"Yes. A great deal of attention."

"Be good enough to examine that paper." (Here the usher handed to Thorndyke the memorandum slip.) "Have you seen it before?"

"Yes. I saw it at Scotland Yard."

"Did you examine it thoroughly?"

"Very thoroughly. The police officials gave me every facility, and with their permission, I took several photographs of it."

"There is a mark on that paper resembling the print of a human thumb?"

"There is."

"You have heard two expert witnesses swear that that mark was made by the left thumb of the prisoner, Reuben Hornby?"

"I have."

"Do you agree to that statement?"

"I do not."

"In your opinion, was the mark upon that paper made by the thumb of the prisoner?"

"No. I am convinced that it was not made by the thumb of Reuben Hornby."

"Do you think that it was made by the thumb of some other person?"

"No. I am of opinion that it was not made by a human thumb at all."

At this statement the judge paused for a moment, pen in hand, and stared at Thorndyke with his mouth slightly open, while the two experts looked at one another with raised eyebrows.

"By what means do you consider that the mark was produced?"

"By means of a stamp, either of India rubber or, more probably, of chromicized gelatin."

Here Polton, who had been, by degrees, rising to an erect posture, smote his thigh a resounding *thwack* and chuckled aloud, a proceeding that caused all eyes, including those of the judge, to be turned on him.

"If that noise is repeated," said the judge, with a stony stare at the horrified offender—who had shrunk into the very smallest space that I have ever seen a human being occupy—"I shall cause the person who made it to be removed from the court."

"I understand, then," pursued Anstey, "that you consider the thumb-print, which has been sworn to as the prisoner's, to be a forgery?"

"Yes. It is a forgery."

"But is it possible to forge a thumb-print or a finger-print?"

"It is not only possible, but quite easy to do."

"As easy as to forge a signature, for instance?"

"Much more so, and infinitely more secure. A signature, being written with a pen, requires that the forgery should also be written with a pen, a process demanding very special skill and, after all, never resulting in an absolute *facsimile*. But a finger-print is a stamped impression—the finger-tip being the stamp; and it is only necessary to obtain a stamp identical in character with the finger-tip, in order to produce an impression which is an absolute *facsimile*, in every respect, of the original, and totally indistinguishable from it."

"Would there be no means at all of detecting the difference between a forged finger-print and the genuine original?"

"None whatever; for the reason that there would be no difference to detect."

"But you have stated, quite positively, that the thumb-print on this paper is a forgery. Now, if the forged print is indistinguishable from the original, how are you able to be certain that this particular print is a forgery?"

"I was speaking of what is possible with due care, but, obviously, a forger might, through inadvertence, fail to produce an absolute *facsimile* and then detection would be possible. That is what has happened in the present case. The forged print is not an absolute *facsimile* of the true print. There is a slight discrepancy. But, in addition to this, the paper bears intrinsic evidence that the thumb-print on it is a forgery."

"We will consider that evidence presently, Dr. Thorndyke. To return to the possibility of forging a finger-print, can you explain to us, without being too technical, by what methods it would be possible to produce such a stamp as you have referred to?"

"There are two principal methods that suggest themselves to me. The first, which is rather crude though easy to carry out, consists in taking an actual cast of the end of the finger. A mold would be made by pressing the finger into some plastic material, such as fine modelling clay or hot sealing wax, and then, by pouring a warm solution of gelatin into the mold, and allowing it to cool and solidify, a cast would be produced, which would yield very perfect finger-prints. But this method would, as a rule, be useless for the purpose of the forger, as it could not, ordinarily, be carried out without the knowledge of the victim; though in the case of dead bodies and persons asleep or unconscious or under an anesthetic, it could be practiced with success, and would offer the advantage of requiring practically no technical skill or knowledge and no special appliances. The second method, which is much more efficient, and is the one, I have no doubt, that has been used in the present instance, requires more knowledge and skill.

"In the first place it is necessary to obtain possession of, or access to, a genuine finger-print. Of this finger-print a photograph is taken, or rather, a photographic negative, which for this purpose requires to be taken on a reversed plate, and the negative is put into a special printing frame, with a plate of gelatin which has been treated with potassium bichromate, and the frame is exposed to light.

"Now gelatin treated in this way—chromicized gelatin, as it is called—has a very peculiar property. Ordinary gelatin, as is well known, is easily dissolved in hot water, and chromicized gelatin is also soluble in hot water as long as it is not exposed to light; but on being exposed to light, it undergoes a change and is no longer capable of being dissolved in hot water. Now the plate of chromicized gelatin under the negative is protected from the light by the opaque parts of the negative, whereas the light passes freely through the transparent parts; but the transparent parts of the negative correspond to the black marks on the finger-print, and these correspond to the ridges on the finger. Hence it follows that the gelatin plate is acted upon by light only on the parts corresponding to the ridges; and in these parts the gelatin is rendered insoluble, while all the rest of the gelatin is soluble. The gelatin plate, which is cemented to a thin plate of metal for support, is now carefully washed with hot water, by which the soluble part of the gelatin is dissolved away, leaving the insoluble part (corresponding to the ridges) standing up from the surface. Thus there is produced a *facsimile* in relief of the finger-print having actual ridges and furrows identical in character with the ridges and furrows of the finger-tip. If an inked roller is passed over this relief, or if the relief is pressed lightly on an inked slab, and then pressed on a sheet of paper, a finger-print will be produced, which will be absolutely identical with the original, even to the little white spots which mark the orifices of the sweat glands. It will be impossible to discover any difference between the real finger-print and the counterfeit because, in fact, no difference exists."

"But surely the process you have described is a very difficult and intricate one?"

"Not at all; it is very little more difficult than ordinary carbon printing, which is practiced successfully by numbers of amateurs. Moreover, such a relief as I have described—which is practically nothing more than an ordinary process block—could be produced by any photo-engraver. The process that I have described is, in all essentials, that which is used in the reproduction of pen-and-ink drawings, and any of the hundreds of workmen who are employed in that industry could make a relief-block of a finger-print, with which an undetectable forgery could be executed."

"You have asserted that the counterfeit finger-print could not be distinguished from the original. Are you prepared to furnish proof that this is the case?"

"Yes. I am prepared to execute a counterfeit of the prisoner's thumb-print in the presence of the Court."

"And do you say that such a counterfeit would be indistinguishable from the original, even by the experts?"

"I do."

Anstey turned toward the judge. "Would your lordship give your permission for a demonstration such as the witness proposes?"

"Certainly," replied the judge. "The evidence is highly material. How do you propose that the comparison should be made?" he added, addressing Thorndyke.

"I have brought, for the purpose, my lord," answered Thorndyke, "some sheets of paper, each of which is ruled into twenty numbered squares. I propose to make on ten of the squares counterfeits of the prisoner's thumb-mark, and to fill the remaining ten with real thumb-marks. I propose that the experts should then examine the paper and tell the Court which are the real thumb-prints and which are the false."

"That seems a fair and efficient test," said his lordship. "Have you any objection to offer, Sir Hector?"

Sir Hector Trumpler hastily consulted with the two experts, who were sitting in the attorney's bench, and then replied, without much enthusiasm—

"We have no objection to offer, my lord."

"Then, in that case, I shall direct the expert witnesses to withdraw from the court while the prints are being made."

In obedience to the judge's order, Mr. Singleton and his colleague rose and left the court with evident reluctance, while Thorndyke took from a small portfolio three sheets of paper that he handed up to the judge.

"If your lordship," said he, "will make marks in ten of the squares on two of these sheets, one can be given to the jury and one retained by your lordship to check the third sheet when the prints are made on it."

"That is an excellent plan," said the judge; "and, as the information is for myself and the jury, it would be better if you came up and performed the actual stamping on my table in the presence of the foreman of the jury and the counsel for the prosecution and defense."

In accordance with the judge's direction, Thorndyke stepped up on the dais, and Anstey, as he rose to follow, leaned over toward me.

"You and Polton had better go up too," said he: "Thorndyke will want your assistance, and you may as well see the fun. I will explain to his lordship."

He ascended the stairs leading to the dais and addressed a few words to the judge, who glanced in our direction and nodded, whereupon we both gleefully followed our counsel, Polton carrying the box and beaming with delight.

The judge's table was provided with a shallow drawer that pulled out at the side and accommodated the box comfortably, leaving the small tabletop free for the papers. When the lid of the box was raised, there were displayed a copper inking-slab, a small roller, and the twenty-four "pawns" which had so puzzled Polton, and on which he now gazed with a twinkle of amusement and triumph.

"Are those all stamps?" inquired the judge, glancing curiously at the array of turned-wood handles.

"They are all stamps, my lord," replied Thorndyke, "and each is taken from a different impression of the prisoner's thumb."

"But why so many?" asked the judge.

"I have multiplied them," answered Thorndyke, as he squeezed out a drop of finger-print ink on to the slab and proceeded to roll it out into a thin film, "to avoid the telltale uniformity of a single stamp. And I may say," he added, "that it is highly important that the experts should not be informed that more than one stamp has been used."

"Yes, I see that," said the judge. "You understand that, Sir Hector," he added, addressing the counsel, who bowed stiffly, clearly regarding the entire proceeding with extreme disfavor.

Thorndyke now inked one of the stamps and handed it to the judge, who examined it curiously and then pressed it on a piece of waste paper, on which there immediately appeared a very distinct impression of a human thumb.

"Marvelous!" he exclaimed. "Most ingenious! Too ingenious!" He chuckled softly and added, as he handed the stamp and the paper to the foreman of the jury: "It is well, Dr. Thorndyke, that you are on the side of law and order, for I am afraid that, if you were on the other side, you would be one too many for the police. Now, if you are ready, we will proceed. Will you, please, stamp an impression in square number three."

Thorndyke drew a stamp from its compartment, inked it on the slab, and pressed it neatly on the square indicated, leaving there a sharp, clear thumb-print.

The process was repeated on nine other squares, a different stamp being used for each impression. The judge then marked the ten corresponding squares of the other two sheets of paper, and having checked them, directed the foreman to exhibit the sheet bearing the false thumb-prints to the jury, together with the marked sheet that they were to retain, to enable them to check the statements of the expert witnesses. When this was done, the prisoner was brought from the dock and stood beside the table. The judge looked with a curious and not unkindly interest at the handsome, manly fellow who stood charged with a crime so sordid and out of character with his appearance, and I felt, as I noted the look, that Reuben would, at least, be tried fairly on the evidence, without prejudice or even with some prepossession in his favor.

With the remaining part of the operation, Thorndyke proceeded carefully and deliberately. The inking-slab was rolled afresh for each impression, and after each, the thumb was cleansed with petrol and thoroughly dried; and when the process was completed and the prisoner led back to the dock, the twenty squares on the paper were occupied by twenty thumb-prints, which, to my eye, at any rate, were identical in character.

The judge sat for near upon a minute poring over this singular document with an expression halfway between a frown and a smile. At length, when we had all returned to our places, he directed the usher to bring in the witnesses.

I was amused to observe the change that had come over the experts in the short interval. The confident smile, the triumphant air of laying down a trump card, had vanished, and the expression of both was one of anxiety, not unmixed with apprehension. As Mr. Singleton advanced hesitatingly to the table, I recalled the words that he had uttered in his room at Scotland Yard; evidently his scheme of the game that was to end in an easy checkmate, had not included the move that had just been made.

"Mr. Singleton," said the judge, "here is a paper on which there are twenty thumb-prints. Ten of them are genuine prints of the prisoner's left thumb and ten are forgeries. Please examine them and note down in writing which are the true prints and which are the forgeries. When you have made your notes the paper will be handed to Mr. Nash."

"Is there any objection to my using the photograph that I have with me for comparison, my lord?" asked Mr. Singleton.

"I think not," replied the judge. "What do you say, Mr. Anstey?"

"No objection whatever, my lord," answered Anstey.

Mr. Singleton accordingly drew from his pocket an enlarged photograph of the thumb-print and a magnifying glass, with the aid of which he explored the bewildering array of prints on the paper before him; and as he proceeded I remarked with satisfaction that his expression became more and more dubious and worried. From time to time, he made an entry on a memorandum slip beside him, and as the entries accumulated, his frown grew deeper and his aspect more puzzled and gloomy.

At length he sat up, and taking the memorandum slip in his hand, addressed the judge.

"I have finished my examination, my lord."

"Very well. Mr. Nash, will you kindly examine the paper and write down the results of your examination?"

"Oh! I wish they would make haste," whispered Juliet. "Do you think they will be able to tell the real from the false thumb-prints?"

"I can't say," I replied; "but we shall soon know. They looked all alike to me."

Mr. Nash made his examination with exasperating deliberateness, and preserved throughout an air of stolid attention; but at length he, too, completed his notes and handed the paper back to the usher.

"Now, Mr. Singleton," said the judge, "let us hear your conclusions. You have been sworn."

Mr. Singleton stepped into the witness-box and, laying his notes on the ledge, faced the judge.

"Have you examined the paper that was handed to you?" asked Sir Hector Trumpler.

"I have."

"What did you see on the paper?"

"I saw twenty thumb-prints, of which some were evident forgeries, some were evidently genuine, and some were doubtful."

"Taking the thumb-prints *seriatim*, what have you noted about
them?"

Mr. Singleton examined his notes and replied—"The thumb-
print on square one is evidently a forgery, as is also number two,
though it is a passable imitation. Three and four are genuine; five is
an obvious forgery. Six is a genuine thumb-print; seven is a forgery,
though a good one; eight is genuine; nine is, I think, a forgery, though
it is a remarkably good imitation. Ten and eleven are genuine thumb-
marks; twelve and thirteen are forgeries; but as to fourteen I am very
doubtful, though I am inclined to regard it as a forgery. Fifteen is
genuine, and I think sixteen is also; but I will not swear to it. Seven-
teen is certainly genuine. Eighteen and nineteen I am rather doubtful
about, but I am disposed to consider them both forgeries. Twenty is
certainly a genuine thumb-print."

As Mr. Singleton's evidence proceeded, a look of surprise began
to make its appearance on the judge's face, while the jury glanced
from the witness to the notes before them and from their notes to
one another in undisguised astonishment.

As to Sir Hector Trumpler, that luminary of British jurisprudence was evidently completely fogged; for, as statement followed
statement, he pursed up his lips and his broad, red face became overshadowed by an expression of utter bewilderment.

For a few seconds, he stared blankly at his witness and then
dropped on to his seat with a thump that shook the court.

"You have no doubt," said Anstey, "as to the correctness of your
conclusions? For instance, you are quite sure that the prints one and
two are forgeries?"

"I have no doubt."

"You swear that those two prints are forgeries?"

Mr. Singleton hesitated for a moment. He had been watching the judge and the jury and had apparently misinterpreted their surprise, assuming it to be due to his own remarkable powers of discrimination; and his confidence had revived accordingly.

"Yes," he answered; "I swear that they are forgeries."

Anstey sat down, and Mr. Singleton, having passed his notes up to the judge, retired from the box, giving place to his colleague.

Mr. Nash, who had listened with manifest satisfaction to the evidence, stepped into the box with all his original confidence restored. His selection of the true and the false thumb-prints was practically identical with that of Mr. Singleton, and his knowledge of this fact led him to state his conclusions with an air that was authoritative and even dogmatic.

"I am quite satisfied of the correctness of my statements," he said, in reply to Anstey's question, "and I am prepared to swear, and do swear, that those thumb-prints which I have stated to be forgeries, are forgeries, and that their detection presents no difficulty to an observer who has an expert acquaintance with finger-prints."

"There is one question that I should like to ask," said the judge, when the expert had left the box and Thorndyke had reentered it to continue his evidence. "The conclusions of the expert witnesses—manifestly *bona fide* conclusions, arrived at by individual judgement, without collusion or comparison of results—are practically identical. They are virtually in complete agreement. Now, the strange thing is this: their conclusions are wrong in every instance." (Here I nearly laughed aloud, for, as I glanced at the two experts, the expression of smug satisfaction on their countenances changed with lightning rapidity to a ludicrous spasm of consternation.) "Not sometimes wrong and sometimes right, as would have been the case if they had made mere guesses, but wrong every time. When they are quite certain, they are quite wrong; and when they are doubtful, they incline to the wrong conclusion. This is a very strange coincidence, Dr. Thorndyke. Can you explain it?"

Thorndyke's face, which throughout the proceedings had been as expressionless as that of a wooden figurehead, now relaxed into a dry smile.

"I think I can, my lord," he replied. "The object of a forger in executing a forgery is to produce deception on those who shall examine the forgery."

"Ah!" said the judge; and *his* face relaxed into a dry smile, while the jury broke out into unconcealed grins.

"It was evident to me," continued Thorndyke, "that the experts would be unable to distinguish the real from the forged thumb-prints, and, that being so, that they would look for some collateral evidence to guide them. I, therefore, supplied that collateral evidence. Now, if ten prints are taken, without special precautions, from a single finger, it will probably happen that no two of them are exactly alike; for the finger being a rounded object of which only a small part touches the paper, the impressions produced will show little variations according to the part of the finger by which the print is made. But a stamp such as I have used has a flat surface like that of a printer's type, and, like a type, it always prints the same impression. It does not reproduce the finger-tip, but a particular print of the finger, and so, if ten prints are made with a single stamp, each print will be a mechanical repetition of the other nine. Thus, on a sheet bearing twenty finger-prints, of which ten were forgeries made with a single stamp, it would be easy to pick out the ten forged prints by the fact that they would all be mechanical repetitions of one another; while the genuine prints could be distinguished by the fact of their presenting trifling variations in the position of the finger.

"Anticipating this line of reasoning, I was careful to make each print with a different stamp and each stamp was made from a different thumb-print, and I further selected thumb-prints which varied as widely as possible when I made the stamps. Moreover, when I made the real thumb-prints, I was careful to put the thumb down in the same position each time as far as I was able; and so it happened that, on the sheet submitted to the experts, the real thumb-prints were nearly all alike, while the forgeries presented considerable variations. The instances in which the witnesses were quite certain were those in which I succeeded in making the genuine prints repeat one another, and the doubtful cases were those in which I partially failed."

"Thank you, that is quite clear," said the judge, with a smile of deep content, such as is apt to appear on the judicial countenance when an expert witness is knocked off his pedestal. "We may now proceed, Mr. Anstey."

"You have told us," resumed Anstey, "and have submitted proofs, that it is possible to forge a thumb-print so that detection is impossible. You have also stated that the thumb-print on the paper found in Mr. Hornby's safe is a forgery. Do you mean that it *may* be a forgery, or that it actually is one?"

"I mean that it actually is a forgery."

"When did you first come to the conclusion that it was a forgery?"

"When I saw it at Scotland Yard. There are three facts which suggested this conclusion. In the first place, the print was obviously produced with liquid blood, and yet it was a beautifully clear and distinct impression. But such an impression could not be produced with liquid blood without the use of a slab and roller, even if great care were used, and still less could it have been produced by an accidental smear.

"In the second place, on measuring the print with a micrometer, I found that it did not agree in dimensions with a genuine thumb-print of Reuben Hornby. It was appreciably larger. I photographed the print with the micrometer in contact and on comparing this with a genuine thumb-print, also photographed with the same microm-eter in contact, I found that the suspected print was larger by the fortieth of an inch, from one given point on the ridge-pattern to an-other given point. I have here enlargements of the two photographs in which the disagreement in size is clearly shown by the lines of the micrometer. I have also the micrometer itself and a portable micro-scope, if the Court wishes to verify the photographs."

"Thank you," said the judge, with a bland smile; "we will accept your sworn testimony unless the learned counsel for the prosecution demands verification."

He received the photographs which Thorndyke handed up and, having examined them with close attention, passed them on to the jury.

"The third fact," resumed Thorndyke, "is of much more impor-tance, since it not only proves the print to be a forgery, but also fur-nishes a very distinct clue to the origin of the forgery, and so to the identity of the forger." (Here the court became hushed until the si-lence was so profound that the ticking of the clock seemed a sensi-ble interruption. I glanced at Walter, who sat motionless and rigid at the end of the bench, and perceived that a horrible pallor had spread over his face, while his forehead was covered with beads of perspiration.) "On looking at the print closely, I noticed at one part a minute white mark or space. It was of the shape of a capital S and had evidently been produced by a defect in the paper—a loose fiber which had stuck to the thumb and been detached by it from the paper, leaving a blank space where it had been. But, on examining the paper under a low power of the microscope, I found the surface to be perfect and intact. No loose fiber had been detached from it, for if it had, the broken end or, at least, the groove in which it had lain, would have been visible. The inference seemed to be that the loose fiber had existed, not in the paper which was found in the safe, but in the paper on which the original thumb-mark had been made. Now, as far as I knew, there was only one undoubted thumb-print of Reuben Hornby's in existence—the one in the 'Thumbograph.' At my request, the 'Thumbograph' was brought to my chambers by Mrs. Hornby, and on examining the print of Reuben Hornby's left thumb, I perceived on it a minute, S-shaped white space occupying a similar position to that in the red thumb-mark; and when I looked at it through a powerful lens, I could clearly see the little groove in the paper in which the fiber had lain and from which it had been lifted by the inked thumb. I subsequently made a systematic comparison of the marks in the two thumb-prints; I found that the dimensions of the mark were proportionally the same in each—that is to say, the mark in the 'Thumbograph' print had an extreme length of 26/1000 of an inch and an extreme breadth of 14.5/1000 of an inch, while that in the red thumb-mark was one-fortieth larger in each dimension, having an extreme length of 26.65/1000 of an inch and an extreme breadth of 14.86/1000 of an inch; that the shape was identical, as was shown by superimposing tracings of greatly enlarged photographs of each mark on similar enlargements of the other; and that the mark intersected the ridges of the thumb-print in the same manner and at exactly the same parts in the two prints."

"Do you say that—having regard to the facts which you have stated—it is certain that the red thumb-mark is a forgery?"

"I do; and I also say that it is certain that the forgery was executed by means of the 'Thumbograph.'"

"Might not the resemblances be merely a coincidence?"

"No. By the law of probabilities which Mr. Singleton explained so clearly in his evidence, the adverse chances would run into untold millions. Here are two thumb-prints made in different places and at different times—an interval of many weeks intervening. Each of them bears an accidental mark which is due not to any peculiarity of the thumb, but to a peculiarity of the paper. On the theory of coincidences it is necessary to suppose that each piece of paper had a loose fiber of exactly identical shape and size and that this fiber came, by accident, in contact with the thumb at exactly the same spot. But such a supposition would be more opposed to probabilities even than the supposition that two exactly similar thumb-prints should have been made by different persons. And then there is the further fact that the paper found in the safe had no loose fiber to account for the mark."

"What is your explanation of the presence of defibrinated blood in the safe?"

"It was probably used by the forger in making the thumb-print, for which purpose fresh blood would be less suitable by reason of its clotting. He would probably have carried a small quantity in a bottle, together with the pocket slab and roller invented by Mr. Galton. It would thus be possible for him to put a drop on the slab, roll it out into a thin film, and take a clean impression with his stamp. It must be remembered that these precautions were quite necessary, since he had to make a recognizable print at the first attempt. A failure and a second trial would have destroyed the accidental appearance, and might have aroused suspicion."

"You have made some enlarged photographs of the thumb-prints, have you not?"

"Yes. I have here two enlarged photographs, one of the 'Thumbograph' print and one of the red thumb-print. They both show the white mark very clearly and will assist comparison of the originals, in which the mark is plainly visible through a lens."

He handed the two photographs up to the judge, together with the 'Thumbograph,' the memorandum slip, and a powerful doublet lens with which to examine them.

The judge inspected the two original documents with the aid of the lens and compared them with the photographs, nodding approvingly as he made out the points of agreement. Then he passed them on to the jury and made an entry in his notes.

While this was going on my attention was attracted by Walter Hornby. An expression of terror and wild despair had settled on his face, which was ghastly in its pallor and bedewed with sweat. He looked furtively at Thorndyke and, as I noted the murderous hate in his eyes, I recalled our midnight adventure in John Street and the mysterious cigar.

Suddenly he rose to his feet, wiping his brow and steadying himself against the bench with a shaking hand; then he walked quietly to the door and went out. Apparently, I was not the only onlooker who had been interested in his doings, for, as the door swung to after him, Superintendent Miller rose from his seat and went out by the other door.

"Are you cross-examining this witness?" the judge inquired, glancing at Sir Hector Trumpler.

"No, my lord," was the reply.

"Are you calling any more witnesses, Mr. Anstey?"

"Only one, my lord," replied Anstey—"the prisoner, whom I shall put in the witness-box, as a matter of form, in order that he may make a statement on oath."

Reuben was accordingly conducted from the dock to the witness-box and, having been sworn, made a solemn declaration of his innocence. A brief cross-examination followed, in which nothing was elicited, but that Reuben had spent the evening at his club and gone home to his rooms about half-past eleven and had let himself in with his latchkey. Sir Hector at length sat down; the prisoner was led back to the dock, and the Court settled itself to listen to the speeches of the counsel.

"My lord and gentlemen of the jury," Anstey commenced in his clear, mellow tones, "I do not propose to occupy your time with a long speech. The evidence that has been laid before you is at once so intelligible, so lucid, and so conclusive, that you will, no doubt, arrive at your verdict uninfluenced by any display of rhetoric either on my part or on the part of the learned counsel for the prosecution.

"Nevertheless, it is desirable to disentangle from the mass of evidence those facts which are really vital and crucial.

"Now the one fact which stands out and dominates the whole case is this: the prisoner's connection with this case rests solely upon the police theory of the infallibility of finger-prints. Apart from the evidence of the thumb-print there is not, and there never was, the faintest breath of suspicion against him. You have heard him described as a man of unsullied honor, as a man whose character is above reproach; a man who is trusted implicitly by those who have had dealings with him. And this character was not given by a casual stranger, but by one who has known him from childhood. His record is an unbroken record of honorable conduct; his life has been that of a clean-living, straightforward gentleman. And now he stands before you charged with a miserable, paltry theft; charged with having robbed that generous friend, the brother of his own father, the guardian of his childhood and the benefactor who has planned and striven for his well-being; charged, in short, gentlemen, with a crime which every circumstance connected with him and every trait of his known character renders utterly inconceivable. Now upon what grounds has this gentleman of irreproachable character been charged with this mean and sordid crime? Baldly stated, the grounds of the accusation are these: A certain learned and eminent man of science has made a statement, which the police have not merely accepted but have, in practice, extended beyond its original meaning. That statement is as follows: 'A complete, or nearly complete, accordance between two prints of a single finger . . . affords evidence requiring no corroboration, that the persons from whom they were made are the same.'

"That statement, gentlemen, is in the highest degree misleading, and ought not to have been made without due warning and qualification. So far is it from being true, in practice, that its exact contrary is the fact; the evidence of a finger-print, in the absence of corroboration, is absolutely worthless. Of all forms of forgery, the forgery of a finger-print is the easiest and most secure, as you have seen in this court today. Consider the character of the high-class forger—his skill, his ingenuity, his resource. Think of the forged banknotes, of which not only the engraving, the design, and the signature, but even the very paper with its private watermarks, is imitated with a perfection that is at once the admiration and the despair of those who have to distinguish the true from the false; think of the forged check, in which actual perforations are filled up, of which portions are cut out bodily and replaced by indistinguishable patches; think of these, and then of a finger-print, of which any photo-engraver's apprentice can make you a forgery that the greatest experts cannot distinguish from the original, which any capable amateur can imitate beyond detection after a month's practice; and then ask yourselves if this is the kind of evidence on which, without any support or corroboration, a gentleman of honor and position should be dragged before a criminal court and charged with having committed a crime of the basest and most sordid type.

"But I must not detain you with unnecessary appeals. I will remind you briefly of the salient facts. The case for the prosecution rests upon the assertion that the thumb-print found in the safe was made by the thumb of the prisoner. If that thumb-print was not made by the prisoner, there is not only no case against him but no suspicion of any kind.

"Now, was that thumb-print made by the prisoner's thumb? You have had conclusive evidence that it was not. That thumb-print differed in the size, or scale, of the pattern from a genuine thumb-print of the prisoner's. The difference was small, but it was fatal to the police theory; the two prints were not identical.

"But, if not the prisoner's thumb-print, what was it? The resemblance of the pattern was too exact for it to be the thumb-print of another person, for it reproduced not only the pattern of the ridges on the prisoner's thumb, but also the scar of an old wound. The answer that I propose to this question is, that it was an intentional imitation of the prisoner's thumb-print, made with the purpose of fixing suspicion on the prisoner, and so ensuring the safety of the actual criminal. Are there any facts which support this theory? Yes, there are several facts which support it very strongly.

"First, there are the facts that I have just mentioned. The red thumb-print disagreed with the genuine print in its scale or dimensions. It was not the prisoner's thumb-print; but neither was it that of any other person. The only alternative is that it was a forgery.

"In the second place, that print was evidently made with the aid of certain appliances and materials, and one of those materials, namely defibrinated blood, was found in the safe.

"In the third place, there is the coincidence that the print was one which it was possible to forge. The prisoner has ten digits—eight fingers and two thumbs. But there were in existence actual prints of the two thumbs, whereas no prints of the fingers were in existence; hence it would have been impossible to forge a print of any of the fingers. So it happens that the red thumb-print resembled one of the two prints of which forgery was possible.

"In the fourth place, the red thumb-print reproduces an accidental peculiarity of the 'Thumbograph' print. Now, if the red thumb-print is a forgery, it must have been made from the 'Thumbograph' print, since there exists no other print from which it could have been made. Hence we have the striking fact that the red thumb-print is an exact replica—including accidental peculiarities—of the only print from which a forgery could have been made. The accidental S-shaped mark in the 'Thumbograph' print is accounted for by the condition of the paper; the occurrence of this mark in the red thumb-print is not accounted for by any peculiarity of the paper, and can be accounted for in no way, excepting by assuming the one to be a copy of the other. The conclusion is thus inevitable that the red thumb-print is a photo-mechanical reproduction of the 'Thumbograph' print.

"But there is yet another point. If the red thumb-print is a forgery reproduced from the 'Thumbograph' print, the forger must at some time have had access to the 'Thumbograph.' Now, you have heard Mrs. Hornby's remarkable story of the mysterious disappearance of the 'Thumbograph' and its still more mysterious reappearance. That story can have left no doubt in your minds that some person had surreptitiously removed the 'Thumbograph' and, after an unknown interval, secretly replaced it. Thus the theory of forgery receives confirmation at every point, and is in agreement with every known fact; whereas the theory that the red thumb-print was a genuine thumb-print, is based upon a gratuitous assumption, and has not had a single fact advanced in its support.

"Accordingly, gentlemen, I assert that the prisoner's innocence has been proved in the most complete and convincing manner, and I ask you for a verdict in accordance with that proof."

As Anstey resumed his seat, a low rumble of applause was heard from the gallery. It subsided instantly on a gesture of disapproval from the judge, and a silence fell upon the court, in which the clock, with cynical indifference, continued to record in its brusque monotone the passage of the fleeting seconds.

"He is saved, Dr. Jervis! Oh! surely he is saved!" Juliet exclaimed in an agitated whisper. "They must see that he is innocent now."

"Have patience a little longer," I answered. "It will soon be over now."

Sir Hector Trumpler was already on his feet and, after bestowing on the jury a stern, hypnotic stare, he plunged into his reply with a really admirable air of conviction and sincerity.

"My lord and gentlemen of the jury: The case which is now before this Court is one, as I have already remarked, in which human nature is presented in a highly unfavorable light. But I need not insist upon this aspect of the case, which will already, no doubt, have impressed you sufficiently. It is necessary merely for me, as my learned friend has aptly expressed it, to disentangle the actual facts of the case from the web of casuistry that has been woven around them.

"Those facts are of extreme simplicity. A safe has been opened and property of great value abstracted from it. It has been opened by means of false keys. Now there are two men who have, from time to time, had possession of the true keys, and thus had the opportunity of making copies of them. When the safe is opened by its rightful owner, the property is gone, and there is found the print of the thumb of one of these two men. That thumb-print was not there when the safe was closed. The man whose thumb-print is found is a left-handed man; the print is the print of a left thumb. It would seem, gentlemen, as if the conclusion were so obvious that no sane person could be found to contest it; and I submit that the conclusion which any sane person would arrive at—the only possible conclusion—is, that the person whose thumb-print was found in the safe is the person who stole the property from the safe. But the thumb-print was, admittedly, that of the prisoner at the bar, and therefore the prisoner at the bar is the person who stole the diamonds from the safe.

"It is true that certain fantastic attempts have been made to explain away these obvious facts. Certain far-fetched scientific theories have been propounded and an exhibition of legerdemain has taken place which, I venture to think, would have been more appropriate to some place of public entertainment than to a court of justice. That exhibition has, no doubt, afforded you considerable amusement. It has furnished a pleasing relaxation from the serious business of the court. It has even been instructive, as showing to what extent it is possible for plain facts to be perverted by misdirected ingenuity. But unless you are prepared to consider this crime as an elaborate hoax—as a practical joke carried out by a facetious criminal of extraordinary knowledge, skill, and general attainments—you must, after all, come to the only conclusion that the facts justify: that the safe was opened and the property abstracted by the prisoner. Accordingly, gentlemen, I ask you, having regard to your important position as the guardians of the well-being and security of your fellow citizens, to give your verdict in accordance with the evidence, as you have solemnly sworn to do; which verdict, I submit, can be no other than that the prisoner is guilty of the crime with which he is charged."

Sir Hector sat down, and the jury, who had listened to his speech with solid attention, gazed expectantly at the judge, as though they should say: "Now, which of these two are we to believe?"

The judge turned over his notes with an air of quiet composure, writing down a word here and there as he compared the various points in the evidence. Then he turned to the jury with a manner at once persuasive and confidential—

"It is not necessary, gentlemen," he commenced, "for me to occupy your time with an exhaustive analysis of the evidence. That evidence you yourselves have heard, and it has been given, for the most part, with admirable clearness. Moreover, the learned counsel for the defense has collated and compared that evidence so lucidly, and, I may say, so impartially, that a detailed repetition on my part would be superfluous. I shall therefore confine myself to a few comments which may help you in the consideration of your verdict.

"I need hardly point out to you that the reference made by the learned counsel for the prosecution to far-fetched scientific theories is somewhat misleading. The only evidence of a theoretical character was that of the finger-print experts. The evidence of Dr. Rowe and of Dr. Thorndyke dealt exclusively with matters of fact. Such inferences as were drawn by them were accompanied by statements of the facts which yielded such inferences.

"Now, an examination of the evidence which you have heard shows, as the learned counsel for the defense has justly observed, that the entire case resolves itself into a single question, which is this: 'Was the thumb-print that was found in Mr. Hornby's safe made by the thumb of the prisoner, or was it not?' If that thumb-print was made by the prisoner's thumb, then the prisoner must, at least, have been present when the safe was unlawfully opened. If that thumb-print was not made by the prisoner's thumb, there is nothing to connect him with the crime. The question is one of fact upon which it will be your duty to decide; and I must remind you, gentlemen, that you are the sole judges of the facts of the case, and that you are to consider any remarks of mine as merely suggestions which you are to entertain or to disregard according to your judgement.

"Now let us consider this question by the light of the evidence. This thumb-print was either made by the prisoner or it was not. What evidence has been brought forward to show that it was made by the prisoner? Well, there is the evidence of the ridge-pattern. That pattern is identical with the pattern of the prisoner's thumb-print, and even has the impression of a scar which crosses the pattern in a particular manner in the prisoner's thumb-print. There is no need to enter into the elaborate calculations as to the chances of agreement; the practical fact, which is not disputed, is that if this red thumb-print is a genuine thumb-print at all, it was made by the prisoner's thumb. But it is contended that it is not a genuine thumb-print; that it is a mechanical imitation—in fact a forgery.

"The more general question thus becomes narrowed down to the more particular question: 'Is this a genuine thumb-print or is it a forgery?' Let us consider the evidence. First, what evidence is there that it is a genuine thumb-print? There is none. The identity of the pattern is no evidence on this point, because a forgery would also exhibit identity of pattern. The genuineness of the thumb-print was assumed by the prosecution, and no evidence has been offered.

"But now what evidence is there that the red thumb-print is a forgery?

"First, there is the question of size. Two different-sized prints could hardly be made by the same thumb. Then there is the evidence of the use of appliances. Safe-robbers do not ordinarily provide themselves with inking-slabs and rollers with which to make distinct impressions of their own fingers. Then there is the accidental mark on the print which also exists on the only genuine print that could have been used for the purpose of forgery, which is easily explained on the theory of a forgery, but which is otherwise totally incomprehensible. Finally, there is the strange disappearance of the 'Thumbograph' and its strange reappearance. All this is striking and weighty evidence, to which must be added that adduced by Dr. Thorndyke as showing how perfectly it is possible to imitate a finger-print.

"These are the main facts of the case, and it is for you to consider them. If, on careful consideration, you decide that the red thumb-print was actually made by the prisoner's thumb, then it will be your duty to pronounce the prisoner guilty; but if, on weighing the evidence, you decide that the thumb-print is a forgery, then it will be your duty to pronounce the prisoner not guilty. It is now past the usual luncheon hour, and, if you desire it, you can retire to consider your verdict while the Court adjourns."

The jurymen whispered together for a few moments and then the foreman stood up.

"We have agreed on our verdict, my lord," he said.

The prisoner, who had just been led to the back of the dock, was now brought back to the bar. The gray-wigged clerk of the court stood up and addressed the jury.

"Are you all agreed upon your verdict, gentlemen?"

"We are," replied the foreman.

"What do you say, gentlemen? Is the prisoner guilty or not guilty?"

"Not guilty," replied the foreman, raising his voice and glancing at Reuben.

A storm of applause burst from the gallery and was, for the moment, disregarded by the judge. Mrs. Hornby laughed aloud—a strange, unnatural laugh—and then crammed her handkerchief into her mouth, and so sat gazing at Reuben with the tears coursing down her face, while Juliet laid her head upon the desk and sobbed silently.

After a brief space the judge raised an admonitory hand, and, when the commotion had subsided, addressed the prisoner, who stood at the bar, calm and self-possessed, though his face bore a slight flush—

"Reuben Hornby, the jury, after duly weighing the evidence in this case, have found you to be not guilty of the crime with which you were charged. With that verdict I most heartily agree. In view of the evidence which has been given, I consider that no other verdict was possible, and I venture to say that you leave this court with your innocence fully established, and without a stain upon your character. In the distress which you have recently suffered, as well as in your rejoicing at the verdict of the jury, you have the sympathy of the Court, and of everyone present, and that sympathy will not be diminished by the consideration that, with a less capable defense, the result might have been very different.

"I desire to express my admiration at the manner in which that defense was conducted, and I desire especially to observe that not you alone, but the public at large, are deeply indebted to Dr. Thorndyke, who, by his insight, his knowledge, and his ingenuity, has probably averted a very serious miscarriage of justice. The Court will now adjourn until half-past two."

The judge rose from his seat and everyone present stood up; and, amidst the clamor of many feet upon the gallery stairs, the door of the dock was thrown open by a smiling police officer and Reuben came down the stairs into the body of the court.

CHAPTER SEVENTEEN

AT LAST

"We had better let the people clear off," said Thorndyke, when the first greetings were over and we stood around Reuben in the fast-emptying court. "We don't want a demonstration as we go out."

"No; anything but that, just now," replied Reuben. He still held Mrs. Hornby's hand, and one arm was passed through that of his uncle, who wiped his eyes at intervals, though his face glowed with delight.

"I should like you to come and have a little quiet luncheon with me at my chambers—all of us friends together," continued Thorndyke.

"I should be delighted," said Reuben, "if the program would include a satisfactory wash."

"You will come, Anstey?" asked Thorndyke.

"What have you got for lunch?" demanded Anstey, who was now disrobed and in his right mind—that is to say, in his usual whimsical, pseudo-frivolous character.

"That question savors of gluttony," answered Thorndyke. "Come and see."

"I will come and eat, which is better," answered Anstey, "and I must run off now, as I have to look in at my chambers."

"How shall we go?" asked Thorndyke, as his colleague vanished through the doorway. "Polton has gone for a four-wheeler, but it won't hold us all."

"It will hold four of us," said Reuben, "and Dr. Jervis will bring Juliet; won't you, Jervis?"

The request rather took me aback, considering the circumstances, but I was conscious, nevertheless, of an unreasonable thrill of pleasure and answered with alacrity: "If Miss Gibson will allow me, I shall be very delighted." My delight was, apparently, not shared by Juliet, to judge by the uncomfortable blush that spread over her face. She made no objection, however, but merely replied rather coldly: "Well, as we can't sit on the roof of the cab, we had better go by ourselves."

The crowd having by this time presumably cleared off, we all took our way downstairs. The cab was waiting at the curb, surrounded by a group of spectators, who cheered Reuben as he appeared at the doorway, and we saw our friends enter and drive away. Then we turned and walked quickly down the Old Bailey toward Ludgate Hill.

"Shall we take a hansom?" I asked.

"No; let us walk," replied Juliet; "a little fresh air will do us good after that musty, horrible court. It all seems like a dream, and yet what a relief—oh! what a relief it is."

"It is rather like the awakening from a nightmare to find the morning sun shining," I rejoined.

"Yes; that is just what it is like," she agreed; "but I still feel dazed and shaken."

We turned presently down New Bridge Street, toward the Embankment, walking side by side without speaking, and I could not help comparing, with some bitterness, our present stiff and distant relations with the intimacy and comradeship that had existed before the miserable incident of our last meeting.

"You don't look so jubilant over your success as I should have expected," she said at length, with a critical glance at me; "but I expect you are really very proud and delighted, aren't you?"

"Delighted, yes; not proud. Why should I be proud? I have only played jackal, and even that I have done very badly."

"That is hardly a fair statement of the facts," she rejoined, with another quick, inquisitive look at me; "but you are in low spirits to-day—which is not at all like you. Is it not so?"

"I am afraid I am a selfish, egotistical brute," was my gloomy reply. "I ought to be as gay and joyful as everyone else today, whereas the fact is that I am chafing over my own petty troubles. You see, now that this case is finished, my engagement with Dr. Thorndyke terminates automatically, and I relapse into my old life—a dreary repetition of journeying amongst strangers—and the prospect is not inspiriting. This has been a time of bitter trial to you, but to me it has been a green oasis in the desert of a colorless, monotonous life. I have enjoyed the companionship of a most lovable man, whom I admire and respect above all other men, and with him have moved in scenes full of color and interest. And I have made one other friend whom I am loth to see fade out of my life, as she seems likely to do."

"If you mean me," said Juliet, "I may say that it will be your own fault if I fade out of your life. I can never forget all that you have done for us, your loyalty to Reuben, your enthusiasm in his cause, to say nothing of your many kindnesses to me. And, as to your having done your work badly, you wrong yourself grievously. I recognized in the evidence by which Reuben was cleared today how much you had done, in filling in the details, toward making the case complete and convincing. I shall always feel that we owe you a debt of the deepest gratitude, and so will Reuben, and so, perhaps, more than either of us, will someone else."

"And who is that?" I asked, though with no great interest. The gratitude of the family was a matter of little consequence to me.

"Well, it is no secret now," replied Juliet. "I mean the girl whom Reuben is going to marry. What is the matter, Dr. Jervis?" she added, in a tone of surprise.

We were passing through the gate that leads from the Embankment to Middle Temple Lane, and I had stopped dead under the archway, laying a detaining hand upon her arm and gazing at her in utter amazement.

"The girl that Reuben is going to marry!" I repeated. "Why, I had always taken it for granted that he was going to marry you."

"But I told you, most explicitly, that was not so!" she exclaimed with some impatience.

"I know you did," I admitted ruefully; "but I thought—well, I imagined that things had, perhaps, not gone quite smoothly and—"

"Did you suppose that if I had cared for a man, and that man had been under a cloud, I should have denied the relation or pretended that we were merely friends?" she demanded indignantly.

"I am sure you wouldn't," I replied hastily. "I was a fool, an idiot— by Jove, what an idiot I have been!"

"It was certainly very silly of you," she admitted; but there was a gentleness in her tone that took away all bitterness from the reproach.

"The reason of the secrecy was this," she continued; "they became engaged the very night before Reuben was arrested, and, when he heard of the charge against him, he insisted that no one should be told unless, and until, he was fully acquitted. I was the only person who was in their confidence, and as I was sworn to secrecy, of course I couldn't tell you; nor did I suppose that the matter would interest you. Why should it?"

"Imbecile that I am," I murmured. "If I had only known!"

"Well, if you *had* known," said she, "what difference could it have made to you?"

This question she asked without looking at me, but I noted that her cheek had grown a shade paler.

"Only this," I answered. "That I should have been spared many a day and night of needless self-reproach and misery."

"But why?" she asked, still keeping her face averted. "What had you to reproach yourself with?"

"A great deal," I answered, "if you consider my supposed position. If you think of me as the trusted agent of a man, helpless and deeply wronged—a man whose undeserved misfortunes made every demand upon chivalry and generosity; if you think of me as being called upon to protect and carry comfort to the woman whom I regarded as, virtually, that man's betrothed wife; and then if you think of me as proceeding straightway, before I had known her twenty-four hours, to fall hopelessly in love with her myself, you will admit that I had something to reproach myself with."

She was still silent, rather pale and very thoughtful, and she seemed to breathe more quickly than usual.

"Of course," I continued, "you may say that it was my own lookout, that I had only to keep my own counsel, and no one would be any the worse. But there's the mischief of it. How can a man who is thinking of a woman morning, noon, and night; whose heart leaps at the sound of her coming, whose existence is a blank when she is away from him—a blank which he tries to fill by recalling, again and again, all that she has said and the tones of her voice, and the look that was in her eyes when she spoke—how can he help letting her see, sooner or later, that he cares for her? And if he does, when he has no right to, there is an end of duty and chivalry and even common honesty."

"Yes, I understand now," said Juliet softly. "Is this the way?" She tripped up the steps leading to Fountain Court, and I followed cheerfully. Of course it was not the way, and we both knew it, but the place was silent and peaceful, and the plane-trees cast a pleasant shade on the graveled court. I glanced at her as we walked slowly toward the fountain. The roses were mantling in her cheeks now and her eyes were cast down, but when she lifted them to me for an instant, I saw that they were shining and moist.

"Did you never guess?" I asked.

"Yes," she replied in a low voice, "I guessed; but—but then," she added shyly, "I thought I had guessed wrong."

We walked on for some little time without speaking again until we came to the farther side of the fountain, where we stood listening to the quiet trickle of the water, and watching the sparrows as they took their bath on the rim of the basin. A little way off another group of sparrows had gathered with greedy joy around some fragments of bread that had been scattered abroad by the benevolent Templars, and hard by a more sentimentally minded pigeon, unmindful of the crumbs and the marauding sparrows, puffed out his breast and strutted and curtsied before his mate with endearing gurgles.

Juliet had rested her hand on one of the little posts that support the chain by which the fountain is enclosed and I had laid my hand on hers. Presently she turned her hand over so that mine lay in its palm; and so we were standing hand-in-hand when an elderly gentleman, of dry and legal aspect, came up the steps and passed by the fountain. He looked at the pigeons and then he looked at us, and went his way smiling and shaking his head.

"Juliet," said I.

She looked up quickly with sparkling eyes and a frank smile that was yet a little shy, too.

"Yes."

"Why did he smile—that old gentleman—when he looked at us?"

"I can't imagine," she replied mendaciously.

"It was an approving smile," I said. "I think he was remembering his own springtime and giving us his blessing."

"Perhaps he was," she agreed. "He looked a nice old thing." She gazed fondly at the retreating figure and then turned again to me. Her cheeks had grown pink enough by now, and in one of them a dimple displayed itself to great advantage in its rosy setting.

"Can you forgive me, dear, for my unutterable folly?" I asked presently, as she glanced up at me again.

"I am not sure," she answered. "It was dreadfully silly of you."

"But remember, Juliet, that I loved you with my whole heart—as I love you now and shall love you always."

"I can forgive you anything when you say that," she answered softly.

Here the voice of the distant Temple clock was heard uttering a polite protest. With infinite reluctance we turned away from the fountain, which sprinkled us with a parting benediction, and slowly retraced our steps to Middle Temple Lane and thence into Pump Court.

"You haven't said it, Juliet," I whispered, as we came through the archway into the silent, deserted court.

"Haven't I, dear?" she answered; "but you know it, don't you? You know I do."

"Yes, I know," I said; "and that knowledge is all my heart's desire."

She laid her hand in mine for a moment with a gentle pressure and then drew it away; and so we passed through into the cloisters.

THE END